Up Roystonhill

Up Roystonhill

Rosaleen Orr

Kennedy & Boyd

Kennedy & Boyd
an imprint of
Zeticula Ltd
The Roan
Kilkerran
KA19 8LS
Scotland.

http://www.kennedyandboyd.co.uk
admin@kennedyandboyd.co.uk

First published in 2014
Copyright © Rosaleen Orr 2014.

Cover Design Copyright © Rosaleen Orr 2014

ISBN 978-1-84921-145-1

to my loving husband, Robert Mulhern

Contents

Dawn Over Mirkhill

First Light

At first light, heavy raw-boned Mother Agnes of the
Holy Child woke up screaming in her narrow bed, her
legs cramping as she tried to free herself from both her
nightmare and her old-fashioned suffocating patchwork
covers. She didn't panic, though, but threw herself
out of bed, and stamped her feet in a certain way that
usually restored her circulation and released her from
cramps. She had grown used to the constraints of her
narrow bed, as much as to the limitations of convent
life. And she took a grim delight in her nightmares, with
which she sometimes terrified the other Sisters over
recreation.

Today she couldn't remember her nightmare
properly. Something had been gnawing at her legs, and
at her poor swollen feet. She understood that her mind
had been trying to make sense of the pain she endured
towards morning, before the central heating came
on again. Agnes didn't shower first thing because the
water wasn't warm either. She waited till she had dealt
with the animals, both rescued and domestic, housed
in the outhouses and sheds in the convent's grounds.
As well as a little flock of pretty ewes nearby that she
helped tend. She was still thumping around in a kind of

ludicrous stamp dance, and her large face creased into an ironic smile that deepened the lines engraved on it.

"Awkward old Biddy! Silly old girl. Fit for the knacker's yard," she seemed to be saying, not so much to herself, but to an invisible companion. Which in fact she was, even giving sideways glances at a non-person to her right.

Then she recalled her nightmare and blushed through the weather-beaten thickening skin. Because someone had been trying to release her from the frantic gnawing animal. Caressing her heavy legs and feet. Murmuring endearments. She remembered who the murmurer was.

"Jesus, Mary and Joseph!" she sighed. "I thought I was beyond all that, finally!"

She sat down again, heavily, on the crumpled bed, which creaked despondently, and ran her callused hands through her pepper and salt, wiry, hair. She reckoned Father Harry would get a shock if she confessed that dream to him. Not that she was stupid enough to consider doing that. Dreams and nightmares were beyond conscious human volition. Strictly one's own business. Though she struggled to regain her dignity and composure as she clumped her feet, still in their bed socks, into the capacious green wellington boots that stood ready on the bedside handmade rag rug (the horrible object that her old friend Sister Philomena had been trying to make for her, and which Sister Mary of the Angels had unpicked and finished).

Mother Agnes thanked God that the nuns in the Convent of the Bleeding Heart at least had their own cells, even if they did not have the en-suite bathrooms with showers enjoyed by the orphans and quasi orphans in the west wing, and that Mother Superior Benigna had promised to install when cash flow improved.

At least the motley crew of holy women did not embarrass each other if shouting out the names of beloveds present and past. Agnes thought of the respectable mother she had got through a difficult childbirth, when she was a midwife in Ireland. The poor woman was roaring and yelling for Geordie all through. And it turned out her husband's name was Mike. God, they'd all had a good laugh over that! And butter wouldn't have melted in the poor woman's mouth, Agnes remembered. The lady had wondered why the young nuns stood round giggling when she confided she was going to call the tiny girl baby Georgianna.

Mother Agnes smiled as she remembered the newborn faces, usually so comically like the mothers that you wondered how mix-ups ever occurred. God help any child she might have had, then, she thought, avoiding looking at herself in the small mirror over the washbasin. But as she washed quickly in the tepid water, the feel of her fingers over her face and shoulders reminded her just how ungainly she had become, perhaps always was.

Although she had been quite proud of herself when she was young. Da always telling her what a fine big girl she was, and Mammie admiring her then rosy complexion. And her older brothers, all much bigger than her, making a pet of her. It hadn't been till she went to primary school that she had realised the other kids were much smaller and daintier and cuter than herself. Even the boys. And that was when she had started cracking jokes about herself. Till Sister Bernadette had forbidden her, and threatened her with the cane if she continued the placatory self-ridicule. And finally, when the teenage Agnes had broken down in tears, cuddled her instead, and drew both Agnes's large hands into her wide brown sleeves. And told her she had a beautiful soul, and an amazing aura.

And that, Agnes supposed, was what had led her into becoming a nun, and to choosing the Franciscan order.

That and her persistent desire to look after the poor, the wounded, and the neglected, both human and animal, like their Saint Francis of Assisi. And as a young nun she had nurtured the ambition to become a saint like him. Saint Agnes of the Holy Child! She had practically swooned with delight at the very thought. They'd make medals with her imposing profile on them. Miraculous medals to cure all ills. Of course she had got over her megalomania. Or medalomania, she thought.

Sister Bernadette would have been cross with her. She was beginning to make jokes about herself again, even if only to herself.

The rescued animals, anyway, worshipped Mother Agnes, not as a saint, but as a God. They were all waiting for her, donkeys, sheep, ponies, and dogs, calling to her in their own familiar languages, as she made her way towards their pens and outbuildings, crunching through the frosted puddles of the leaf strewn rutted tracks.

No-one else was stirring yet, in the house or in the surrounding grounds. Just as well, she thought. Her get up was strange, though based on the old fashioned religious attire that the convent had been privileged to adopt. She had the skirts of her brown habit kirtled up under her hempen belt, revealing baggy jeans and her green wellies. She had an old anorak over her mantle, guimpe and wimple. And she was wearing a cook's pristine white apron over her habit. The effect was of a mediaeval peasant. Her image would not have been out of place in the Bayeux tapestries.

The landscape she took her place in gave a similar effect in the uncertain dawn light. The distant tower blocks up Roystonhill, shrouded in mist, looked like ancient battlements, and the deciduous trees that had been protected and had survived in the mansion house convent's parks were really ancient, noble specimens.

"Like meself, maybe!" quipped Agnes to her unpresent companion.

A strange pain twisted in Mother Agnes's gut, as she pushed on towards the outbuildings. She wondered if it was the sign of some mortal illness that would test her equanimity and fortitude to bear with dignity. She thought she could. She hoped she would. The water in the flax ponds, where lesser souls, over the decades had drowned themselves, gleamed in soft flickers among the reeds as the mist started to disperse.

The shut in dogs were kicking up an awful din. She wondered if some of her tramp people had called by, looking for a handout, in return for some unskilled labour.

Something about the gently sloping prospect was making her feel uneasy. A frisson ruffled the landscape at the edge of her vision, where the beech hedges divided the slopes like strung out copper lines.

It was Mother Agnes's vanity not to wear spectacles. But she had a pair of lady's field glasses in the pocket of her habit, and these she brought to her eyes and focussed. Focussed on the little trembling flutter of motion, russet against copper, white against grey. She let the breath out that she had been holding, in a low groan, rising to a sob, and she broke into a ragged trot, as fast as she could, towards the moving blobs of colour.

Finally she managed to get out a guttural roar, and the large dog fox which was ripping open the belly of another animal, paused and looked up, bloody snout in the air. The white fleecy animal shuddered and lay still; a hogget, a half grown ewe, it was. Not just any ewe, she was somehow certain, but Maillie, her pet lamb, that she had hand-reared. Who had followed her about like a puppy. From being around humans, Maillie had got smart assed, up to all sorts of tricks. Had run away from the dipping. Had got out of pens and gates the other sheep would not have looked at. And answered to her name. Even when back in the flock, she still answered to her name. So it must be Maillie, right enough, Agnes thought, her breath coming in gasps as the contemptuous dog fox went back to his wicked work.

When Mother Agnes finally got to the crime scene, what was left of Maillie, after the fox had dragged off the best bits, in steaming trails, looked quite weird. A bit like those funny big slippers with animal ears. Only just the one. And four pretty hooves, which Agnes had used to polish. The rest was a bloody mush of still-palpitating organs. Agnes tried to drag the remains of her pet out of the bloody puddles, but found herself unequal to the grisly task. Worse still, she found she could not get herself up from the ditch, as Maillie's blood stained her white apron in a gruesome imitation of the red dawn that was reeking through the wisps of mist.

"Never mind, Maillie!" she said stupidly, stroking the torn ears, "Never mind, wee lamb!"

How ridiculous she was, Agnes pondered, still on her knees. It wasn't as if she was even a vegetarian! Her facial muscles again contracted into their usual pathways, making her face twist into its usual stiff wide grimace.

"But she came to her name when I called!" she burst out, in spite of herself.

She felt rather than saw a figure standing over her, a person who had approached from the field gate, unseen and unheard in the mist.

Then she recognised the masculine scents of cigars and aftershave, as the man leant over and dragged her up unceremoniously. She gasped and complained as his arms crushed her bosom as he accomplished this, after a struggle. She started to roar and bawl.

"Hush now, Macushla! Hush now, Alanna!"

She recognised the gruff tones of her old friend Father Henry Xavier. Father Harry, as he was known, always spoke mock Irish in moments of stress. Her sobs diminished as Father Harry led her to his car, an old green Volkswagen, parked on the roadway outside.

"What a mess he made of her, poor Maillie, that old dog fox! Poor innocent animal!" Agnes cried in outrage, disgracing herself as she clung to Father Harry, her tears and snot baptising the new waistcoat he was wearing that day. He was in good tweeds but still sported his dog collar.

Father Harry brought out a large coarse linen handkerchief. The hanky was so large it looked like a duster. He mopped Agnes's streaming eyes and nose with it and gave it to her, then swung her down into the passenger seat of his car, and brusquely but affectionately swung her stricken legs in after her.

"Wait there!" he said. "I'll put the carcase in the hut to bury later. I'll say a De Profundis over the creature, too. I'll see to the other animals, then I'll come back for you and drive you home by the roadway. Okay, Mother Agnes?"

But Mother Agnes still could not let him go, hanging on to his lapels.

"Come on now, Mother Agnes, get off of me!" he shouted, "People will think we're out courting!" he laughed as he extricated himself from her frantic embrace.

Finally he produced his hip flask of whisky and held it to her lips. She grasped the warmed flask, as the curved silver vessel gleamed in a ray of light, and drank copiously.

"Poor innocent creature!" she complained again as she collapsed into the passenger seat.

"And the poor hungry hunted fox, is he not innocent too? Remember Brother Fox!"

Before he left, Father Harry switched on a tape for her. Mozart, she thought, Sacred stuff. He walked off, whistling the air of the Agnus Dei that was playing.

Had he no heart, Agnes wondered, just for a second, till the whisky warmed her frozen sluggish blood and set it coursing through her violet, thickened, veins. Which swelled as they tried their best to deal with it.

She watched Father Harry as he walked briskly away from her, taking off his jacket, and unbuttoning his waistcoat jauntily. The rising sun picked out points of light on the tops of the far off trees, and on the spiders' webs of the nearby half stripped hedgerows, and suddenly made a corona of light round Father Harry's springing red gold hair.

He looked like a Gainsborough, Agnes mused, like a country gentleman, as clouds divided in the morning sky and let through slivers of light to spotlight him dramatically.

All at once, reacting to the intricacies of the eighteenth century music, Mother Agnes's large hollowed eyes closed. And she suddenly rejoined the world of her special recurring dream, languishing and loving, that had earlier that morning carried her to her special, recurring and agonisingly sensuous nightmare.

Mother Agnes did not wake up till Father Harry drew up in the driveway, having taken the long way round the convent's spread out, patched together, estates.

He woke her up gently, and was rewarded by a beatific smile, which Agnes only just managed to transform into her usual sardonic grin.

As she got out, young Rory O'Donnell leapt in to take her place. He'd heard that Father Harry was around, and had jumped out of bed to try and intercept him, and beg a lift into Saint Jude's. Rory squealed in horror when Father Harry explained what had happened, and asked him if he would like to help bury the remains of poor Maillie. Rory was Agnes's favourite 'orphan', as well as Father Harry's. Rory's mother had been jailed for drug dealing, and his father was unknown, or so his mother said. Mother Agnes was quite shocked at how strict Father Harry was being with the boy, telling him to be a man, and come and help dispose of the sheep's carcase. Agnes could see the boy going white and his lip trembling. The boy, who was a bit babyish, perhaps, and looked younger than his eleven years, had a toy fluffy chicken clasped in his delicate long hand. Agnes watched in amazement as Rory made the little toy chick shout abuse at the priest in a gabbling chicken voice.

"I don't think so!" the chicken was squeaking. "Try to make me, Harry! Go on, try!" and he made the chicken poke at Father Harry's arm as he was switching on the ignition.

Mother Agnes went over to the passenger seat window, and Rory rolled it down. His large blue eyes were fearful and touched Agnes's tender heart. She reached in to ruffle his blonde spiky hair, which, as he had coated it with gel, surprised her by being hard beneath her fingers.

"Never mind, son!" she cried, a bit fuddled with the whisky, and quite prepared to be annoyed with her saviour, Father Harry. "You don't have to go if you don't want to. It might be too disgusting for a little lad! Don't you think, Father Harry?"

But Harry was crimson in the face, and sweating with rage.

"He's not such a little lad! You're turning him into a milksop. A mummy's boy! You're tying him to those apron strings of yours, Agnes! For goodness sake let the boy grow up!"

There was an undignified tussle then, as Agnes tried to wrench open the door, and Father Harry, pushing Rory aside, leant over the boy to lock it manually.

As Father Harry slammed into gear, gravel spurted under his wheels as he spun away. Mother Agnes was distraught, as she peered in, to glimpse Father Harry's still furious face. She stood at a loss, on the house steps, watching the car as it swooped down the curving drive. Then she saw it swoop up the opposite side of the driveway and draw up just beneath where she was standing, clutching at the gory stained apron with her blood caked hands.

Father Harry jumped out of the car right away, went round to the passenger seat, and laughingly pulled Rory out, tickling him, and swiping at his bottom as Rory escaped indoors.

Harry looked up at Agnes, his hands in his pocket, hanging his big handsome head.

"You were right, Mother Agnes." he stated quietly. "And I, as usual, was wrong! The boy had skipped his breakfast, and of course he's too young to come to terms with the death of a pet. One killed in such a brutal way. I'll go and bury the poor body, and say a couple of prayers over it. I'll be back later to drive Rory to Saint Jude's. He hates that school bus."

As he was about to step into his car, he had second thoughts, and went and stood on the step below Mother Agnes.

"And what would we do, poor male creatures, without saintly women like you, Agnes, to keep us right? My own Mammy was just such a saint. Rory's Ma is no saint, but she's the best he's got and he adores her," he said, grinning up at Agnes charmingly, as she blushed.

Then his face straightened suddenly. He reached up, and grabbed the large crucifix which hung low around her neck, and pressed his lips briefly to it.

"Go and rest now, Agnes, my mother in Christ, and my superior in charity!"

Agnes felt herself go dizzy with sensual and spiritual delight.

Later, watching from her window for his promised return, she mused that Harry had not been entirely in the wrong, as far as wee Rory O'Donnell was concerned. She had begun to think perhaps the Sisters had been molly-coddling Rory. She supposed boys did need a father figure, however stern he could sometimes be. She threw up her window, as she heard the sound of Harry's car. To her surprise, it hardly stopped, the door being flung open as it slowed down. Rory jumped in quickly and obediently, and the old Volkswagen crunched off down the drive and through the wrought iron security gates. Looking out over the grounds in Mirkyknowes, overcast now by cloud, Mother Agnes shivered in the sudden cold.

Dawn over the Schemes

Though storm clouds were stacking over the convent in Mirkyknowes, down in Low Mirkhill the sun was flashing from behind the far Royston tower blocks, colouring the cloud and mist. Dawn flared blush pink amid swirls of smoky grey over blocks of sixties built quick fix Mirkhill tenements. Bands of clouds streaming over these low rises, like a time enhanced film, lent the enclave a kind of glamour. As yet the motorways looping round the school of Saint Jude's and the housing alongside were comparatively empty and peaceful, with just a few scary covered trucks rumbling to the meat market, and a few white vans scooting out of the flower market to shops in nicer bits of the city.

Varrie came to life slowly, under her Japanese-lettered duvet, in the 'hole in the wall' bed recess in the kitchen of her un-converted Victorian sandstone tenement (one of the few that had been retained in the scheme). Varrie was naked, but still made-up, and had been sleeping like the dead till her radio alarm sounded with news of wars in far off lands. Considering the life Varrie had endured, her body had held together quite well, as last night's boyfriend had gratefully discovered. Her inky black hair, escaping from a 'pompadour' pinned up by a jet comb, made her look Japanese, too. Her parchment skin, with its various tattoos, some shop bought, some home-made (from her time in a secure youth unit), gave her a kind of graphic novel look. Or as if from a woodcut of 'the floating world' of Japanese courtesans.

The bed reeked of gin and patchouli and spliffs and sex. But another aroma made itself gently felt, a perfume of attar of roses or dolly mixtures, as the duvet was thrown back, and an exquisite young girl lying so far unseen and spoon fashion with the woman, lashed out in her sleep. She wore a candy striped pyjama suit, and as she tossed and turned, the electric mass of her bright red curls splashed out on the pillow and spoiled the monochrome effect.

Varrie, becoming conscious of her daughter, leapt to her feet in horror. She usually kept the kitchen door latched when she had a boyfriend over. Liam must have left it open when he took off in a bit of a hurry. (She had been winding him up that her partner was due out of Barlinnie jail that morning.) She dived into the white raincoat he had left on a hook in panic. She dashed into the unreconstructed bathroom, where a mixer tap had been fitted over a white rust-stained bath, and yanked the erratic shower on full blast. Under the warm spray Varrie relaxed, in spite of herself. She still felt guilty that Kansas had crept into her bed of sin. She'd confess it to Father Harry at her next Confession, and she was bound to get absolution from him. He was very nice and easy going. And she sometimes thought her Confessions were the one bright spot in his dreary hard-working day, dealing with all those winos and junkies that gathered in the Roystonhill graveyard. Her heart warmed to him as she recalled the little services he sometimes gave to the derelicts among the grey tombstones from which the shy half-tamed roe deer peeked. Sometimes she joined him there, in the role of a penitent sinner (a glamorous

Mary Magdalene), and as a helper and distributor of the nourishing sandwiches she had helped him make.

Under the shower her body warmed too, with more carnal memories, as her heavy breasts felt the comfortable flow of the water. Any young rural artist would have been inspired to capture the dappled landscape of her body, where the marbling of pregnancy varied her heated flesh tints against the antique off-white of the old bath. Like a tragic Klimt female, perhaps. Varrie knew about the Secessionist painters from her time as a life model at Glasgow School of Art. She had patterned her old bathroom in gold in their honour. She would have painted herself in it, in the steamy yellow light, if she had had the skill.

She had been very popular as a model, and had offered private posing sessions to only the very best artists. Her first real love affairs had been with them. They'd all been after her, and not being able to choose between them, she had gradually become promiscuous.

She had come slowly to the realisation that the handsome artists, who used her as model and mistress (sometimes borrowing money they never paid back), all considered themselves, once the first flush of passion had worn off, to be her superiors. Not just in talent and wit, but somehow, morally too. That was when she'd packed in the modelling game, and taken up another game. One no less demanding, as it turned out.

Varrie ran some umber henna over her head to give the blue black dye warmer tones, and the rinse, dripping down, spread like sandy tributaries and rivers over the sad hilly terrain of her body. It splayed out and grew paler as it floated over her drooping bosom and over her stretch marked stomach, becoming nearly transparent as it trailed over the tracks of injections in the past, down her thighs. Which were now muscular and toned from her aerobics sessions, (not taken, given), and were smooth and hairless. Varrie was no coward and regularly suffered if not a full Brazilian on her pubic hair, a radical pruning, in a great wee waxing salon tucked away down crowded London Road. (Handy for the Prince's Infirmary, if razor wielding hands should slip, or wax strip ripping off pain should give a client a heart attack.) So the streams of foaming water drained poetically through formal copses of darkened hair, down her scarred thighs, to the chipped plum coloured nail varnish on her bunched up toes.

The water stopped suddenly, and as quickly started again, nearly scalding her before it evened out. That was Kansas playing games with the kitchen taps to get her out of the bath. Varrie was going a bit goose pimply and pruney anyway. So she turned off the taps and slid back the shower screen (attached to the wall by Frankinstein-esque fitments). She caught her image in the steamy long mirror on the opposite wall, as she stepped out reluctantly from the bath. She looked rather like an early Monet, Varrie thought, or a late Renoir.

On second thoughts, as she examined her face close up, it wasn't sort of round and soft like the Impressionists' wifely or servantish models. No, she really was more like a Klimt. Or a Schiele, with her edgy features, aquiline nose, dark, well marked eyebrows, and fierce black almond shaped eyes. Her 'Ice cream Tally' (to use the racist term) blood had given Varrie her Wicked Madonna-like features and also her harmonious surname, Valentino.

As she dried herself lovingly in the bathroom, lavishing orchid scented talcum all over, she recalled fondly Liam's words of passion before she had decided to spook him out, and send him on his way, back to his single person's top floor high rise flat.

"You're a lovely lassie!" he had gasped. "A lovely big lassie!"

Not very original, she thought, for someone who had such a big tip for himself. And who was actually thinking of setting himself up as a gigolo. He would have to have a good few lessons before then, she thought. And in case he hadn't realised, he'd have to be prepared to pay a good price for them too.

When Varrie had squeezed herself into her skimpy black leather top and mini skirt, and sneaked back into the kitchen, Kansas had already boiled the dodgy electric kettle, made the Earl Grey tea, and decanted the luxury muesli Varrie favoured. At ten years old, although preternaturally mature from looking after Varrie, she was still kid enough to choose a fresh Variety packed sugary cereal herself. Spookily, she didn't like fizzy pop, or tea or coffee and was sipping a bottle of plain ungassy water. She would have drunk tap water, in the interests of bio-degradability and carbon footprints. But her biology teachers had taught her that the water pipes in old tenement houses were made of lead, made soluble and leaky by the soft fresh water from Loch Katrine that her geography teachers were always boasting about.

"I'll make the toast, hen," said Varrie generously. "Away and pack your PE kit. I've laid it out in your bedroom. I'll bring your highland dance costume. I'll see you after school."

"Does that mean you're not going into work this morning, Mama?" Kansas asked frostily.

Varrie indicated her tight leather gear. "Do I look as if I was going in to work, darling? Listen Kansas, I've got loads to do today, pet. Don't go all funny about it. My pal Martha will cover up for me again. Listen, honey, could you phone her?"

"She'll be on the road already, Mama. And you know she doesn't believe in mobiles. She thinks they leak into your brain. I'll phone the jannie instead."

"But if you phone him, he'll know! Maybe dock my wages! Oh, alright then! But make sure you describe how ill I am!" Varrie made a vomiting face, clutching her tummy dramatically, even going so far as to roll about on the new mock parquet floor in pretend agony, finishing up stretched out pretend dead.

Kansas gave a small reluctant giggle and went into the hall to phone jannie Knightley on the tatty land-line phone. Varrie could hear her begin, loyally, in a little panicky hoarse voice. She was probably giving him a tale about asthma, and asking him if she should phone up a scary medical advice hotline.

While Kansas was elaborating, Varrie whipped the minging sheets off the bed and threw them into the machine, with loads of fabric softener. She bunged in a capful of Dettol too. Sometimes she agreed with Martha that her present lifestyle wasn't all that healthy. If any half decent guy came along, who could at least pay his way, she'd give it up, she promised herself, getting out her fags and lighting up. Puffing and gasping, she went out into the hall to make background noises to convince the jannie.

"Will I get her to talk to you herself?" she heard Kansas mischievously asking. "No, Mr Knightley, sir? Will I not bother? Right, right, I'll tell her. Thank you, jannie. Thanks loads!"

Kansas grabbed the cigarette out of her mother's hand and, slipping into the kitchen, tossed it into the sink. She turned to confront her mother. "The jannie says to be sure to look after yourself. Wrap up warm in bed. And if you're not feeling any better tonight, you've not to dream of coming in. He says be sure and use your Ventolin inhaler, and if you need any wee thing from the chemist, he'll pick it up for you and bring it round himself."

"I knew you were overdoing it, hen," Varrie grumbled. "Well I suppose I'll definitely be back at work after school, swabbing out those putrid art rooms. Anything but let that wee guy get his foot over the door!"

It was as yet only a quarter to eight. They could both have had an hour longer in bed, she thought, yawning. She'd lie down for five minutes after Kansas had gone. Before she tackled credit cards, the bank, and the tallyman. The latter, she thought she could get round just once more. But she knew it would take another class of tart to get round the bank manager. And the credit card guys, apart from sounding ultra respectable, and having names like Ewan and Hamish, all seemed to operate from India. She remembered when she was a wee girl, when an honest shag by one of her mammy's buxom friends could usually purchase a hundredweight of nutty slack. Her mammy herself had been very straight-laced and good living, going to mass every morning, never mind every Sunday. But still and all, Mammy used to giggle too, when hard up coalmen used to cry their wares,

"Coal just for money! Coal for cash only!"

As she watched Kansas, from the window, making her way demurely down the hill to Saint Jude's, her hair neatly plaited and tied with double ribbons in the school colours (the only service she was allowed to perform for her daughter now, and it was a good job she was great at it), she thought how like her granma Kansas looked. Same pointed nose, and aggrieved expression. She wondered if Kansas had ever told tales on her. Before her granma had gone gaga. What would that skinny Holy Mary have said if she'd discovered that her pious daughter was a part time lady of the night? Not really of the night, usually, Varrie mentally corrected. Most of the professional jobs were accomplished in the late afternoon, when Kansas was at school. Between her morning and evening shifts as a cleaner. And before she took the occasional community aerobics classes in the further education wing of Saint Jude's. Talk about multi-tasking, Varrie thought wryly, as she got out her mobile phone. She reckoned she'd better get started after all, and, plastering an appealing smile to her carmine lipsticked lips, started to dial. She still looked out, tracking Kansas on her schoolward trek as she did so, she wasn't sure why.

Kansas hurried on, feeling her mother's eyes on her, determined not to turn round. She overtook her little friend Dakota, who had much in common with her. They had both perfect school uniform, and homework neatly completed, though they both went in to the breakfast and homework clubs just to get away from their mothers a bit earlier.

"Race you, Dakota!" shouted Kansas as they turned the corner away from their homes.

"Race you, Kansas!" agreed Dakota, pushing back a wisp of her carefully plaited hair.

By the time the two schoolgirls had run round the playground a couple of times and made their way into the club rooms, where they cheerfully sat down to a second breakfast each, they looked just as carefree as the other kids. And by that time, Varrie had put the phone down, relieved, the rigid smile gone from her lips. The tallyman had refused her kind offer. He said he was getting to be an old guy, and didn't want special favours, but he'd give her another week to find the extra interest. And at that point, to Varrie, it seemed like plenty of time.

She started to giggle and dance, remembering the song her mother used to sing.

"What do you want if you don't want briquettes?
What do you want if you don't want coke?"

Those were the days, when Mammy and the other devout women in her family could feel superior to lassies who exchanged sex for coal. Varrie opened her purse, and started counting out her cash into little piles. She'd maybe have to fit in another wee job.

Varrie was beginning to think of giving up the cleaning game totally. It was starting to get on her nerves that the kids undid every day what you cleaned up in the evening before. She wondered why that big clown of an art teacher, Miss Wallace, didn't realise that her pet, wee Rory O'Donnell, was one of the worst for making a mess, and for stealing anything that wasn't tied down. Just because he looked like a wee angel, and had a nice genteel voice, how he'd acquired it, nobody knew. And now he'd been cast as a munchkin in the school adaptation of "The Magical Wizard of Oz", along with Kansas and her best pal Dakota, just as though he was every bit as good as them. She was sure Father Harry, out of the kindness of his heart, had vouched for the rascal. He was even giving him a chance as an altar boy.

Varrie groaned, trying to decide which lucky punter's call to answer for the next wee job. Lounging with a fag, and looking lazily out of the living room window, putting off returning a punter's call, Varrie Valentino was surprised to spot Father Harry's old car lurch round the corner. The battered motor drew up at the side entrance to Saint Jude's (the gate that was kept open to admit latecomers). She was more surprised when Rory O'Donnell scrambled out of the car.

"What the hell is he doing, that sneaky wee rascal?" she murmured, stubbing out her fag and leaning against the window to peer out. "The school bus won't be good enough for him!"

Just then, Rory dashed back, as if called from the car. He stuck his head in the window. For a minute it looked as if Father Harry was kissing him goodbye. Then she made out that Rory had just had his designer wire glasses looped round his ears. Must have forgotten them.

"Allow him, the wee bugger!" Varrie said to herself. "Just like him to get Father Harry to give him a lift. Good job Harry doesn't have to clean up after him! Mucky wee devil!"

She started reluctantly picking out numbers on her phone pad with one false fingernail.

Dusk Over Mirkhill

Limbo Hour

It was now limbo hour in scarred Mirkhill, the time after the school kids had scooted up the stairs of their liftless high-rise flats. When the teachers had locked themselves into their cars for scary cross-town journeys to their houses in the leafy west end. The hour before the autumn gloaming darkened, and the winos woke up ugly from their beauty sleep among the toppled angels of the Necropolis. When genteel school cleaners glanced at their watches and sighed, switching off 'Countdown' reluctantly.

Martha Dearie prepared to leave her sixth floor flat in the Brick Road block. She did a last-minute tidy up, and a quick hoover. Her tabby cat, called Tabby, retired to an arm-chair and gave Martha a funny look. She wasn't supposed to sit in that chair, and she knew it.

"Bad Tabby!" said Martha, flinging her off. "You know that's Daddy's chair!"

Tabby gave her another funny look and yawned as if to say. "And who'll make me when you're away to your work, then, Missus?" Then she sneakily scrambled back onto the chair.

It seemed as if the flat was empty, it was so silent, but before she left, Martha opened the big bedroom door a crack and whispered, "Well, I'm away, Jimmy! I'll see you later!"

She waited a minute, and, there being no response, threw on a man's anorak, and laced up her white trainers. She went through her many-zipped shoulder bag, making sure she had her private cleaning utensils that she took home every day to wash properly. Then she took a deep breath, and opened the numerous locks on the front door, checking that she had all the right keys, and that they still worked.

"Cheeriebye well!" she called in a soft sweet voice, and Tabby for an instant looked as if she meant to get off the armchair. As the front door closed behind Martha, the cat relaxed.

Martha squeaked down the perpetually damp stairways, gallus in her ridged rubber soles. As usual on her grim journey to work, Martha sat down on the top step of the first floor, and had a sip from the bottle of water she always carried, before getting up her courage to scurry down the last flight and make her exit quickly. She picked up her newspapers the paper boy had dumped on the bottom steps before the kids hanging about the lifts saw her.

But hardly had she crossed the graffitied threshold of the flats, when large drops of icy autumn rain threw themselves at her in flurries of sudden winds. She tied her large grey anorak hood under her chin, lowered her head, and marched on, her step still springy, but her neat, small featured face going a little wan.

On paper, the distance between the tower blocks and the school seemed like nothing, but paced out through deepening puddles, and with garbage blowing about head high, from all directions, it seemed like miles. By the time she got to Saint Jude's playground, she couldn't keep the bulky anorak hood on, and the rain had soaked her tight permed curls.

And the playground, which was down a small flight of steps on one side, and hemmed in by hedges on the others, had become like a swimming pool.

The large windowed art classrooms of Saint Jude's, which were Martha's particular remit, were unlit, and appeared deserted. The life-sized, crude, papier maché figures hanging from the ceiling lights were attempting to take over the rooms, until the cleaners clocked on. They each had the benefit of a real, if cheap, guitar strapped to them. And as they swayed in the draught from a couple of open windows, the guitar strings vibrated. A further illusion of life was given when the radio in the store room switched itself on, programmed to do so by Varrie and tuned in to her favourite Country and Western station. It sounded as if the restless figures were singing, as well as playing the guitars their paper fingers plucked.

There were hardly any kids about. School had been dismissed twenty minutes earlier, but the large flabby art teacher, Lena Wallace, was still mooching round her disgustingly untidy classroom, trying vainly to make it less shamefully messy before those snidey cleaners turned up. She was being 'helped' by a young slender boy who was rushing around crashing paint trays together, and actually making the mess worse.

"Come on, Rory! Let's go." she called to the boy. "We've done our best. The cleaners will be clocking on soon. And they'll start complaining again. They don't have horrible kids to contend with while they do their job. I would manage perfectly fine without the kids."

The gawky fair haired lad was busy emptying jars of coloured papier maché down the sink, which he stirred about, as if in a trance, before coming to his senses as the sink blocked up and made gurgling sounds.

"Sorry, Miss!" he said, staring up hopelessly at Lena's bulk as she put her hands gently on his shoulders to turn him away from the sink, his glasses steaming up, concealing tears about to trickle down his small elfin face. "I was only trying to help."

"Come on and I'll walk you to the bus." Lena offered. "In case that gang is waiting."

"No, that's alright!" said Rory, cheering up instantly, "I'm off to the Emerald City! Do you not remember I'm a munchkin, Miss? I'll tidy up a wee bit more for you."

Miss Wallace gave up and left Rory in possession of the classroom.

She exited by the door near the janitor's house, a conserved little Victorian dwelling that looked like a Wendy House as it stood in the playground of the slab-like sixties built school. From within the cosy house the janitor's bulldog barked and growled as she hurried past, her long skirts trailing through the greasy puddles, as she battled to the windswept bus stop.

In the swimming pool of a playground, two boys were relentlessly practising kick boxing as the moisture flew off their leather gear, and flattened the blonde spikes of their hair. As little Martha paddled in through the open gateway, she recognised the pair, and instantly started to slap them with her mittened hands. Then she grabbed first one, and then the other and tried to push and pull the lads indoors, as a small mother cat might try to deal with her large obstreperous tom kittens. She finally succeeded, and her cries could be heard in the corridor outside the art rooms.

"Wayne!" came the weak protesting cry, accompanied by the boys' thumps, "Darren!"

The lads ran in backwards to the classrooms, still doing karate kicks.

Martha followed her twin sons in meekly, and disappeared into the art base, ripping off her sodden anorak, and reappeared almost instantly in a short-sleeved pinny over a long-sleeved jersey and droopy skirt, her Marigolds already on her hands. She tried to make herself heard over the boys' random shouts.

"Will you listen a wee minute?" she pleaded as Wayne launched a super-kick, only just missing her face. "Will you stop it, son?" she requested reasonably.

"Why, Mammy?" the boys asked in unison, genuinely puzzled.

"Cos I've told you, boys!" Martha smiled, pleased at her own strictness.

"But why, Mammy?" they asked again.

"You two are going to get told off in a minute!" Martha sighed in resignation, and turned to dampen her wash cloths at the sink. Wayne climbed on top of the sink to get her attention.

"Maa-aamy?"

"What, son?"

"Maa-aamy?" Darren sprawled at her feet, catching at her overall.

Martha gave in, put her cloths down, and opened her handbag. She put two pound coin pieces in each boy's outstretched hand. "And take the papers to your daddy. I picked them up. He'll be wantin' them, and the paper boys'll not climb the stairs. Don't go and get them crushed..."

The boys aimed kicks at the papier maché figures, which started to swing crazily, then ran out, slapping each other over the head with the rolled up newspapers.

"Or wet!" Martha called after them, as they loped into the torrent, each holding a paper over his head.

"I told you not to do that!" Martha stood wringing her hands as her two sons roared off.

Saving face in case any of the other cleaners were listening, she called out, from the open window, "Cheerio, boys! See you later!"

She opened another large window, to let out the pong from the stinky sinks. Instantly the room was invaded by pungent coffee fumes, from Mirkhill's one surviving factory. You could get high from these acrid fumes, she thought, choking. And the papier maché figures started moving again, obviously agreeing with her. Martha hastily banged the windows shut. She stood at the windows staring out. There was something funny in the air tonight, she thought.

The view from the wide metal windows was urban chic, the dereliction partly obscured, and at the same time glamorised, by big blotchy pretend stained glass panels. Torrents of rain suddenly lashed down against the glass, probably sent by the displaced farming gods of that Dear Green Place, Glasgow. The coffee fumes abated, and the classroom pong increased in proportion. A flash of lightning enhanced the garish daubs pinned to the wall. It also sparked off a pair of kid's specs abandoned under the teacher's desk. Next to them was a doughnut shaped splodge of brown, at which Martha screamed, taking it to be shit. She sighed with relief when she saw an upended bottle of sepia poster paint beside it, and another of vermillion, masquerading as blood.

"That's that wee villain Rory O'Donnell," Martha mouthed grimly to herself. "Up to his old tricks again." Still, she supposed it could have been worse. Sometimes he spread around real bodily fluids, not their substitutes. Even after they'd given him the part of the king rat in the school panto, at the recommendation of his social worker. Martha thought it was a waste of a good fur suit, which she, as a matter of fact, had helped to make. Although she had to admit he'd been brilliant in it. Brought the house down with his ad lib gags.

"See that Rory O'Donnell!" Martha muttered, "the mingin' wee toerag! I'll get him!"

It was a good job there was no-one about to hear Martha's heated outburst. It wasn't like her at all to speak like that. If she'd thought anyone could overhear her, she'd have been black affronted. If she'd thought that Father Harry, for example, had witnessed her losing her temper in such a way, she would have wished the ground to open up and swallow her, she thought, getting on with her work. She would have got a right red neck!

Martha had suffered from Rory's paint spraying before, which the big art teacher lady didn't seem to be able to stop. They could have floated a Govan battleship on the amount of paint Rory O'Donnell had stolen. If they'd had any battleships left to float.

Martha hoped her co-worker Varrie would turn up tonight to give her a hand with the horrible messy art rooms. The big empty classrooms were beginning to spook her out. She wondered if Wayne and Darren would come back to see her home. She wondered if they'd taken Jimmy's newspapers up to him.

At that moment Big Jimmy's papers were lying crumpled at the feet of Darren and Wayne. They were seated comfortably in a shed in the back yard of the wee newsagents off Mirkfield Square. The twins had been casing the joint for a future break in, when the weather was a bit better. The little shop didn't look as if it would be much bother to two strong boys like them. The wood of the back door was nearly rotten, and it didn't look as if anyone came round that way much anyway. It was getting too dark to see.

"You comin'?" Wayne asked his twin.

"Aye, sure!" Darren answered.

They made their way round the front to suss out the shop itself, though they should have known it well enough, being in and out of it most days.

"Dearie's papers!" Darren demanded from the Indian shopkeeper. "Never come. Ma Da gets upset when they never come!"

"And give us twenty Players for the old guy. And a Racing Times!"

When they left, Mr Mac (short for Mahksood) thought what good boys they were. Good to their old father, in their fashion, although a bit rough and tough. Nothing like his own tall, handsome boy, Ahmed, who was at that moment stacking baked beans for his father, reaching the second top shelf, without having to use the stepladders. Up his Tower Block, Jimmy Dearie heard the double rattle of bovver boots on the stairs. He sat up in bed, and fished for his glasses. That would be the twins with his papers. He found a stub of a pencil. Wayne and Darren loped into the room, chucking his papers on the quilted bedspread. Licking his pencil, he started making his predictions for next day's racing.

"Do you know a big guy called Sky?" Jimmy asked. "Give him these slips to put on for me tomorrow, boys. He can wait till the odds are right. Did you mind to buy my Thunderball?"

"No, Da! Sorry, we forgot!"

Jimmy looked from one to the other, trying to stop his top lip from trembling.

"Yiz forgot!"

"Sorry, Da!" They hung their heads penitently, sneaking looks at each other.

"Aye, Da, we forgot! At first! Then we remembered and went back for it!"

Wayne and Darren jumped into the old man's bed, on either side of him. They cuddled him and butted him with their spiky heads, leaving their father with a euphoric expression of relief and delight. Jimmy's head suddenly rolled back on his pillow, as he fell into one of his sudden unpredictable dozes, his lips still drawn up into a surprised smile. The boys took charge of the betting slips, tidying his covers.

Some pound coins tumbled out from underneath the pillow. Wayne counted out two to Darren and two to himself, and put the rest back carefully.

Big Jimmy, now thin and shrunken, opened his eyes again as the boys shut the door of the flat carefully. Propping himself up, blinking, on his many pillows, he stared out over the Mirkhill scheme, as the rain stopped suddenly and the swept clean fiery skies made the neighbouring tower blocks stand out majestically. Lights blazed from nearly all the windows and television sets glowed so clear in each front room that he felt he could almost watch the identical programme to which they were all obediently tuned.

From the convent attics, Mother Agnes stared out at the apocalyptic clouds hanging over far Mirkhill, suggesting weird figures, reminding her of the Sistine Chapel ceiling.

Love in the Afternoon

The 'wee job' that Varrie had been forced to fit into her busy schedule had turned out to be a bit of a drag. In her tenement flat, at the other end of the scheme from Martha's high rise, she was still trying to get rid of her last punter. An idea had slowly fixed itself in her mind. He would be her last punter, full stop. She didn't think she'd ever had such an annoying client. Even the message he'd left on her mobile had been exasperating.

"Zac here! Seen your advert. Be over this aftie! Okay?"

He referred to the postcards she'd left in smelly phone boxes, and in the Tartan Arms bar. If he didn't get a move on, Kansas and her wee friend would be here for their tea. (Kansas had phoned her on her mobile to say Dakota wanted to change into her highland dancing kit in Kansas's bedroom, because they were supposed to use the boys' changing room after four, and it was pure, pure stinky.) Varrie got the point. When she taught her aerobics class at Saint Jude's, her poor athletes had to change there too, and many of them chose to arrive fully kitted out, and depart in their sweaty exercise togs. Anyway, it would save her having to carry all her daughter's highland dancing gear over to Saint Jude's. As well as her cleaning stuff. She always brought her own dainty cloths and sponges. That was when she turned up at all.

Meanwhile, Varrie got on with the job in hand, as best she could. He'd have to look sharp, usually no bother with such a strong young guy. When she'd opened the door to him, her first thought had been what was such a fit young man doing requiring her services. But when he took off his grease stained leather work jacket, reeking of motor engines, she discovered that underneath, he was still reeking sweaty and minging. She suggested a wee shower as a kind of foreplay, at no extra cost. And that turned out to be the best of the sexual encounter. She resisted his invitation to climb into the old bath and shower beside him, and contented herself with playing the spray over his rather nice, muscular, body. He reacted like a little boy, doubling up in fits of laughter, cupping his hands over his private parts.

Varrie didn't know if it was like Samson's hair, the guy seemed to lose his strength without his garage stained clothing, and sweaty grime on his body. He said his girlfriend liked to make love to him straight from work. She thought he smelled manly. Varrie shook her head in rueful appreciation. What some women will do to keep a man! Varrie herself had a hard time getting him into gear at all, and when he lost power totally she washed her dainty hands of him. She loitered in the bathroom while he got back into his clothes, putting on her orchid scented hand cream and sympathising with herself in the mirror.

As he sat on her newly washed duvet pulling on his working boots, Varrie shuddered as the sight of the oil from his raggy jeans staining her flashy new cover. He brought out his wallet and produced a roll of greasy fivers, and also some photos of his family. There was his nice little fair round faced wife, which he at last admitted her to be. Why did guys always say 'girlfriend' to her? The wife had her arms around two blonde angels whom she presumed to be the young man's. He looked towards Varrie for appreciation and praise.

Varrie didn't say a word, but there was something in the way she handed him back his wallet that made him think he had to explain himself. It seemed that his mates at work were having a go at him because he had only slept with the one lassie, the one in the photo, his wife. They said he should get some experience before he got too old for girls to fancy. And that was why he had come to Varrie. He didn't like chatting up girls in pubs. And they might turn out to be his wife's friends, and she might hear, and might divorce him because she'd never had another boyfriend since him in primary school. And then what if she took the kiddies away and went off to stay with her mother away up north where there were hardly any jobs for garage mechanics? And he needed his wife's wages as a care worker to pay for the council flat, so he might get put out and end up on the street with no job. His pals had all clubbed together to pay for his sexual education, which they said would be to his wife's advantage in the long run. And now he'd just wasted the money.

Varrie looked at the roll of oily notes in distaste. She shoved them back into the wallet he was still holding, next to the images of his wife and kids. He looked as if he might cry.

At the door he tried to kiss her.

Varrie blushed with rage and shame and vexation.

Then he made it much worse.

"I think I might know you." he whispered shyly on the doorstep. "Did you used to be Varrie Valentino in primary seven? I was only wee but I always fancied you rotten! No offence, but could I take you out for a drink some night? No strings attached. I'll tell the wife I'm on overtime. You're a brilliant listener, so you are. And you're still a lovely girl!"

His last words reminded her of Liam MacNee.

"See if somebody tells on you, one of your pals, maybe? Maybe somebody who fancies your nice wee wife, and wants to get his mitts on her? See if she finds out you've been here and she divorces you and goes to live with her mother, up north? Tell you what you could do! With your looks and your sexual powers, have you never fancied being a gigolo?"

Varrie slammed the door so hard behind him, that it was a wonder that Kansas and Dakota, running out of the playground with the hoods of their anoraks up, and under one umbrella, didn't hear it. Then Varrie battered around, cleaning the flat, demented, slungeing the bath, changing the sheets. The only ones left were Kansas's favourites, Barbie ones, usually kept for special occasions. Maybe when Paddy, Kansas's Daddy, got a home visit from Barlinnie.

Kansas and Dakota had got diverted at the sweet shop, buying old fashioned type sweeties, humbugs and mint imperials and bullseyes, which were the latest thing. So Varrie had time for a quick fag so that her heart slowed down and the flush faded from her cheeks. She should have taken that other guy, the wee plumber, instead of 'Zac' as he called himself, the garage mechanic. She remembered why she hadn't. The wee plumber was the kind of funny wee man who was ferociously sexually endowed. He could do it all night, to a band playing, in spite of being short and tubby. No wonder he had to pay for it. And the smell off his breath! And she'd never have got finished in time for her evening cleaning at Saint Jude's.

Varrie began to do some mental arithmetic, to see if she could actually manage to live on what she could earn as a cleaner, an aerobics instructor, and the odd wee job she still got modelling at the Glasgow School of Art, where the tutors still loved her. (Some of them remembered her intellectual aspirations when she'd first been directed there from the DSS.) Nothing was worth what she'd just been through, and without earning a bean. And some of the girls, her friends she hung

32

about within the Tartan Arms, had had knives pulled on them, when punters hadn't fancied paying, and had turned on them, insulting their charms. And some of them got beaten up by their pimps if that happened and they couldn't produce the cash. At least Varrie had no pimp. She had guarded her amateur status fiercely. But she knew it was only a matter of time till one of the ponces tried to move in on her.

And then there was Kansas. It wouldn't be long till Kansas noticed. Till she really noticed that the guys visiting her mother weren't proper boyfriends. Lots of other kids' mothers had boyfriends. Maybe some big kid would tell her. Varrie thought she would really and truly chuck it for good. Dabbling with vice, Varrie was vulnerable, as Father Harry had often remarked. Especially as she was getting beyond the first flush of youth. She made her mind up. She would make a true confession to Father Harry, with a real purpose of amendment, meaning she would intend never to commit the sins again. She had never done that before, resorting to the childish device of keeping her manicured fingers crossed behind her back. She'd get hold of Father Harry as soon as she could, and make a clean breast of it.

Then another thought occurred to her. If Paddy got parole from jail, he'd be snooping around her to find out how she was doing. Their divorce wasn't absolute yet, and Kansas still adored her big red-haired comical daddy. Varrie had always put the frighteners on her punters, mentioning Paddy and his incarceration. But Patrick John Doig would never have hurt a fly. He was in jail for fraud and money laundering on a large scale, which were, after all, quite genteel occupations for criminals in Mirkhill and Royston.

Varrie stubbed out her spliff, and got the highland dance kit out for Kansas. Then it occurred to her! How would she pay for all Kansas's classes? They meant a lot to her, and she met nice kids there. Varrie started noting down columns of figures, and got out her calculator to make a job of it, just as Kansas, giggling and shouting, let her wee pal Dakota in the door with the key she always kept on a ribbon round her neck.

The two schoolgirls chased each other all round the flat, ignoring Varrie totally, but when they dashed into the kitchen, Kansas stopped in her tracks, and a suspicious look that Varrie knew all too well came over her face.

"How come you've got my good sheets on the bed?"

Then the little girl's expression changed to one of delight. She danced up and down, her elfin face flushed and beaming. She grabbed her friend and made her dance too.

"It's Paddy, isn't it? He's a got a home visit, and he's staying over, in my bed. And I've to sleep with you in here! That's it, isn't it?"

Varrie was shaking her head energetically, trying to get through to her daughter. Kansas at last twigged, and also noted a shame faced look on her mother's face.

"Do you mean you two are back together? He's due in here, with my good Barbies? Never mind, Mama! I'm pleased anyway. After all, you're still married, just! Different if it was another horrible boyfriend!"

"Is he your Mum's Ex?" Dakota asked.

"More than that, Dakota! He's my Daddy! That I got my red hair from. And he's lovely!"

Like the coward she was, Varrie left explaining till after Kansas had made her friend her speciality of peanut butter and strawberry jam sandwiches. Her daddy's favourites, she told Dakota. Which, although it may not have been strictly true, was so much part of the legends Kansas had built up round her Dad, Paddy, that it seemed true, to both Kansas and Varrie.

"I sometimes make him Chicken Maryland, don't I, Mama?" Kansas enlisted her mother's help in convincing

Dakota. "Dad got to like that Stateside, when he was touring his band."

But Varrie had some stories she wished to tell herself. She had brought her mobile phone into the kitchen.

"Oh, Darling!" She put her arms round Kansas. "My poor little darling. You're never going to believe this. What rotten luck! I've just got a text from Paddy. Not even from him, from his social worker. All home leave is cancelled till they sort the riot out!"

"What riot?" Kansas asked, her face going pale, her lips looking drawn and thin.

"The lady says it will be on the six o'clock news tonight. But we're not to worry about Paddy, she says. He was in the library studying for his degree when the gangsters took the warders hostage. He locked himself in the warders' bay, and it was him that raised the alarm. So the minute the jail is back to normal he'll get his home leave. Not like those gangsters, Kansas, darling! They'll lose their remission."

"And will the gangsters not get annoyed with Daddy for giving the game away?"

"How the hell should I know? I managed to stay out of jail, not like your Daddy. Hurry up you two, get your costumes on, or I'll be late for my shift and they'll dock my wages."

Her text messager sounded.

Kansas pounced on Varrie's mobile, but wasn't able to decipher the text before Varrie grabbed it back and switched it off. It wasn't from Paddy anyway, but from 'Zac', who seemed to be trying to apologise. Varrie had noticed before that it often happened that if you made yourself obnoxious to a bloke, they were all over you. If you were as nice as ninepence, you got dumped.

Just as they were going out the door, Varrie and her daughter gave each other a look. A long look they both understood. When either of them had got carried away making up untruths, wee porky pies, as Varrie called them, they occasionally came down to earth before too much harm was done. Kansas, though not for a moment taken in by the tales of a prison riot, recognised that Varrie was trying to save face in front of Dakota. And Varrie never let on about Kansas's fantasy cooking either. So they were kind of quits.

Varrie had had a real scare, though. Kansas was so clever, she'd soon suss out totally about her mother's profession. And then the skies would fall in.

Skipping across the puddles in the uneven cobbled roadway in her high heeled boots, the two little girls giggling and trying to see who could jump furthest, Varrie suddenly took off in a tremendous leap, to show she could still cut it. She made it across the deepest puddle, and managed to land on both feet, but was alarmed when she heard a sickening crunch as she lost her balance. She staggered on till Kansas and Dakota fielded her, and helped her limp on, one arm over each girl's shoulder.

"Christ, my poor friggin' ankle!" she gasped, remembering the horrible crunching sound.

"Mama!" Kansas suddenly let her go so she staggered again. "I think you'll find that was the heel of your stupid boot!" The two girls danced round her in triumph, as Varrie's face fell. She had quite fancied being off work with a slightly sprained ankle. And the boots were new.

But she was beginning to feel better. She could stick the squidgy heel on with superglue, of which there was plenty in the art room. (Miss Wallace used it all the time). And she began to relish her new chaste resolution. She'd begun to think she'd give up sex totally, not just its commercial aspect. If she could convince her pal Father Harry of that when she honoured him by letting him hear her Confession, maybe he'd give her a wee loan to tide her over. He'd done that before when the tallyman had been on her trail. And he'd just pinched her cheek and tweaked her ears playfully, before giving her a quick sympathetic cuddle. Still, she didn't want to push her luck with Father Harry. She had a funny feeling about him. He was a lovely man, of course, but Father Henry Xavier of the Society of Jesus was nobody's fool!

As they entered the school, Dakota dashed off to her chanter lesson, a preliminary for the school pipe band, and Kansas reluctantly went into the art department with her mother. The poor child instantly got something sticky from the door handle on the ruffled sleeve of the white blouse she had washed and ironed herself.

"It's that Rory O'Donnell again! I'll murder him, the stinky sleekit rat!" Kansas shrieked, having suffered from his messing up door handles before. "Oh, I hope it's not snotter!"

"Sneaky wee bastard!" Varrie joined in. "You alright, Kansas pet? Look, it's only chewing gum! Auntie Martha will get it off. She's brilliant at that. I suppose she'll manage to glue my friggin' heel on properly, too. So have you got your chanter, Kansas, precious?"

"I don't need my chanter, Mama! You couldn't pay the Pipe Major's fees! Remember?"

Varrie turned away huffily. "Don't forget who pays the fees for the highland dancing! And the elocution, too! And the bloody ballet!"

She slowly turned to Martha with a long suffering smile.

"Kids, Martha, kids!"

Martha was attacking a filthy sink, quite out of breath from wielding a plunger among the rancid papier maché and poster paint. Red in the face, she stopped for a moment.

"Aye, Varrie! Kiddies! Right enough! You never said a truer word!"

Girl Talk

The glow had died totally from the storm cleared sky over Saint Jude's. Lights blazed in every room of the large art department, making the ugly building look like a light house, or a space ship come to rest by mistake on the tired-out old district. Martha was mopping the floor, not in such a cleansing frenzy now; she moved in a rapt relaxed way, as she swung the mop round in exact figure of eight sweeps. Some of the desks had been removed, and Kansas was practising a sword dance fiercely at the far end of the room, where the freshly washed floor was nearly dry. Scottish country dance music was playing on the radio in the store room. Varrie was redoing her finger nails, sitting on a sink top, and taking little puffs from a spliff. She put the fag down carefully on a clean paint tray.

"So I goes, 'Are you effin' plyin' for hire, or are you effin' not?'"

Without stopping her rhythmic mopping, Martha interrupted,

"Did he have his wee yellow light on?"

"Yeah sure, Martha! Turned it off but, when I came waltzin' out the pub!"

"Is that a fact, Varrie? Taxis are not supposed to do that! Did he think you were tiddly?"

"I wasn't but, Martha! So I goes 'Are you wantin' business or are you not?'... He goes. 'It all depends what you mean!'... I goes 'How?'... He goes 'I've had a few offers.'... I goes 'What kind of effin' offers?'...He goes 'That's right! Them kind! From lonely women wantin' a wee bit of attention!' he goes."

"Did he mean, like..." Martha had to pause, to pick her words. "Like haughmagandy?"

"If that means what I think it means, yeah. That's what he meant!"

Varrie took another couple of drags from her fag.

"And you should've seen him too, face all scarred from zits."

"Darren's got awful bad zits the now. Teenage acne."

"Aye, but Darren's a bit of a boy! This idiot's supposed to be a big man! Or so he says!"

"Varrie! What was it he said?"

"Well, Martha..." Varrie jumped down nimbly off the sink, to whisper in her friend's ear. "He says he's thinkin' of startin' up as a gigolo! He's seen a programme about it on the TV!"

"Oh, I saw that! It was brilliant! This wee Italian guy says..."

Varrie interrupted. "Well, it seems he's had a lot of offers...from the lonely women. It seems it would be no bother at all to him, so he says!"

"How do you mean, Varrie?"

Varrie lit another fag, and blew out a smoke ring. "God's gift to women, Martha!"

"Oh, I see!"

"He goes... 'How come you've never pulled tonight? Nice lookin' lassie like you?'"

Martha clapped her hand over her mouth, to register amusement.

"I says... 'The only guy wi' nice wheels had funny eyes, and I live away out the scheme.'... And he's like... 'I'll drive you for nothin!'...I'm like... 'I thought you were a gigolo!'... He's like... 'Sure, but I quite fancy you, babes!'...I goes... 'Hell, that's a shame, so it is! I'm gay, you see! Helluva sorry!'... He nearly drove off the road! Then he goes... 'See if you ever decide to try a guy, gonnae try me first?' he goes."

"And you with the wean too!"

"A virgin birth, but, Martha! Get on with your practising, Kansas!" Varrie called as the child stopped dancing and looked around. "A virgin birth, it might as well have been, for all the money either of us got out of her father!"

"Then he goes... 'Right enough, babes? Are you gay? Tell me what you do, will you? Can't figure it out. How you wouldn't want a big strong guy like me!' says he, flexin' his muscles."

"Did he have muscles, Varrie?" Martha asked. "My Jimmy was well built as a young man."

A funny look came into Varrie's eyes. "I suppose I'd have to admit he did. Although the face spoiled it for me. But, seeing I'm gay anyway..."

Martha dropped her mop, and it splashed the newly dried bit of the floor. "Is that a fact? Well, I want you to know, Varrie, it won't spoil our friendship. I'll always be there for you. Not in any sexual way, of course. What is it youse do, anyway? I've never been able to figure it out either, Varrie. Oh, sorry, I shouldn't have asked that." She picked up her mop and started singing along to the Scottish tune on the radio. Which was, unfortunately for her, a version of the famous Scots comedian Jimmy Logan's old time hit, 'I Love a Lassie.'

Varrie stood it as long as she could, with a straight face. Then she took another look at Martha's wee dismal eyes, and burst out laughing, going over to hug her over the pinny, the plastic apron and the rubber gloves, to Martha's vague alarm. "Sorry, hen! Only kidding!" She resumed her story, after checking that Kansas was occupied. "Anyway, I paid his fare, plus a quid. Then

I got to thinking. In the interest of scientific research. Was he God's gift?"

Martha tried to look unshockable. "And was he, Varrie?"

Again that odd expression flitted across Varrie's face. She blew a few more smoke rings.

"Well, like Judy Garland's Minnie from Trinidad, he wasn't good, but he wasn't bad! But I think he was a wee bit put off, thinking I was gay. And I kept shouting out for Maggie at the psychological moment. I may have hurt his feelings!"

Varrie roared with laughter. Martha joined in with a snigger. Suddenly Varrie stopped.

"Hell, I'll have to rush to the loo! Stress incontinence. See when I laugh! Not be a minute!"

She picked up her fags, then felt in the pocket of her skirt and produced a white card.

"Gave me his business card, too!"

"Liam MacNee. Social Escort Services. No job too big, no job too small." Martha read aloud from the card, as Varrie lurched for the door, limping on her still squint heel.

"Oh God, I'm pure bursting!" Martha and Kansas heard her cry as she stumbled along the corridor towards the staff toilets.

"Auntie Martha! Mrs Dearie!"

"Yes, Kansas?" Martha looked over to where Kansas was standing, in the store room doorway, balanced on one leg, her face bright pink. "What is it, sweetheart?"

"Could you come over here quick? There's something awful dirty in here!"

"What is it, dear? A wee mousie's nest?"

"No, worser!"

"Is it sickness, pet?"

"No, worser!"

"What is it, dear? You can tell Auntie Martha."

"Oh, Auntie Martha, it looks a hell of a lot like shite!"

"Shush, Kansas, it'll be brown paint, hen. You know that!"

Kansas started to sob. "But maybe it is shite! It's pure stinky!"

Varrie re-appeared shortly afterwards, taking in the situation, holding her nose.

"I see the Phantom Bum has struck again! See that wee messer Rory! I thought he'd stopped since he's been away under the educational psychologist. I thought he had taken to paint. I could bloody murder him! C'mere Kansas." She hoisted the tear stained little girl onto her lap. "Come and recite your nice poem to us, darling."

Kansas jumped down, though, and took up her poetry reading stance, reciting bravely in her posh voice, with appropriate actions.

> "If I were a Maouse
> And I wanted a Haouse
> I think I would Chuse
> My new red Shuse
> Furry Edgings!
> Fur in Syde!
> What a Lovely place to Hyde!"

And she finished with fur against face actions.

Varrie managed to catch her and kiss her. "You're a pure credit, darling." she said.

But Kansas scrubbed the kiss off her face ferociously.

"So you are, dear. A pure credit to your Mammy!" Martha called, trailing a pail of sawdust across the floor.

"Want a hand with that bucket, Martha?"

"No, Varrie, it's okay! But see that manky wee bugger! I'd have him killed!"

She came out of the store room carrying a pail of soiled sawdust. Varrie and Kansas turned aside, putting their hands over their faces with exactly the same expression.

Varrie thought Martha looked shocked, and they'd better take a wee tea break. And for once Varrie made the tea and toast. Though she left the teabags floating in the sink.

Kansas was drawing on the blackboard with coloured chalks, a rainbow over a cat and a mouse, in huge assured lines. Her white jabot was covered in multi-coloured speckles when she scampered off, late for her highland dance class in the school assembly hall. But Varrie was too stressed to check her out and notice. Martha kept staring into the tea leaves at the bottom of her cup, where the tea bag had burst. The radio had worked its way back to a Country and Western station. The song being belted out was a favourite, about being loyal to your spouse. Suddenly the two women felt like crying.

"Pay day the morrow!" Varrie blurted out brightly.

"I know, Varrie, it's the only pay I'll get this week!"

"How is that? Big Jimmy laid off?"

"Lyin' off, more like!"

"That's not like your Jimmy! He was always a worker!"

"That's what I told them!"

"Energetic too. Wasn't he always out playin' darts and dominos?"

"He was never in, Varrie! Now he's never out!"

Martha's small face began to crumble, and Varrie dived in her skirt pocket for her usual remedy. "Smoke?" she offered hopefully.

"Why not?" Martha gave in, but had a job lighting up. Varrie had to steady her friend's hand, which held the match, with her own. "Thanks, hen." said Martha, putting the fag down.

"What happened, Martha?" Varrie scraped her stool nearer.

"Nothing, really! Jimmy just started sitting down a wee minute before he went to work. Then he's sitting half an hour. The next thing..." Martha's voice had started to slow down. "The next thing, he gets up early, makes his piece, puts on his working boots, and sits down again. When I came back from my work, he was still sitting there. I'd to take his big tacketty boots off for him." Martha picked up her cigarette and saw it had gone out.

"Couldn't have been feeling well, Martha."

"But next day he pulled himself together!"

"That was good, Martha!"

"Didn't last, but!" Martha lapsed into silence.

Varrie waited a bit, and then asked, "How was that, Martha?"

"Well, the lifts went off. He says, 'Martha, I'm no gonnae manage thae stairs.'"

"They still off?"

"They were back on for a bit, but it was no use. Never had his foot over the door from that day to this. Six weeks ago."

"Did your doctor give him those..."

"Tranquillisers? Yes."

"And those..."

"Anti-depressants too. Never did any good, but. I've got to shave him now. I even have to fill in his lottery ticket, the numbers he was so keen on, of all our birthdays. And I do his pools, and phone the Bookie for him."

"You must be pure demented!"

"Now the DSS says he's skiving. Wants to reduce his benefits."

"That's a dead liberty, so it is!"

"And Jimmy was always a good worker, just like us two, hen. Loved his joinery. And big planks of wood. Loved the smell." She got up in a dream and floated over to the sinks, her nose wrinkling in disgust. "Talk about smells, this sink's still putrid. Would you go and get more of that bleach from the jannie's store? Take an empty bleach bottle to put it in."

But Martha still couldn't get rid of the stink. She thought it must still be in the store room. No wonder, she thought, looking around. That pile of old clothes brought in for school plays and jumble sales was still cluttering up the space at the back. Martha herself had brought in some decent clothing that had begun to swamp her husband's now fragile frame. She'd never seen any sign of them since. She reckoned the better clothes were picked out quickly for wee private enterprise deals involving Paddy's Market down by the Clyde.

That latest daft art teacher was keen to hang onto the stinky leavings, to clothe her paper people, poor soul. She didn't have many real people in her life, and the kids gave her a terrible time of it. And there seemed to be some new rancid stuff there, that smelled really atrocious.

Martha gingerly poked in the topmost pile with a ripped parasol lying to hand. Instantly the odour became worse as the pyramid of bundles came tumbling down and flying open. At the top, an ancient long black coat threw wide its ragged arms. Embraced in them was the slight pathetic form of Rory, the boy they had each cursed, looking as if the curses had worked pretty well. A gash above the boy's blonde eyebrow was spurting blood, made, no doubt, by the metal edge of the large wall crucifix that Rory appeared to be clutching.

"Jesus, Mary and Joseph!" Martha cursed piously, "He's been trying to steal that rusty old crucifix!" She remembered that some kids did small lines in scrap metal. She could see where the shelves had been disturbed as he'd used them to climb up to it. It must have given way suddenly, and the metal edge had battered into the boy as it came off the wall. The piles of old clothing had concealed his injured body.

He was now exposed sprawling on top of them, blood still running down his pallid face, his stick-like limbs thrown out at strange angles. As Martha watched in shock, waiting for him to move, she saw that the little boy's gym shorts were stained and reeking. That was where the stink came from. Maybe Rory had something medical wrong with him. Maybe he suffered from fits.

And how in God's name had she not noticed him when she'd come in to clean out the room before? Was it just terrible luck that the junk had hidden him from her eyes when she could have helped him? She wondered if he was beyond all human help now. His frail little hand, when she nerved herself to touch it, seemed terribly cold.

From the wall phone in the store room, she phoned for police and ambulance. By mistake, she asked for the fire brigade too. And then she got Father Harry on the line, from the drama department where he was practising for his role in the school play. It was a good job, Martha thought, that Father Harry Xavier had a 'box of tricks' (as he called it) which he kept stashed in a locker he used in the art store room. It held the sacerdotal water and chrism for emergency Extreme Unction (the rite for the dying). She got the box out and took out the phials, smearing oil on the boy's brow.

Martha had heard that Extreme Unction still 'took' if there was any warmth left in the body. She convinced herself that there was, as she put her hand on his ash blonde hair, usually aggressively fashionably styled, now streaked with blood and dust and, she noticed, little feathers from somewhere.

Rory's blood had started to spurt again, mixing into the holy oil she had just put on. Surely that meant he was still hanging on, still clinging to life.

Martha started to recite the Confiteor. She knew it well. She was fond of Confession.

"I confess to Almighty God," she started, "and to you, my brothers and sisters."

She stopped suddenly, and instead, put her lined mouth carefully on Rory's pale lips, breathing in and sucking out air the way she had seen on the telly. Rory's throat swelled and a piece of chewing gum shot from his rigid gaping mouth through her thin feeble lips. She nearly panicked, but then recalled from the programme that pounding on the chest was really the thing to do. She pulled up the child's polo shirt, revealing his skinny chest, where the delicate ribs stood out. Calculating a spot just between the small rosy nipples, she clasped her hands together to make one fist, and set to as ferociously as she did when wielding her sink plunger. She hoped she wasn't damaging him even more, but was reassured as his breast bones seemed quite elastic and springy. Then the final instructions from the telly programme came back to her. What was it you were supposed to be singing at the same time, to give the right beat? Her mind went blank. Not 'Stand by your Man'! Wait, she had it! When the ambulance men got there, after having pushed their way through the rush hour crowds, Martha, now on her knees from exhaustion, was still pounding with both fists on the chest of the slender, groaning, boy. And still gasping out 'Stayin' Alive' in her funny croaky wee voice.

A cleaner, rushing in with the paramedics, not recognising Martha's out of tune rendition of the song, thought it was a hymn she was singing. So Martha was turned into a saint, one with miraculous powers. And a heroine into the bargain.

Wanderers

Up Roystonhill

There used to be an old wooden shed at the back of Royston cemetery, next to the gate house. It has only recently tumbled down totally, which it did quite quickly and suddenly when the down-and-outs who had squatted there were finally got rid of. At the time I'm telling you about, there had been a lot of interest in keeping up old graveyards, and a brief flurry of renovation had taken place, funded by European Union money. When that dried up, the derelicts crept back, the prostitutes who fancied it used the groves and marble monuments unharassed, and the little shy roe deer, who had reached it who knows how (it must have involved some dangerous planting of dainty hoofs on tarmac) had become a prized ecological feature of the place. The council gardeners ripped over the larger areas, but the nooks and hollows were left to the homeless. Some of them were not exactly homeless, and these vagabonds, and sometimes some troubadours, lived there from time to time, as a rest from the homes and Homes they despised.

The day after the latest wintry storm had swept over Mirkhill, the gods of the Dear Green Place had laughingly offered a bright sunny day, with balmy breezes that hardly dislodged the bronzed leaves ready to tumble from the beeches that encircled the recently restored bronze Royston Cemetery gates. The storm which had lashed the high rise (where Martha was now sleeping blissfully late) had made it tremble and sway. Now it was solid as a rock, not a Spanish tile on its lately added pitched roof in danger.

And the workman's hut where the unemployed now dossed down was more or less waterproof too. The Wanderers who gathered there had taken a pleasure in cadging or nicking the materials to keep it repaired. That day the group had left the comfort of their cabin rather early, as the sun stole through the paint-splashed sheets pinned up at the windows. I'll admit that the shed, full of people who habitually slept in their outer clothing, sometimes had a funny smell about it. But there were showers on offer in drop in centres in the district. And sometimes Father Harry actually let the tramps use his own Spartan shower room, to the resentment of his housekeeper. The paraffin stove, though, usually overpowered these human scents, as well as adding the thrill of danger to an otherwise almost too cosy environment for the brave or despairing souls who used it. Plenty of stone bothies used by healthy hikers have smelled much worse, I suspect, once the hiking boots have come off. The Wanderers – as I'll now go on calling them, since the other terms such as tramps and down-and-outs are so incorrect, and homeless, too, is a term coming into disrepute, and not well liked by the ladies and gentlemen of the road – the Wanderers never took their boots off, except occasionally for a sexual encounter, or for crossing the little burns that ran through the graveyard in the rainy season.

Like Bedouin (except without camels, or indeed any other form of transport), the Jaikies, as our Wanderers sometimes admitted themselves to be, were crouching in a half circle round a bright fire blazing against a boundary wall, with a smoked-up kettle merrily on the boil, well-balanced on a tripod. The four guys and one lady Wanderer were breaking their fast with tea, and then coffee, just like the nomads. But unlike the Bedouin of the explorer Thesiger's day, the Jaikies got up at dusk, not dawn, to get ready for the working, Wandering, day. Their journeys would take them round separate pubs and shebeens. Maybe a drop in centre for a shower and a meal if they were too rank to be accepted into the pubs.

They all had their own special ports of call, and all worked them separately and jealously. But at the moment it was share and share alike, with bits and pieces of food being brought out of various hiding places for the first meal of the day. Cold sausages were heated in foil in the outer ashes and toast making with special forks was a ritual that was valued in binding relationships. Sky was at that moment making a nice piece of toast for his special girlfriend Imelda.

The group of guys took a last leak behind some derelict gravestones, and waited with courtesy, in a discreet, comradely way, for Imelda to visit the little girls' room behind the big holly bush, where she was making heavy weather of unsnagging her heavy bulky clothing. Then Sky gave her a kiss and cuddle before releasing her to go her own way. That day she had decided to call in at the Convent of the Bleeding Heart, where in her innocent youth she had been a kitchen maid. She knew a shortcut across scrubland from the cemetery.

When she had gone, the guys indulged in a little rest and dreaming by the fire. The cemetery was perched on a hilly place overlooking Royston, and on such a clear day the city was spread out like Toy Town in front of them. Drug dealers were already jouking in and out closes, Sky noticed, where wee lassies were playing Ring a Ring a Roses. He noticed the rhyme and wondered if there was a poem in it. Or maybe he could include the phrase in his latest one, the one he had called 'Up Roystonhill'.

"Guys!" Sky cleared his throat.

His comrades looked a bit uneasy, and looked round them for an interruption. They had a good idea what was coming.

"Guys!" Sky began again. "Compadrillos! I was inspired to write a... I mean, to immortalise our little paradise on earth here."

Some of the Wanderers were on their feet, ready to wander off. Almost absentmindedly, Sky produced from his rucksack three bottles of Guinness. His mates sat down again. Rab, after glugging most of one of the bottles ungratefully started singing his party piece, 'Rosita, my sweet! Do you hear the drums beat?' It always went down well, especially the bit with the drums, which Tam and Toalie had got off to a fine art on some old tin pans. Sky joined in, gamely, too. But Millsie reckoned he had a kind of funny look on his face.

"Now!" said Millsie, sitting down again from where he had been acting out firing a rifle. He put his arm round Sky's shoulders. "What about that poem, Sky, the one about our camp? Come on, lads, fair doos! Silence for Sky. One singer, one song!"

"Well, if you really want to hear it." Sky suddenly leapt to his feet. "And what the hell, even if you don't! You'll like it well enough, when you do!"

Sky struck a heroic pose, one arm outstretched, grey bearded, in his slouch hat, with his lady's fur coat round his shoulders. On the hill's edge against the sunset, he looked dashing.

"I've called this one 'Up Roystonhill', and if you listen carefully, you may recognise a few names of my beloved compadres. No ladies in this poem. I hope Imelda won't mind. I'll write the dear thing another, in a different vein!" he leered around him, wolfishly.

"Keep to the point!" Tam complained. The other guys smirked. It was common knowledge that Tam was a bit sweet on Imelda himself.

"Certainly, certainly old chap, you're quite right." Sky acknowledged Tam's right to be grumpy, since he was crossed in love. "Shall I give you a tune on my fiddle instead? No?"

He took up his pose again, but then couldn't find his good copy of the poem he had just finished the day before, in Father Harry's little library. He started feverishly searching for it in his pockets, and his friends began to fidget and exchange looks. No wonder, they were all thinking. No wonder Sky got kicked out of his job at the University. No wonder his students had gone on the rampage and locked themselves in and him out. If he was always so bloody boring as this, no bloody wonder.

Then Sky found it in his fur coat, and they breathed a sigh of relief, as the Guinness did its work, and the dusky clouds floating up from the town made them all feel poetical. He began.

"Up Roystonhill
Up Roystonhill where the foxes cry
Rab Tam Toalie Millsie and Sky
Kings of the castle on the lookout
Where grey girners girn and blackbirds shout.
Where the vans ding dong and the magpies gab
Sky Tam and Toalie Millsie and Rab.
Drinking and dreaming in the half dark
As the lights come on and the wild dogs bark
As the night comes on and the hoolit kills
Sky Rab and Tam, Toalie and Mills."

Sky was amazed to be greeted by applause at the end. There was usually an embarrassed silence after he'd read, and then the gang would say things like 'very nice', and 'not bad at all'. But the applause was being led by a figure who had just appeared, like a ghost, from behind a marble monument. Father Harry, still wearing his black soutane from benediction, stepped forward to clasp Sky's not very dainty body in his chunky arms.

Sky reeled, almost losing his footing on the edge of the hillside. His old body was not what it had once been when he rowed for Oxford. He held on to the priest and hauled himself up.

"Well done, man!" Father Harry said, clapping him heavily on top of the ratty fur coat, "You're a real poet!" He turned and grinned at the rest of the gang, winking at them cheekily, "Whatever anyone may say to the contrary!"

The Wanderers had been almost crying, moved at the clever way Sky had worked in their names. They were actually a bit sorry for Imelda, who had been left out. But now, they burst out laughing again, their wide open mouths showing their stumpy teeth, and their raucous bellows making even the bold Father Harry flinch away from their rancid breaths.

Sky had sat down on the child's monument he considered his. The little stone body had been detached from the pedestal, and it was on this slab that Sky habitually sat. After his triumph, or in spite of his triumph, Sky was obviously shaking. Father Harry went and sat down with him, putting his arm round his shoulder, and murmuring in his hideous ear. Sky's breathing began to get more even, and the shaking stopped. It went very quiet.

The pale roe deer came nosing, smelling the air for titbits, or for quarrels. Just as one had decided to emerge from the shadows, Father Harry leapt in front of them, swinging his hands in the cold. The small buck leapt for cover.

"How about a hymn, to keep up our spirits?" he asked, "or will we have the spirits first?" He gallusly produced a silver hip flask from under his cassock, and passed it round the men, taking the last nip of whisky himself without wiping the rim of the flask.

Suddenly, he seemed to catch sight of someone coming up from the terrace below, and started to leap down the hill, with cries of welcome.

It was Varrie he was welcoming, Varrie not in her church helpers' plain clothes, but in her tartish leather gear. She was upset. She wanted to talk to him about young Rory's accident, and to be reassured by him that the boy was still alive. She hadn't managed to get in touch with him since the ambulance had taken the boy off, the priest going with him, reciting prayers over the little stretchered body, already fitted up with oxygen. But it seemed that Harry couldn't bear to talk about him yet. Maybe Rory had been a little favourite of his. He kept up a stream of comical patter, as he playfully dragged her up the hill, to where the gang of men sat shyly, embarrassed by the banter, and by Varrie's revealed comeliness

But Father Harry must have had it on his mind. Still keeping his arms round Varrie, he started up a hymn in his ringing tenor. A hymn, it turned out, more suited to the little children under the tussocky grass, with their toppled monuments listing the childish illnesses that had cut short their lives, than to the injured but breathing child. Harry's voice swelled with emotion at the repeated last line, as the gruffer, quavering voices of the Wanderers joined in the bit they remembered. 'Requiescant in Pace'. May they rest in peace.

Above them rang out the vibrant mezzo of Varrie's young woman's voice, till, still singing, and shaking off the priest's encircling arm, she walked off downhill, in the dusk, shivering and trying to close her skimpy black leather jacket. Not having got a serious word out of him.

Before she had followed the pathway to the bottom of the hill, the breeze brought her a change in the melody. They were back with 'Rosita', Father Harry's resonant voice drowning out all the others.

After Varrie had made it to the bus routes, the peace of the graveyard was again disturbed. The jackdaws held a committee meeting to complain. Sky was rehearsing Monty's Czardas, on his battered old fiddle, for his debut outside the Rex Picture Hall, sometime maybe. He'd quite a bit of practising to do first, he was quite prepared to admit.

But Sky's gnarled fingers in their fingerless mittens couldn't manage the double stopping. And when he had a go at Massenet's Meditation, the old fiddle just didn't have it in its poor cracked heart to respond to stopped harmonics.

Sky shook the fiddle in a rage, and then had to retune it.

This would never do for the Rex, which had such a genteel class of customers, and where they even got into queues for the first screenings of avant garde films. He'd try something a bit easier, maybe some jigs and reels.

Ah, that was better. He could just endlessly reprise, and let his mind wander. He'd set his compradrillos' toes atapping.

But when Sky left the lee of the hut, Royston cemetery was deserted. The long pathways and hillocks were as quiet as the grave. He snatched the old fiddle from under his chin, and stared down the braes despondently. Beyond the bronze gates, the traffic was beginning to growl and then to roar round Mirkshields interchange. The party-going, pub-going traffic, that zoomed off with lucky socialising people, and left other poor souls high and dry.

As home going Varrie Valentino was waiting for a number eleven bus, an old green Volkswagen scooted past the stop, then reversed back to her again. Her heart lifted as Father Harry leant to open the door for her, and she jumped in, feeling tearful and grateful. But for some modest reason, she managed to get into the back seat, not the one beside him. She wondered if she should tell him about her resolution to give up her life of profitless sin, and take to the straight and narrow. Somehow she was sure he'd guessed something of the kind, anyway, as she caught his concerned blue eyes seeking hers in the car mirror.

As they passed the Rex Picture House, that Sky had his eye on for career advancement, Father Harry sighed and turned towards her.

"Wouldn't it be lovely now, to nip into the cinema, and see a nice romantic film. Black and white would be nice. An old one like 'Brief Encounter'. I've seen that seven times. Think of the lovely warm dark. With Rachmaninov! Maybe a Cornetto in your hand!"

"I like 'Notting Hill'." Varrie said dreamily. "They still show that sometimes. Do you not think I look a wee bit like Julia Roberts, Father Harry?" She leaned over him, laughing.

"You wish!" said Harry, a bit cross about the back seat business. "I'm going to have to sling you out here, at the end of your street. I've a poor tired old donkey to go and visit at the Convent of the Bleeding Heart... And Mother Agnes hates to be kept waiting!"

Varrie didn't seem to get the joke. She didn't laugh, anyway. And instead of leaping out of the car, she questioned him again about Rory. She said she didn't like to phone, she'd been so nasty about him before. He told her wearily that the boy was still on the critical list.

Father Harry felt the blood drain from his face. He felt his lips go like putty, as if he could never again use them to speak. He actually laid his head against the steering wheel, sounding his horn by mistake. He jumped upright. What was the woman saying now?

Varrie was asking if Rory's mother in Cornton Vale had been informed. Harry had been unaware people knew about Rory's awful mother. It was one secret he was keen on keeping, Rory's parents. He gave Varrie a sideways look and then put on a pious air.

"And if he doesn't make it, Varrie, we've one more wee saint to pray to in Paradise!"

Harry was ashen pale as he drove off, wondering if Varrie Valentino was getting at him. He wondered if she knew more about himself than she was letting on.

Under the Bridges

On an impulse, Father Harry decided to go and visit Mother Agnes at the convent, to make up for the heartless joke he had made about her to Varrie. But Agnes was not at home when he called at the imposing Bleeding Heart Convent to inquire for her.

She had been summoned to the travellers' encampment under the bridges. The camp was a temporary one. Most of the travelling folk who sometimes stayed there had other domiciles too, elsewhere, nice mobile homes or real houses, and the camp was a makeshift affair of semi-derelict vans and trailers. There were even one or two traditional gypsy caravans, with the ponies to draw them tethered and exercised in the nearby fields. The men worked seasonally with local farmers, or excavated in the local scrapyards for spare parts to restore old motors. The women and girls made and dressed clothespeg dollies and sold them door to door, in their best gypsy-looking gear.

One of the young married gypsy women was in a wee spot of bother, as her mother had explained to Agnes. She had missed several ante natal appointments at the Prince's Infirmary, because she was terrified of hospitals. Now she had gone into premature labour, and the lassie was screaming at the mention of an ambulance.

As a matter of fact, it was no simple matter to summon an ambulance to the encampment under the old, now disused, railway bridges. The dispatchers checked and checked again, before sending large vans into the labyrinthine pathways that approached it, where they might well be ambushed by kids while attempting to reach the camp. The mercy vehicles were usually attended by police cars, which the itinerant workers thought were unnecessarily intrusive. The girl's mother had done the sensible thing and sent for Mother Agnes, with her black midwife's bag that she had brought with her to the convent. Surely the one place she would have no call to use a speculum or forceps.

But the traveller baby had birthed himself with gallus ease, and Mother Agnes had found that no intervention had been necessary. She had used a method of helping the mother that she had learned from an African Sister, in which the midwife supports the woman's body in a low chair, holding the swollen abdomen, and accommodating and providing a resistance to the play of muscles and the contractions during labour. She had been told it was much more secure and comfortable than being perched on top of a hard delivery trolley, with nothing to hold on to. In this case, the small baby shot out even faster than Agnes had expected, and was expertly fielded by his granny. Agnes clamped the umbilical cord, and then cut it, before she herself summoned an ambulance, while waiting for the afterbirth to be expelled.

Sister Mary of Perpetual Succour, who had driven Agnes in the convent jeep, turned out to be no succour at all, although the eldest of six siblings, and retired to wait in the jeep.

Father Harry, following Agnes to the camp, found himself scarily in the middle of a cavalcade of emergency vehicles, and, panicking, nearly drove off the road and down an embankment. When he pulled himself together, he turned, with some difficulty, and drove himself straight home to the priest's house next to Saint Jude's church, where his housekeeper, at least, was pleased to see him.

Later, when the ambulance had stretchered off mother and baby, Agnes had a distinct triumph. Dressed in her magnificent white ceremonial habit, just back from the dry cleaners, she made a spectacular effect as she sat enthroned in a tall chair that had been dragged to the campfire for her. The new baby's relatives sat on oil drums and stools. Mother Agnes had just been about to take part in a sung service for the recovery of little Rory, which Mother Benigna had organised. Luckily, as it happened, because her white habit was the most sterile garment of hers she could have possibly laid her hands on. Now, having discarded her plastic apron and gloves, she was quaffing a few tots of whisky, to the admiration of the assembled travellers, and showing off just a bit.

The baby's granny had read Agnes's hand, telling her she was a good woman, strong in spite of her creaky legs, but that unfortunately she would never have any children. The granny said she couldn't puzzle out whether Agnes had a sweetheart or not.

But Agnes turned the tables on her when she snatched up the gypsy's hand and then accurately enumerated her children. (Although she admitted she wasn't quite sure if there were four boys and two girls, or four girls and two boys. The crowd of relatives set up a roar at this, and said it was the latter.)

And as for sweethearts, Agnes bent over the scrawny palm. She saw one, two, three, and then the two others made five. And all before the granny was seventeen. The woman's husband looked relieved at this. He hadn't married her till she was all of eighteen.

Agnes explained she had seven older brothers and this it was that gave her the second sight. She could also read Tarot cards. But after shuffling them expertly for a bit, and when all that was coming out was the Hanged Man and the Jester upside down, she threw the pack down and resumed her palmistry. She hunched over the hand of the young father, as he knelt beside her. She looked into his eyes quizzically, after tracing his lines of Life and of Heart, and the mounts of Jupiter and Saturn and their interconnecting pathways.

"You've been up to some high jinks!" she accused him. "Some scam involving multiples of twenty. Either you're insider trading on the stock market, or you're selling Russian fags! Now which is it?"

Her audience murmured uncomfortably at this, and the young guy moved away. But Agnes called him back, to look at his hand again.

"You're afraid you're going to be found out. Not this time! But don't push your luck!"

There was a sudden rush to bring tea to Agnes, served in a beautiful bone china cup and saucer. She noted that it was made with loose tea leaves, not teabags. So she knew she was expected to do her stuff. She sipped her tea and swilled the small remainder round the bottom of the cup, so that the tea leaves made a pattern round the sides and base.

"I'd be on your guard!" she said. "It looks to me, as if a fox will be about the camp. Maybe after your pullets."

She swished the tea and that pattern dissolved and another replaced it. She frowned, her broad brow creasing into folds as it jutted over her narrowed eyes.

"And here's a funny old fella for you! A big wild man, like a wolf or a bear. Wait now, he has a fiddle under his chin." she looked up at her audience crowding round her, eyes bright with enquiry. "But I'd advise ye, one and all, not to dance to his tune!"

Sister Mary of Perpetual Succour ventured from the jeep where she had been waiting for Agnes, her mobile phone in her hand.

"For you, Mother Agnes." Sister Peppy (as Agnes called her) handed her the phone, which Agnes managed to get the right way up and listen to.

"Father Harry!" she said, surprised and pleased, and turned away to continue. "Yes, I'm feeling okay! You're going up to visit the boy? Well, let me know how he is. The Sisters are offering sung vespers for him tonight, the poor wee soul. He, and you too, Father Harry, will be in my prayers, through the night, when I keep my vigil."

She rang off, and, passing the phone back to Peppy, followed her to the jeep.

Peppy eagerly turned the key in the dashboard and the powerful engine roared.

But Peppy's ordeal was not over yet. The new born's grandfather came up to her window and handed in two plastic bags. One contained a splendid bottle of malt whisky. The other contained the remains of two rabbits, still in their fur, dead ears flopping out.

Sister Mary of Perpetual Succour's rosy cheeks turned pale as she manoeuvred the jeep out of the improvised barricade gates of the encampment. But Mother Mary Agnes of the Holy Child flushed with pleasure, even as she grued at the blood. And an extra bottle of whisky would be useful, when she asked Father Harry up for tea, as she boldly intended.

She wondered if she dared boast to him about guiding the feisty tinker baby into the world, or would he, a bachelor and anointed priest, find the details disgusting? Perhaps she should bite her lip, and try to play the lady, for a change.

Homecoming

Striding along Central Station platform, Marie Louise rose above the other passengers, not just by her superior height compared to the average homecoming Glaswegian leaping out of the evening ex London Express. Nor was it only her quite unfashionable and deeply incorrect trailing and voluminous mink coat. Her brown tresses were dressed in exactly the same style as most of the women who had managed to get to a decent hairdresser, either in Chelsea or Castlemilk. Her long hair was perhaps just a smidgen more glossy, and the cut a little more geometric. The make-up she wore was available in all the big name stores, and anyone could have tried their hand. Her Jimmy Choos were just one small cut above the other ladies' best footwear.

So what singled her out for the stares of the passers-by, some of whom rudely stopped passing, to stand and stare? Plenty of the hastening returning exiles were in stranger gear. Young guys in weather-beaten kilts and Doc Martens, without the excuse of a football match. Some odd-looking city gents in perfectly tailored suits trying to hide their bowler hats. Extended families of pickpockets returning from the metropolis with their spoils, hoping to launder the foreign currencies, who could have done with a bit of laundering themselves. Even a few Arabian princesses were returning to their palaces in Pollockshields, their Nubian slaves trammelled by designer carriers from the fashion shows' prêt-a-porter.

Something about her eyes, perhaps, when she was forced to raise them in navigating her way through the crowd. Yes, perhaps what singled Marie Louise out was the searing despair and longing in her hazel eyes, only intermittently glimpsed, mostly downcast, even while outmanoeuvring the evening gaggle to the taxi rank. That, and her effortless loping stride that carried her by a cunning shortcut to the front of the taxi queue. The stride of a thoroughbred race horse, a model, or even a ballet dancer. Although the few balletomanes in the long queue would have realised she was a little too tall for that.

The ordinary folk already waiting for a taxi waited on, uncomplaining, turning round to congratulate each other by grimaces, on having caught a glimpse of the lovely girl. Perhaps not a girl, just a little older than that. A film star playing a girl, she looked like. But she might have been in her middle to late twenties. She leaned in to give the address, heedless of the seething queue she had disturbed.

"Saint Jude's!" she commanded, in an unplaceable accent, "Mirkhill Road! Step on it!"

The driver didn't give her an argument, as he eased into the evening traffic, keeping her in sight in his mirror. But his pock-marked muscular neck reddened.

Fate was kind to him, and his cab was soon stuck behind a vehicle transporter which couldn't make the cut of the traffic lights at a difficult turn off. Only then did the driver feel it safe to turn round, rolling his china blue eyes in sympathy, running a rueful hand through the wiry blonde curls springing from his squarish head.

"I hope you're not in a rush madam!" he said, grinning impishly, flashing his capped teeth. "Liam!" he introduced himself, extending his fist, which his passenger did not appear to see. "Liam MacNee!" he indicated his identification tag swinging from the dashboard.

The great looking girl's eyes widened just a bit, but in annoyance, not interest, and she focussed her gaze on the transporter towering over them. Then she leaned forward.

"You can exit to your left now, and go first right, second left, all the way round the second roundabout, through the scheme, past the church, take the track under the bridges. Then double back onto the dual carriageway to some waste ground that you'll be able to drive over. Or do you want to let me drive?"

Liam did as he was told, but he was getting desperate, and that lent him courage. He didn't want to let this one get away. She looked like a friggin' millionairess, on the run, maybe looking for true love, from an attractive guy like himself. Or maybe even just a quick shag. He'd be up for that too, if the price was right. He squirmed uncomfortably in his driver's seat. Who was he bloody kidding, he reflected, a flush making the scars on his face stand out. This one would count as experience. Let stuck up Varrie laugh that one off! Christ, he was glad he'd applied a little undetectable cover up cream over his scars. Even if he'd been told that scars were manly. Guys really shouldn't have to bother.

He panicked, realising the journey would end soon, as he passed a garage tucked under one of the now derelict single track rail bridges that had carried freight to the now abandoned factories. Usually, he wouldn't have got out there for a pension. But he wasn't the guy to give up easily. Every minute he had for putting her under his spell was precious.

"Jesus Christ!" he grunted "Out of diesel!" And with no more explanation, turned into the space by the only diesel pump.

He filled his tank as suggestively as he could, standing legs apart and crotch stuck out, as he manipulated the nozzle in a macho way. He wanted her to get the benefit of his good build, and the elegance of his retro chic 'Wild Ones' gear. But when he glanced over, he saw, to his annoyance, that his glamorous passenger had rolled down her window and was playing peek-a-boo with a little traveller child who had come to the window. The young girl, looking like a Glasgow Boy 'Goose Girl', had a dolly made from a wooden clothes peg to sell.

Liam unsportingly hurried to pay for his petrol, hoping to spoil the kid's sale. But no-one in the tiny garage shop was in a hurry to serve him, and he had to rattle a long time on the plastic counter with a pound coin till a lady in a head scarf came to serve him. Changing his tack, Liam grabbed several large bunches of flowers, drooping their heads in the shame of the unchosen, from their basket. They perked up instantly, and looked quite pretty as he returned to his cab, and nonchalantly chucked them into the back beside Marie Louise.

"My apologies for the inconvenience, lady!" he said, softly and seriously.

He got just a flicker of interest and amusement from her cool eyes. The serious little girl was still negotiating a deal. Liam was nothing if not adaptable. He went round to her side of the cab, and taking a handful of silver, with difficulty, from the pocket of his tight jeans, he offered the young girl her choice. Thinking there must be some catch, the girl selected only a two pound coin and two single ones. Blowing kisses, Liam backed out of the garage and down the overgrown track. His cuteness must be having some effect, he thought, as they passed the traveller camp site under the scrubby trees. But when he dared to look round, the lady was playing with the silly dolly, undressing it and dressing it again, lost to the world.

Liam was by now simmering with resentment, but his business plan did not allow him to let resentment of a woman put him off. Rejoining the carriageway, he aggressively overtook several vehicles, including a police car, which, to his regret, didn't try to stop him. He recklessly thought he could have worked up quite a scene over that. But the cops, too, had been intimidated by Marie Louise's regal profile as she stared out of the window.

Across the waste ground, Saint Jude's School came into sight. Liam had recovered. "Front or back entry? Which do you prefer?" he asked cheekily.

"Janitors' entrance!" she rebuked him, in her teasingly neutral accent. "Round the side. Make for the football pitch, then turn fast right into the pend marked No Entry. Ignore the bollards, you'll manage to get past okay."

Liam just about managed it, only getting his left front wing scraped a little more than it had been before.

Marie Louise finally let Liam press the flowers on her, and for good measure, he dropped his card into them. He grabbed her travel bag to carry it for her, and she didn't struggle. A change had come over her the minute she put her long elegant foot on the first of the stone steps leading to the janitor's little house in the playground.

No longer in command, her eyes unfocussed, she did not avoid him as, taking advantage of standing on a higher step, Liam turned and, dropping a light kiss on her lips, whispered, "You are the most beautiful woman I have ever seen. I will be there if ever you should call me. And I would give my life to spend one hour alone with you!"

Marie Louise turned the icy fire of her amber eyes on him contemptuously.

"You and the ten million other punters!" she hissed.

Then MacNee witnessed an unaccountable scene.

The door from the janitor's house into the playground opened. Three uniformed jannies dashed out. One wrestled Marie Louise's travel bag off Liam. One took charge of the flowers. And the third, the oldest, ran towards the lady herself, as she leapt up the stairs towards him, and he was received into an embrace in the deepest folds of her mink coat.

Tears splashed down the woman's beautifully made up face, as she clung to the grizzled older guy, and cried her heart out.

"It's me, Mister Knightley!" she sobbed. "It's me! I've come back!"

Then, arms entwined round each other, the lady and head jannie entered the little house.

The one thing no-one had mentioned, not even Liam himself, was the fare. But that wasn't the only, or even the main reason that the cab driver followed the euphoric couple and their attendants over the asphalt, and behind the wrought iron railings to the municipal green painted front door of the wee house.

When he rang the bell, a thin lady with a new perm and a frilled apron answered it.

"How much?" she asked bluntly, opening the purse she held in her hand.

Liam MacNee craned his neck to see beyond her, where, through an open door, he could see figures gathered round an open coal fire. The Beauty was kneeling on the hearth rug, not crying now, but laughing, teasing a fat bulldog. And she seemed to be telling a funny story.

"Well, how much?" said the little lady. Probably the jannie's wife, he guessed correctly.

"It's not that!" Liam tried to explain, and at the sound of his voice, the party inside stopped talking, and put their hands to their mouths. Almost as if they'd been talking about him, even though that, of course, was improbable. However, Liam was delighted to see the girl jump up from the fire and come to the door. She snatched the purse from the janitor's wife, who looked thrilled at this sign of intimacy.

"There!" Marie Louise fished two twenty pound notes out of the purse. "That should cover all your expenses for the trip, the flowers too!"

In spite of himself Liam could not help pocketing them, and feeling dismissed, walked off.

"Oh, and another thing I forgot!" Liam nearly fainted with delight as she called after him.

He came back to stand beneath her in the doorway, and looked up hopefully.

A stinging smack on the face at first shocked then gratified him.

"And that's for your cheek in kissing me!"

And she turned on her heel and slammed the door on him, but not without giving him one swift flirtatious smile.

Liam reeled back to his cab, seeing stars in more ways than one. He was still sitting behind the wheel, stunned, when the older jannie came trotting out, and signalled to him. But Mr Knightley hadn't come to ask Liam in to join the party.

"Prince's Infirmary, son!" the man, ordered, "If it's not too much trouble!"

Reluctantly Liam pulled his handbrake off, and switched his intercom on again. Drifting across town, cars overtook him and cut him up at will.

For the first time in his life, Liam MacNee was in love.

In the bright living room, Mrs Knightley explained apologetically to Marie Louise that a wee boy, Rory something or other, a wee pest, had had a bad accident in the art room. The cleaner who had found him wanted to go and sit with him for a while. But Mr Knightley had decided he would go instead. He had made the cleaner agree not to report for duty next day, either. Just like him. 'Saints' like Martha Dearie could be hard work, though.

When Mr Knightley got back, he said he thought he hadn't done much good. The boy was in Intensive Care, under masses of tubes. With only a shoogly line of light showing he was still alive. And he'd just disturbed Father Harry, whom the nurses had forced to leave when he arrived. Thank goodness, driving home, he'd found one off- licence still open.

Marie Louise was sitting on the sofa beside Mrs Knightley showing her a little album of snapshots. Mostly of herself, a tall young model, holding a tiny flaxen haired baby, her cute little brother Robbie. And there were a few of an impish looking little boy in a toy car.

"Where can he be?" she said, running a bejewelled hand through her multi-toned mane. She sipped the brandy and Babycham the janitor had mixed for her. "I have this feeling something has happened to him. I feel like running mad in the street, calling his name!"

In the cosy little spare room of the janitor's house, Marie Louise at last settled down for the night. Although the room was as warm as her hosts could make it, Marie Louise, being used to overheated studios, felt a little chilled. She draped her mink coat over the pretty rose pink quilt, that Mrs Knightley had got out of moth balls for her. And just then Pinkie, the white bulldog, shoved his way in and bounded up onto her bed. Jamming himself against her feet, he began snuffling and snoring, his dog smell almost overpowering the perfume of the lilies and carnations from Liam's bouquet. Marie Louise's exquisitely arched eyebrows raised as she smiled to herself.

"What a bampot that young guy was!" she said to herself, lapsing into the vernacular of her childhood.

Then she remembered what she had come for, and leapt up, kicking Pinkie aside, to rummage in her many pocketed travel bag.

She set out a little simply framed photo of blonde baby Robbie, trying to take his first steps, and herself, a little plumper than now, leaning over holding his upheld hands. She, a teenaged glamour star. Sure of herself. Earning loadsa money down south. Brown curls tumbling over her smiling face. In a Mirkhill backgreen, on a welcomed visit. That was long before Mammy had gone into a jealous huff with her.

"Never mind, wee Robbie!" she whispered "Marielou is coming to get you, so she is! Your big sister will always take care of you, Robbie, Love."

High Hopes

Pie in the Sky

Martha had a marvellous view from her sixth floor window. She could see out over the whole district, and one of her favourite bits was the hilly Royston cemetery. You could see the plan it had had, from above. The lines of little gravestones for the common people, and the larger monuments for the more prosperous families. There was a statue of a horse, put up by the family of a little boy who had loved horses and had been killed while out riding. That always touched Martha's heart every time she glimpsed it.

Martha was still off work. But she had no intention of letting that go on too long, or she'd find herself in the same state as Jimmy, maybe. Not able to go back to her work. And she had got so used now to walking up and down stairs that her legs felt funny if she didn't. Also, she had to admit that Darren and Wayne were getting to her. Since she'd been made into a heroine for finally finding the injured Rory (whom she should have discovered much earlier, she thought) her twin sons had started trying to help around the house, and kept making her wee cups of tea, although they never got the milk and sugar right. And they'd stopped playing pool and hanging round the Bookies, and were staying in to watch the television with her. Thank God it was a school day, and then they had karate club.

And since she'd become a saint by administering Extreme Unction to the injured lad, Father Harry had started dropping in at unexpected times to congratulate her on her daring action of giving the last rites, which he said it was quite okay for a lay person to do if no priest could be found. As for why he himself had not been found for so long, on the fateful evening, he kept reproaching himself. Martha knew she had spoken to him on the phone, but he said he'd though it was a prank call. From some mammy jealous that he had just chosen Rory as altar boy instead of her own laddie.

The priest always enquired kindly after Jimmy, and would have liked to speak to him too, but Jimmy started panicking whenever he called, and pretended to be asleep, his head hidden under the covers. Martha was beginning to wonder if Jimmy had something on his conscience. Well, everybody had. She herself had been examining her conscience closely since the awful accident. She was feeling guilty about the way she had cursed Rory. You weren't supposed to do that. Martha thought that maybe everybody was hard-hearted and unkind at times, even if they thought they were just being funny.

Sometimes she'd caught some of the elite squad of cleaners, the Polishers, laughing at her. Polishers were paid extra for working the heavy machines. They were all fine big women, Martha admitted. But they didn't need to make out she was a weakling, just because she was smaller and skinnier. Martha had always wanted to be asked to work a polishing machine. But in all the years she'd worked at Saint Jude's, she'd never been asked. And the new improved machines were easier to work than the older models. She'd been given a shot of one of those, way back, and it had run away with her.

Everyone had laughed, she remembered. She wasn't sure, but she wondered if one of the big Polishing lassies had left it on at high on purpose. You had to build up the power gradually, she'd read in the instructions leaflets. Martha's little face grew wistful as she began to think of the extra money the Polishers made, and what she could do with it. She seemed to have less and less left in her purse by the end of the week.

One thing that had given Martha a bit of a shock since the first day she was off, was that she discovered that Jimmy was leading a kind of secret life, having visitors while she was at work. And funny visitors at that.

Martha heard the crank of the lift outside. It would start working, just when she needed a bit of isolation. God, she hoped it wasn't Jimmy's strange old visitor again, but she heard the shuffle of dragging feet coming along the corridor, and was not surprised when the doorbell gave its electric double peal. Sure enough a tramp-like creature stood wiping his desert boots on her door mat, balancing himself on a tattered old umbrella.

"Sky!" he introduced himself, as he always did, "Sky High, to give my full moniker, but you can call me Charles." Martha would have been shocked to find out the amount of effort Sky had put in to getting ready for his afternoon call on Jimmy. For a start, he had left his lady's fur coat stacked under bunks in the Wanderers' hut. He was as clean as Father Harry's shower could make him. He was wearing a 'new' hacking jacket the priest had got him, with a pair of stained flannels. On top of this, he had on a fireman's heavy jacket (which had been stripped off a firefighter called out to a hoax call by the kids, and then jettisoned). Sky was still a tall guy, in spite of his age, and in the jacket he seemed to take up the whole room.

Big Jimmy insisted on getting up and sitting in his dressing gown opposite his guest. For a while silence reigned, broken by only a few remarks. Sky said Father Harry had sent him to see how Jimmy was getting on. Jimmy said he was fine. Then it dawned on Martha that they wanted rid of her so they could talk in peace. So Martha went into the kitchen and sat down with her knitting, but she didn't turn the radio on, and she left both doors open. There seemed to be some discussion going on about a win on the horses. There was talk of lottery tickets.

A light clicked on in Martha's head. She'd been missing money from her purse for ages. She'd suspected the boys, but now it seemed to her that Jimmy was taking the cash. He was pilfering his own money. That was sad and pathetic, because they had always split their cash evenly. She had paid the bills, and Jimmy had paid the rent and bought treats.

Martha boldly walked into the tiny sitting room again. Tabby scuffled in, fur on end.

"Look here, Jimmy!" she said, going to the bureau where she kept the cash. "This money is yours as much as mine. What you want to do with your cash is up to you. Here it is, Jimmy."

"Suppose he wins, Mrs Dearie," Sky interrupted, "I've a feeling he might! He should keep his tickets in a safe place. Sometimes Jimmy is a bit confused where he hides them."

Martha put her arm round his Jimmy's bony shoulders. "We can all get confused, pet!"

Jimmy turned towards her, putting his claw-like hand on her arm.

"But it was all for you, hen," he explained, his voice deep and rasping, as if coming from the bottom of a well. "It was so you could live in comfort when I'm gone. Give up that job!"

It sounded as if he was surprised and indignant that she hadn't known that.

"But I don't like comfort!" Martha objected, only half joking, "And I like my wee job. Gets me out the house." She pushed against him affectionately. "And if you decide to turn a cartwheel out that window, I'll turn a cartwheel out after you!"

"Mr Sky!" Martha turned to confront their dumbstruck guest, "Could you fill me in?"

"Not Mr Sky, Mrs Dearie, madam!" he enunciated. "Sky is the soubriquet I received when I joined the band of Wanderers among whom I live. When I abandoned my family to hide my difficulties from them. Now they have abandoned me. And who can blame them? My name is Charles. Charlie the Toff my students called me. From Dublin by way of Oxford to Glasgow Uni. Not a drop of Scots blood in my body. I must have had a reason for choosing to live here once. But I still have a few pals. Jimmy here, not least."

Jimmy's jaws were working as he tried to say something, but Sky went on.

"Jimmy and I used to meet at the bookies when my giro gave me enough for a small wager now and then. When he couldn't make it down those cruel stairs, I agreed to put his little bets on for him. I hope I have not displeased you, madam. Perhaps we both got carried away. We began, the pair of us to think that we were in for a run of luck. Somebody has to win sometime! We've tried our luck in the lottery too. I'm sure we're bound to win!"

After a pause, in which all three looked for inspiration at the Dearie's brown floral carpet, Sky was off again. "As a matter of fact, Mrs Dearie!" he began with sudden emphasis.

But she interrupted him. "Martha, please, Charles!"

"Martha. It's beginning to prey on my mind. I can't quite remember which numbers I bet for Jimmy, and which for myself. And sometimes I forget to check his.

And I panic when all the numbers are announced on the pub telly. I'm afraid I may have lost a few tickets I bought for Jimmy. Although I have the numbers all written down in a little notebook. Among a few things Father Harry lets me keep in his library."

"Jimmy!" Sky stood in front of his pal. "What do you say? Will we stop all this gambling nonsense, and live like two respectable old gents?"

Jimmy nodded, wordlessly but eagerly, and Martha kissed him. She hadn't done that for ages. Maybe for years.

"You two lovebirds at it again?" a jolly voice called, as, in a sudden draught, Father Harry stood before them. Sky mustn't have shut the door behind him, Martha realised.

"Cup of tea, Father?" Martha rose to the challenge of the unexpected visit, going into a comedy routine she copied off TV. "Just a wee cup of tea? Sure ye will, ye will, ye will!"

At first Father Harry looked as if he hadn't caught on, had something else on his mind.

"I'm fine, really, Mrs Dearie!" catching on, he said in an Irish accent. "No really, I'm fine." Then, "No, Martha," he said in his ordinary Scots voice, "I've just come to see what this one is up to. In the name of all that's holy! What is that you've got on your back, Sky High, my good friend? I heard Mirkhead fire brigade are scouring the city for that jacket. Here, give it to me, and I'll return it. No fivers in it?"

He took the big waterproof coat off Sky, and went through the pockets, grinning. Then he followed Martha into the kitchen, where in spite of the badinage, she was still intent on making the priest a cup of tea. Tabby squeezed in just as Harry was shutting the door.

"Martha!" he went up to her, and put an arm round her aproned waist. "Listen, lovie! I've just taken the jacket off that idiot. It's stolen goods he's wearing, the rogue! But it strikes me, he'll be a bit chilly going home in that old tweed jacket. I don't suppose," he put his head close to Martha's ear so as not to embarrass the old guy. "I don't suppose you'd have a good garment of Jimmy's to lend him? Give. To give him. You wouldn't want it back after it had been in that putrid shed. Maybe I shouldn't have asked."

Martha's watery blue eyes filled with tears. What a gem Father Harry was! Always worried about the lowliest of his parishioners. Sometimes she puzzled over how he'd landed in a dump like Roystonhill, with his stout ruddy good looks, and that wonderful booming voice, not to mention his great sense of humour. He should have been at least a bishop already, Martha reckoned.

Martha opened Jimmy's wardrobe quietly. There was not much left in it, but she pulled out a big black working anorak. It still had the smell of wood and sawdust about it, and Martha sneakily buried her face in it as she was getting it out. But Father Harry quickly snatched it from her, rifling inner and outer pockets skilfully.

"Sorry Father, this is all I have left. I took some into Saint Jude's. I don't know what happened to them."

The priest made a little sign of the cross over her. "I know you did, you fine girl! And I'm sure they've all gone to a good home. They were best quality, my lass. Sure you have the man dressed like a king!"

Martha's heart was still fluttering with pleasure and with high hopes as the elevator containing Sky and Father Harry clanged downstairs. Wasn't it lucky, Martha thought, changing her tune, that the lift had started to work again. Maybe if Jimmy was up to seeing visitors once more, he was on the mend.

"Do you want a wee cup of tea, darlin'?" she asked, "And then we can maybe watch Countdown. Since I don't have to go out to work this afternoon. You were always so good at Countdown, so you were!"

Jimmy looked up and smiled, and set about clicking the remote.

After the programme, Martha saw Jimmy hungrily eyeing the paper Sky had left. It would be tomorrow's runners he would be after. Martha snatched it up and turned to the back page, annoying Tabby, who had settled on her knee for a nap.

Big Jimmy and the cat were equally surprised. Jimmy squeezed nearer Martha to see what she would pick. And Tabby jumped up on her shoulder to stare down too.

"Now let's think, Jimmy!" she said, "What do you fancy for the three thirty at Ayr? Will I pick? Will I pick a wee cuddy? A gee-gee? I'm beginning to feel lucky, so I am!"

Lucky Day

Martha kept that lucky feeling back at her stinky sink. Except it wasn't stinky any more. Talk about miracles! Martha was supposed to be a miracle worker now. But in her own way, Varrie had accomplished the near miraculous. In the few days Martha had been off work, she had got in 'Dyno Rod' for the sinks. Persuaded the two junior jannies to decant the putrid papier maché into the toxic waste tubs. And got round Father Harry to take away all the old clothes (to be sorted out in the church hall and the rubbish dumped, by special treaty with the waste disposal services).

From force of habit, Martha wielded her plunger, but the interest had gone, as the water purled away sweetly down the drains. Martha turned to the paint trays, usually overflowing, now quite neat. But Varrie, her hair scraped back, and wearing a starched white lab coat, elbowed her aside.

"Excuse me! My colour coded trays, I think." In a couple of minutes she had them slotted into their racks.

"But the smell?" Martha asked. "There was always some kinda funny smell."

Varrie pointed to plug in fresheners at power points.

"Not beyond the limit of scientific invention, sure it's not?"

Stunned, Martha looked round her. A few paintings, carefully mounted, decorated the walls. And the layers of ancient stuff that teachers had brought in as 'source material' (that is, fustie stuff they wanted rid of and the bin men wouldn't take) had vanished too.

"Got a guy in from Paddy's Market," Varrie explained. "Some of it was quite valuable. I got a bob or two for the old typewriters, and the bashed trombone fetched a pretty penny." She rubbed her hands in pretend greed. "Of course I owned up to it, hen! What do you take me for, Martha? A wee tea leaf?" But Varrie had her slender fingers crossed behind her back.

"So what did that poor soul, yon big art teacher, make of it. Did she go pure demented?"

"Her, nuh! Pregnant! At her age! The new one's a real gent, wears an artist's smock!"

"Gay, Varrie?"

"What a homophobic remark, but actually, yes."

"Do the weans no, like, kinda..."

"They don't seem to. He happens to have very good discipline. And he just gives them wee toaty bits of coloured paper and felt tipped pens."

Varrie started sorting out squares of coloured papers on the paper shelves, which had never been revealed before.

Martha looked round disconsolately. She would hardly have needed to come out on a cold damp night.

"Does his own dusting, I see." she remarked, running her finger disapprovingly along a pristine work surface. "Well, that just leaves..." her eyes lit up, "the mingin' windows!"

"Sorry, darlin'" Varrie made a warning face, "You'd be tangling with one of the biggest, meanest, unions in the region, if you laid a finger on a school window cleaner's window. With or without a shammy leather."

"Zattafact!" Martha gave up. "Got a fag? Want a cuppa?"

In the distance she could hear the Polishers revving up. Then them singing and polishing at full throttle.

Soon they'd be sending out for fish suppers. Polishers did that. Martha Dearie sighed, trying to blow a smoke ring at the ceiling, where the big figures still hung swaying in the draught from the open interconnecting doors. Inspiration dawned.

"Varrie!" Martha indicated the figures with her glowing cigarette. "What about them?"

"You up for that? Looks pretty dodgy to me!"

"You not game?" Martha's face screwed up with disappointment.

"Me not game? Bring it on! Hold my jacket!" said Varrie, shrugging off the lab coat.

"Now hold yer horses, Varrie! This requires careful thought."

Martha circled the swaying figures as an engineer would, about to blow up a dam.

Varrie waited for instructions.

"It seems to me," said Martha, "that this will require double ladders."

"Like two pairs of ladders? Or one double ladder?"

But there was only one pair of ladders they could get their hands on, without arousing suspicion and putting themselves at odds with Health and Safety. So Varrie had to stand on a stool on top of a table, with a Stanley knife in one outstretched hand, straining upwards, her bosom straining her skimpy top, reaching up, like a Ziegfeld Folly girl in an old movie.

On top of the ladders, Martha snipped the main cord, and as the figure swung sideways, Varrie lurched at it with the cutter, and slashed at the twine supporting the torso. The hollow figure sort of sighed and began to collapse, releasing its paper grip of the guitar.

"Shit!" shouted Varrie, as the guitar bounced off her head, but gamely kept her position. Another couple of slashing lunges, and the first giant had toppled.

You would have thought they would have learned from their first attempt, and everything would have gone smoothly. (It pains me to say this, but I think any two guys would have managed it better.) Anyway the second guitar fell on Martha's head so that meant the two ladies were equal. Now all they had to do was sort out the grungy rubbish.

They had just got the first giant dismembered and were starting on the other one, removing its scruffy garments, when Martha gave a long high pitched scream, maybe more like a long squeak.

"Would you look at this, Varrie? It's my Jimmy's good Crombie coat, that I thought would keep the cold out for some poor soul. She's turned it inside out, and slashed it for her stupid model. It's no use to man nor beast now!"

Absentmindedly, she started to go through the pockets. Nothing, till she tried the inner breast pocket (now, of course, the outer).

"Christ, another one of his lottery tickets, and it's from way back. May twenty-eight."

"Did you say May twenty-eight? They've been advertising for the holder of a ticket for May twenty-eight. I noticed because it's Kansas's birthdate. Check the numbers."

But Martha's feet had gone from under her. "Gonnae you check the numbers, hen?"

A kid in the evening computer class accessed the numbers for Varrie. She didn't even have to write them down. They were the Dearie birthday numbers, that Varrie knew well from when Martha used to check them at bingo.

Somehow Varrie managed to get back downstairs to the first floor. As she got to the art rooms she heard voices. It was Martha talking to someone, putting on a funny voice.

"Ye will, ye will, ye will!" she was saying, switching on the electric kettle. Varrie could see from her sparkling eyes that she was just waiting for an opportunity to tell

Father Harry about the lottery ticket. Somehow, Varrie didn't think it was a good idea to tell anyone.

Varrie switched off the kettle. "No time for tea, pet!" She shoved Martha out of the door. "Big Gemma has slipped on a waxed floor, and the Polishers are short handed. Big Josie said I've to send you along to interview for the job." Varrie had seen some big Polisher limping.

Martha turned pale. All ideas about lottery winnings going out of her head. This was what she'd waited for all these years. The chance of promotion at last.

"But, Varrie," she protested from force of habit. "Are you sure they'll want me? They'll maybe think I'm too skinny or something!"

"Well, you'll never know till you try. The woman that brought the kiddie back from the dead? Sure they'll want you!"

With an anguished look backwards, almost hoping to be stopped, Martha scuttled along the corridor, towards the Polishers' staff room, the scent of fish suppers tickling her nostrils as she went in.

"Yeah?" Big Josie looked up as she entered.

"I heard Big Gemma went and slipped?"

"Well, you heard wrong!"

The off duty cleaners were gathering around, ready for a wee laugh at Martha's expense.

"It was Big Magret, actually!"

Martha gasped but went on. "I heard you wanted to see me!" She finished bravely.

Big Josie looked round her underlings, seeking enlightenment. The women drew nearer.

But one of them suddenly recognised Martha. She whispered in her boss's ear.

"No! Is that a fact?" Big Josie murmured. "She saved a wee boy's life? Fought off a murderer? Her life's under threat till he's in jail? Is that right? Did ye?"

"Kind of," admitted Martha. She hadn't thought of an attacker before, but now she did, it was possible.

Why would the boy have been so well covered up? Why did he shite himself?

Martha reeled, feeling her poor brain was not up to facing the horrible problem.

But Big Josie was talking, breaking into her furious conjectures.

"Excuse me." said Martha. "What was that you said?"

"I said tomorrow." Big Josie repeated. "Will that be alright to start tomorrow?"

"And which will be my machine?" Martha was savvy enough to ask.

"Lorna! You give her your new machine. It'll be light enough for her to handle."

Martha was making her way back to the art classroom, Varrie was fielding Father Harry in more ways than one. Had something happened, he'd asked. Why was there so much junk lying around? Had they come across any more of Jimmy's good clothes that Martha had brought in? Somebody must have nicked them, he didn't like folk to do that. He was going to make inquiries. Someone would have something on their conscience.

"How about you, Varrie?" he asked roguishly. "Have you got anything on your wee conscience? Is it not about time you came back to me for Confession?"

He was chasing Varrie playfully round the teacher's desk as Martha came back in. She caught his last words about Confession.

"Oh, Father!" Martha cried. "I've got an awful sore hell of a thing on my conscience, so I have. Can I come to you for Confession some day next week?"

"Sure, sure." said Father Harry, giving up on Varrie. "It'll be a pleasure! But I hope I won't hear anything to bring a blush to my cheeks! Well, I gotta go! See you, girls!"

"Well?" Varrie asked, enquiring about the job.

But Martha had no need to respond. Because just then, the Polishers were returning from their extended break tending to Big Magret's ankle. As they pushed their huge surly unplugged machines to their next base, they took up the song they'd been singing before, with gusto.

"When you walk through a storm, hold your head up high!"

And some of those big women, Varrie acknowledged to Martha, with a shake of her head and an appreciative squinting of the eyes, had dead brilliant loud voices. The sound reached a ringing climax as the Polishers paused for a moment directly opposite the art rooms. Josie, the Gaffer, waved her hand majestically at Martha before her procession moved on.

"Well allow you, madam!" said Varrie. "Going to be a big Polishing woman tomorrow, are you, lady? Is that a pure fact, Martha?"

For one second, Varrie had forgotten the news she had to give Martha, about the ticket. When she remembered, she nearly pissed herself.

Page Three Girl

The medical room at Saint Jude's was where children used to be weighed and measured and examined for nits. These things were dealt with more sensitively now, and the room was mainly used for vaccinations and inoculations. Some of these 'jags' were just for girls. Why not for boys too, some of them wondered?

But the room had always served another purpose. It had been a kind of refuge for vulnerable kids. Plenty of small bullied boys had sheltered there, under the protection of the jannies, rereading the pile of ancient comics stowed there. (They were relics that were probably valuable by now.) And plenty of little girls, who despite the best efforts of film, booklet and video, hadn't been attending to health education lessons, kidding on with their pals. Or had been too disgusted to attend properly, and had then thought they were bleeding to death, had been put wise by passing dinner ladies. Many otherwise liberal teachers, in practice, still kept Talmudic taboos on menstruation.

And there were other subjects, too, that girls never liked to tell their teachers. And questions that pals had no answer for. Like when did a mammy 'having a few boyfriends over' turn into a sex orgy? What should a lassie do, when her bedroom was being used by paying punters? Would telling the parish priest do any good? And was she just stuck up because she didn't fancy joining in the fun?

Marie Louise, the glamorous model, had in her schoolgirl years had these problems. And had brought them to the jannies and Polishers and dinner ladies as she lay sobbing on the padded examination couch (the same one was still there) in the medical room. Wrapped in a blanket, and given wee cups of tea, and sometimes toast. With aspirin sent out for from the corner shop, not provided by supplies. The excuse she often gave being 'period pains'. But teachers who noted such things realised the girl's pains were not periodic but constant.

Sometimes, Marie Louise had not been in pain, but could not manage to concentrate on her lessons, when an all night 'party' had deprived her of sleep. When the janitors found her after playtime stuck in a corridor looking out of the window, unable to move, they would coax her to the medical room, and summon a dinner lady from scalding her cauldrons.

But these ancillary staff had no power of referral to higher authorities. And if they had, what then? If every little girl whose mammy was on the game had been the subject of a court order, the children's homes would have been full in a week. Mostly the powers on high only acted in cases of 'cruelty', and that was hard to define.

Marie Louise's Mammy was not considered cruel. She was a big tough woman who, along with her sisters, had been herself brought up to the 'oldest profession'. She was usually good natured, though handy with her fists, and never tried to coerce Marie Louise to follow in her footsteps. She looked at the girl in amused amazement sometimes when she came home from Mirkhead public lending library, her arms filled with books. Marie Louise had been the result of a brief encounter with a toff. What Renee, the mother, mockingly called 'The Carriage Trade'. How that virginal university professor had got himself into the Tartan Arms at closing time was a mystery to everyone. Some said he was researching the history of epidemics in Roystonhill graveyard, and had been chased into the pub by banshees. Renee always seemed to have some spare cash on her, after the wee lassie was born. Totally unlike her cousins, tall and straight and gawky as she grew up, the other kids called Marie Louise a big stookie.

Then, quite late in her adolescence, Marie Louise had sprouted a pair of breasts which rivalled any of the Page Three girls reigning at that time. Her breasts became a source of embarrassment to her. And her height increased even more, till she was towering over her companions, many of them from sturdy peasant stock. And she became suddenly pretty, too. Because of her mother's occupation, the big boys would not let her alone, and head janitor Knightley often had to rescue her from some lout's unwanted attentions.

Marie Louise was by no means a show off, and disguised herself as best she could with her school scarf, and was into the bargain a very pious girl. She was always in the chapel, making novenas for her mother's eventual salvation (when they would get a little cottage in the country and take in injured animals, she hoped.) All the same, it seemed like madness to her mother and her aunties in the trade, not to cash in on her valuable attributes.

About that time, the extra money dried up, and the rumour was that the posh guy had lost his job. Been sacked for spending too much time at Roystonhill, both in the graveyard and the Tartan Arms, at the foot of the ancient hilly plot.

So the female members of the clan got together and organised a portfolio of photographs, including, to the girl's humiliation, a few topless shots.

The agent the photographer sent them to in London required no second invitation to take the newcomer on his books. A bidding war ensued. Because not only was Marie Louise well endowed in the mammary department, with a totally natural unenhanced bosom, but she had a most beautiful face, too. Her modest downcast look made her seem like a Madonna. Joe Public was bound to find that titillating.

So Marie Louise allowed herself to be packaged in trendy gear, and sent down to London, where the picture editors discovered that not only was she the Real McCoy for a Page Three, but that her lovely nature made her so easy to work with, and her dislike of booze and drugs made her so punctual, that they booked her time and time again.

So Marie Louise made a mint of money, and some of it she sent back home to Royston. The flat on the Mirkhill scheme there, where Renee still plied her trade, became a wee palace, as they say. Sometimes Renee came down for a shopping spree, and a champagne breakfast with Marie Louise's pals and fellow models, and basked in reflected glory. Her daughter was now a celebrity known by her first names, simply as Marie Louise.

And Marie Louise got used at last, to having rich boyfriends, sometimes the same ones as the other models, which gave them something in common, and something to talk about. And it was nice having pals, and even hangers on that you looked after. But her lifestyle cost cash, there was no denying. Always looking gorgeous can be expensive. And models are supposed to take glamorous holidays, so the paparazzi can be employed by the editors to spy on them.

She had to give up some youthful dreams, of course. Photographers said that kids would ruin her tits, and anyway, the one guy she fancied, a picture editor, a quiet bloke and a family man already, she considered out of bounds. Although she might have got him. She could tell he couldn't help liking her. But the thought of his kiddies put her off. She knew what it was to be constantly yearning for an absent father. (She had been told that it would have cost her father his job to acknowledge her. So what? He'd lost that job anyway!)

She had resigned herself to never meeting her mysterious father only recently. She'd plucked up her courage and got in touch with the Salvation Army to trace him. And the young Salvation Army officer had admitted that her father did not wish to meet her. But she had dared to hint to her that he had come down in the world and had several addiction problems. But she wasn't allowed to give a contact address, or phone number. Marie Louise had left hers, though, and once found a garbled message on her machine, in a posh slightly Irish accent. The entire message had been taken up by a poem.

> *If God that is If God exists*
> *And takes it into his handsome Godhead*
> *To hand me some swift chance of final earthly bliss*
> *A father's kiss upon your sainted lips*
> *My benediction on your hallowed head*
> *I'd count the lonely missed and senseless decades*
> *The life in this dark wilderness I led*
> *My only daughter blessed*

There followed a list of numbers intoned slowly one by one, which sounded like a mobile phone number. But any time she dialled no-one picked up, and a statement brusquely said that a message would not be recorded. The origin of the phone call turned out to be a land line in a pub, and no-one there had ever heard of Charles Lavery.

Marie Louise's mother was no help. She was still angry over the money supply stopping, and Marie Louise had finally fallen out with her mother in an unlikely way. Renee had got pregnant, and opted for an abortion. Marie Louise sent her cash, to persuade her not to. And when the baby was born, she had set up a trust fund in his name, to be used only for his needs in childhood, and the rest to be put aside for his education. This had infuriated Renee, who had called her a snob and an ungrateful bitch. Not trusting her own mother to look after the cash. She vowed the girl would never see herself or the boy, her brother, again. And as a mere sister, it turned out she had no rights under Scottish law to access. Incredibly, Renee obtained a form of power of attorney over the trust fund, which Marie Louise maintained. And she had endowed the little lad with another name, which seemed to be permissible, too. And had taken him out of the boarding school his sister's funds had sent him to. Marie Louise had, however, been informed by the prison services, as the next of kin, that Renee was in custody for drug dealing. But they had not divulged what had happened to the boy.

So the very next morning, instead of schlepping into the studios of a famously randy photographer (who had long been waging a campaign of seduction), Marie Louise set her long foot on the step leading to the Pullman compartment of the London to Glasgow express.

And where better to start looking for her brother than back in Mirkhill? And where better than at Saint Jude's? And who better to stay with than the janitor and his wife, who had been the comfort of her childhood? They had always written to her, rejoicing in what they saw as her good fortune, and being thrilled when she modelled at important events, and even sometimes appeared on the telly.

So there she was, back at Saint Jude's. And even in the medical room, where she had lain on the hard couch so often. She was lying on it again, wrapped in her long mink. She had placed her large bouquet of flowers on the small table, in honour of the comfort she had received there. She had set a match to the fire that had been laid in the small grate, and as it flared and crackled, Marie Louise went to kneel down before it. She was feeding sheets of newspapers to the flames, carefully, one by one. They were the Page Threes of the Daily Globes delivered to the jannies. Her image, looking luscious by the sea (eyes cast down, holding a mass of wet tresses over her head, drops of spray outlining her nude breasts), grew transparent as it succumbed to the flames. The last one of her bundle. And the last one ever, she vowed.

Because Marie Louise had had another childhood dream. And this one she meant to fulfil. She had always wanted to become a nun, in one of the orders which still wore traditional nun's attire of tunic, guimpe, and wimple, preferably in brown or white. So she was going to take a trip to The Convent of the Bleeding Heart, and see if they would accept her. After all, Jesus had washed the feet of the penitent Magdalene. And the feet of the penitent Marie Louise would have been nicer to wash, she felt sure. Slender and elegant, with pearly square cut nails, she was well aware they were another of her most admired and photogenic assets.

The Visit

Convent of the Bleeding Heart

The Convent of the Bleeding Heart used to be called Saint Philomena's. But poor Saint Philomena had been debunked by a Vatican Council, and declared a non saint. And the Sisters who had devoted themselves to her were left high and dry, secluded in the picturesque hinterlands of Royston. Just beyond the defunct railways and factories. Past the waste lands that grew only coarse grasses. Lapped by the beginnings of arable land and small dairy farms. Out of the mainstream in other words, and relicts of the past.

Saint Philomena had always been a popular lady to a certain type of teenage girl, and the convent had never lacked entrants into the novitiate. The image of her in her tomb in the catacombs, her body miraculously preserved, and long golden hair still growing, had caught the imagination of many sad ladies. And the fact that she had preferred slaughter to the advances of a handsome Roman warrior, made each of them feel superior. The Sisters had had cards printed showing scenes from her life, and sold loads of these.

So the downgrading of Saint Philomena, along with Saint George and his dragon, came as rather a blow. Especially to Sister Philomena, who insisted on still making novenas (nine days of certain set prayers) to her namesake. Since Sister Philomena was getting old and a little bit wandered, Mother Benigna, the Mother Superior, wisely turned a blind eye.

But the sudden fate of Saint Philomena had been a wakeup call to the nuns, to get a bit more ahead of the game. And it brought a new lease of life to the convent. First, the new name had been decided on in conclave, with the youngest, silliest, novice's vote counting for as much as any of the learned Sisters, with three degrees, who sat at lecterns above her lowly pew. And they had got on very well with the name, attracting grants and gifts from sponsors worldwide for their charitable works. Americans, especially, seemed to be attracted to the name, and to the pictures posted on the newly devised website. Sister Mary of the Angels had set up the site with all the devices then available, with flicking pages, and cute pictures of the boy orphans in their care. And also the rescued animals that were looked after in the old stables. Sister Angel herself, as she was known, did a super daily blog which, as she was spectacularly pretty, was downloaded widely.

When they gave up their saint, the Sisters had bargained cannily with the Curia. And had been granted the right to revert to the historical nun's garb of a sweeping habit with stiffened gauze collar, and a mantle. Everyone in the House loved it, except for a few malcontents who, instead, insisted on wearing their usual Marks and Spencer's cardigans and skirts. This they were allowed to do, but they did not have half so many members of the public request to see them as the old-fashioned nuns. The convent had started retreats, where pious guild members could hide away for a few days of quiet to examine consciences, and give up the booze, perhaps. And the retreatants were beginning to ask if there was a special uniform they could wear to single them out from casual visitors (they said they'd be happy to pay more for this). And people were also eager to fast, the nuns found, when they did their opinion polls, and they would like to have some sort of physical punishment for their sins as well. But Mother Benigna drew the line at this. She thought it smacked of perversity, and that only a fully ordained religious should be allowed to wear an itchy hair shirt or scratchy scapula.

The Sisters of the Convent of the Bleeding Heart were lucky to own the mansion that they occupied, and to have an income in trust that paid the council charges, which were hefty and unfair, they thought, considering their charitable status. But local councils had begun referring problem boy orphans to them, and they always seemed to do brilliantly with them. And the capital expenditure on the conversion of the west wing to single rooms with en-suites could be put against taxable income till profits increased.

But the east wing, where the nuns themselves lived, had been left ungutted, and as basic as when the little doomed Marchioness had brought it to them as a dowry in the eighteenth century, and died almost immediately, before her wicked relatives could devise a way of snatching it back. The nuns held a vigil in her honour on the anniversary of her death. And some young nuns were sure they heard the rustle of the wings of the angels which were reputed to have swooped down, in full view, to carry the poor lady off to paradise. The vigil this year had been dedicated to supplication for the recovery of young Rory O'Donnell.

The anniversary had taken place only the night before, and the Sisters felt invigorated and uplifted by the experience. Gregorian chants and incense had always been a feature of the vigil, and lent the chapel mystery and magic. Even after just a few hours sleep, the nuns were flying around the convent on their duties, as if they had wings on their feet. Marie Louise, at that moment, was being driven at speed along the motorway towards the slip road that would take her along the Mirkyknowes road to the convent; the road she knew so well. Although she had never dared to approach the convent itself, as a schoolgirl. She would have chosen Philomena as her confirmation name, but her snidey form teacher had forbidden it. (The writing had already been on the wall for poor Saint Philomena.) She had chosen Aquinas instead, as an earnest of her academic ambitions. She had always fancied herself in a heavy unisex Glasgow University blazer, a garment which would have concealed her stupid bosom. It was not her fault that she had been sent off to be a topless model, and condemned to wear skimpy halter tops instead.

Liam was driving Marie Louise in his cab, which she had booked the night before. He was a bit disappointed that she had only wanted that service, and not a more intimate one in his new role as a self employed gigolo. And she had refused to sit in the cab with him too, and had her nose buried in some old fashioned prayer books she had found in the medical room at Saint Jude's.

An uneasy feeling began to creep over him.

"You're not thinking of..." he searched for the right word, "joining up?"

"Joining up?" she repeated icily. "Do you mean joining the Foreign Legion? Or the Marines? And if I did, what's it to you? Look, I'm paying you to drive! So just drive!"

Liam couldn't believe his rotten luck. One lassie gay, and the other going to become a nun. But he perked up again, thinking that Varrie had not really seemed all that gay. Maybe he was having an effect on her. Maybe he would begin to get to this big lassie too.

"See if you decide not to become a nun, gonnae..."

"Gonnae shurrup? Gonnae drive?" Marie Louise shocked Liam by dropping her stateless accent and reverting to Mirkhill dialect. Behind her polaroids and prayer book she smiled.

When Marie Louise jumped out at the massive front door, it was opened by Sister Philomena, who wasn't supposed to answer the door, but was so nosey she often did. She had some difficulty pulling the heavy door open wide enough. So instead of going round the back to wait, Liam jumped out and put his shoulder to the door gallantly. Sister Philomena seemed delighted to see him.

"Oh good, son! You've turned up! Well, better late than never. This way!"

She led him towards the basement, leaving Marie Louise standing in the hallway. She heard screams from the corridor, and a young rosy cheeked nun in old-fashioned brown garb, pulling a gangling boy by the jersey, passed through the hall, shouting at him as she did.

"Yes you will! Yes you will, Joseph! You made the mess! You will clear it up!"

But the boy had caught a glimpse of the glamorous visitor, and he pulled back, dragging the little nun back into the hall. She too noticed Marie Louise, and let go of the boy. They both stood there rooted to the ground. The boy was dumbfounded by Marie Louise's beauty and her big fur coat. His eyes went misty and he sighed. His long body appeared to go bendy. The little nun screamed, then collected herself, and ran off down the far corridor, knocked at a door, went in, and came out again dragging an elderly nun behind her. The older woman was still attaching the full sleeves to her white habit.

"White!" breathed Marie Louise. "Brilliant!"

Marie Louise had an uninterrupted view down the long corridor (which the young nun didn't seem to realise). She was making hour glass shapes with her hands, and pointing to Marie Louise. It was plain she had had a squint at page three of that day's Daily Globe.

"I'm Mother Benigna!" the elder nun floated up, and introduced herself sweetly. "I spoke to you on the phone. You wish to see round our convent. Are you a journalist?"

"Well, I'm connected with the newspaper industry." Marie Louise replied, blushing in spite of herself as the plump young nun doubled up with a fit of the giggles.

"You'll have to excuse Sister Mary of Perpetual Succour! She's not used to meeting the Press. But she'll show you around. Come on, Joseph!" Mother Benigna gestured to the tall child, and he trotted after her, meek as a lamb.

"Call me Sister Peppy! Everyone does!" the young nun said in a 'jolly hockey stick' voice. "Do you like our new habits? We only voted by the narrowest of margins not to wear black. I was all for those guimpes with the big sticky out wings, like the Sisters of Charity, but the stick in the muds banded against me, and I was outvoted. Coffee?"

Marie Louise followed her into the kitchen, where coffee was bubbling in a percolator. A short dumpy lady in a pinny, with a pudding bowl haircut, was rinsing dishes in the big square sink, although a gleaming new dishwasher stood idly by.

"This is Imelda." Peppy introduced her.

"Sister Imelda?" Marie Louise asked, smiling over at her.

The little lady looked panicky and shook her head violently.

"Not quite, although there's no reason why not. At the present Imelda is a Wanderer, and just comes in to help us out the odd day. Sugar? No, you wouldn't, I thought not."

"Are you short of staff?" Marie Louise asked.

"Not as short as we are of novices, to take over the chores like teaching and nursing."

"Oh, I would rather like that. I think it would be nice!"

"You must be mad! Did you see that Joseph? Butter wouldn't melt in his mouth when he's with Benigna. But you should see what he gets up to on the fly! You're surely not thinking of ... Do you think you have a late vocation? I know, it sounds like a gynaecological disease. But you wouldn't, would you. I wouldn't really recommend it to you. Think what you'd have to give up. The haircuts, the shopping, the guys!"

"But that's what I hate about my present life, Peppy! Especially the guys! Here you have orphans and injured animals. Oh, I've always dreamed of that!"

"They're not all exactly orphans. They're just in need of carers, and some of those stray rabbits can be vicious!" Peppy, with her round eyes and buck teeth, looked bunny-like herself.

"Would you like to visit the stables with me? I'm about to take a few snaps of Mother Agnes for our website. She's wonderful with the animals, you'll see, and a right laugh!"

Marie Louise was thrilled to see, at the convent outbuildings, just the kind of set up she'd always dreamed of. Injured animals crowding to receive titbits from Peppy and herself. Of Mother Agnes herself there was no sign, till Peppy found her mucking out the donkeys' stalls. Peppy took the opportunity to take a few quick snaps, and Marie Louise was tempted into producing her own state of the art camera she kept in her leather shoulder bag. The scene was like a Rembrandt, she thought, The brown habit against the shadowy stable, gleams of light picking out Mother Agnes's noble if craggy features.

"Look out for that good coat!" Mother Agnes shouted, as Marie Louise tried for a close up. "How many wee beasts gave up their life for that?"

Mother Agnes did not seem such a laugh, as she threw down her pitchfork noisily.

Marie Louise blushed under her glamorous make up. The minks had already given up their lives for it decades before. And it had been pressed upon her as a fee, when she had done a gig in Moscow, and the gangsters who had hired her hadn't wanted to pay her in cash. So why not use the coat? She had endured enough to get it, one way and another.

From the inner tack room, another fur-coated figure was peering out, pale and riveted by shyness, as he paused in the middle of wolfing down a cheese sandwich. He had a school jotter in his hand, from which he had been reading aloud, through his full mouth. Mother Agnes, respecting his modesty, forbore to introduce her tramp poet to the big rich lady.

Going outside, Mother Agnes was soon playing up to the camera in her usual way, and she waved them off with her wide shy grin, poetic against the farm background.

As Marie Louise and Peppy wiped their feet on the huge doormat at the front door of the mansion when they got back, Peppy decided to invite her to explore further.

"Have you time to see the kids' accommodation? Far better than ours. I hear rattling from the basement. I take it your driver has been roped into servicing the boiler. Why Philomena does that I really don't know. It's usually poor Father Harry she snaffles. He's such a decent soul. But we really should get rid of the whole kit and caboodle, and claim scrappage. Well, here we are! I'll show you this one because it's empty at the moment. The poor kid who was here has had a nasty accident. He's in the Prince's Infirmary. But what a mess he's left!"

The nun instantly started tidying up, shaking out the duvet, putting the tops back on rows of poster paints on shelves, and scooping up piles of photos that had fallen from a tin box.

Marie Louise stared round the room. Larger than most institutional rooms, but in spite of various attempts with rugs and posters to make it homely, nevertheless it had a pathetic air of serial occupancy. Her eye was caught by a toy train track on the floor. She bent to pick up a derailed toy train. So someone had bought the poor kid a train set, anyway.

And that's when Marie Louise saw it, the photo of herself as a girl, with pigtails, looking miserable, standing outside Saint Jude's. And then another of her, all glamorous now, and thrilled, with a tiny blonde baby in her arms. With a cry she fell on the snapshots, hungrily turning them over.

"Why, what on earth's the matter with you?" Peppy looked from the dog eared photo held up to her, to the face of the glamorous visitor.

"That's you!" Peppy gasped. "And do you know the wee boy, Rory? Rory O'Donnell? Look, I'm so sorry you're upset!"

"Robbie, he was called. And not O'Donnell. He was called Robbie Lavery!"

Marie Louise sprang up from the rose-coloured carpet.

"And what in God's name did you let happen to him, my poor wee brother?"

Sister Mary of Perpetual Succour didn't take offence, though. The kids had to go to school, and it was someone else's responsibility then.

"It was an accident at Saint Jude's. A head injury. I'm really very sorry!"

Summoned from the basement, Liam was wiping his sooty hands on a linen cloth. He didn't think he'd done the boiler any good. He wasn't brilliant with boilers. His talents lay elsewhere, he consoled himself. Sister Philomena followed him to the car.

"Gone to get parts, son?" she asked him. She turned to Sister Mary of Perpetual Succour. "They always seem to have to go and get parts, heating engineers nowadays."

Liam MacNee held the rear door open for Marie Louise, and she threw herself in, without giving him a backward glance.

"The Prince's Infirmary!" she ordered.

Peppy came up to the car, and pressed some objects into her hand. Some medals, a little brooch and some cards, all with the image of a pretty blonde child on them.

"Saint Philomena's artefacts!" Peppy explained. "You might think they're just rubbish, but some people swear by them, who've had sick kids. Sometimes they can be a comfort!"

As the cab sped off, Marie Louise clutched the medals in her hand so tightly that she scratched her fingers on a rough edge, and bled over her hanky.

Visiting Hour

Liam MacNee was forced to wait in the car park at the Infirmary. Marie Louise left him in charge of her mink coat, and dashed through the main visitors' entrance in her slim black dress. She didn't want the coat, knowing well the blasts of hot stuffy air that would greet her in the hospital. She still clutched the medals she didn't at all believe in.

She wasn't quite sure how to get to Intensive Care. But one casual polite enquiry to a young medic rushing off for his lunch was enough to make him stop in his tracks and lead her gently and tenderly to the very threshold of that terrifyingly quiet and ordered place.

It happened to be visiting hour, but he managed to detour the streams of visitors rushing to be first in the wards as if it was some kind of competition.

"Thank you!" Marie Louise turned to him in gratitude and dismissal.

The very young man went on his way with his now soggy brown paper bag of salad baguettes. (He'd been trying to lose weight, and now he wished he'd tried harder before.)

But it wasn't so easy to be admitted to visit a patient in Intensive Care. On the corridor outside she had to give proof of her identity, which, even when she did, did not help much. The boy she was enquiring for was named Robbie Lavery. The young patient was labelled Rory O'Donnell. A bustling dour Sister told her she'd have to take it up with the Almoner. The Sister was the exception that proved the rule of Marie Louise's universal attractiveness. She confronted the Beauty with an almost sneering officiousness.

But seated outside the ward was a dapper young man in a pin stripe suit, striped shirt and red braces. A detective, he said. He spoke quietly. He believed Rory was the lady's brother, he told the nurse. His research had shown he had an older sister. He would himself vouch for her.

Tut-tutting, the nurse swept aside curtains and screens to admit Marie Louise to the bay where the little boy was stretched out, looking tiny in the adult sized bed. Under the oxygen mask his small face was waxy, like a statue of an angel, his blonde hair gleaming against the pillow like a halo. Marie Louise sat down on the chair beside the bed, nearly passing out with the heat and the emotion.

She took the little boy's hand in hers.

"Robbie! Robbie!" she said. "Can you hear me, darling?"

Because it was certainly Robbie in the bed; although she hadn't been able to see him for years, she recognised his narrow face and delicate features right away. Not at all like their mother, or even like herself. He must take after their mysterious father.

Robbie - Rory twitched as she stroked his slim hand, and his pale eyelids fluttered under their long golden lashes. The lights on his monitors began to move erratically, making the computerised bay seem even more like a space station.

His sister hung over his bed, feasting her eyes on his face. Stroking his cheek. Murmuring to him softly. As if she had just come into his bedroom at home to waken him for breakfast, and he was playing a game with her, pretending to be still asleep.

"Come on. sleepy head!" she cooed. "Time to waken up!"

Amazingly, the boy's eyelids fluttered and his eyes opened. He was struggling hard to form words. Hardly any sounds could be heard from underneath the transparent mask, but Marie Louise knew what the words were he was repeating.

"Marielou! Marielou!"

His pale lips relaxed as his eyelids began to close again, just after his eyeballs rolled back in his head, as he relapsed into unconsciousness.

As she sat on beside his motionless slight figure, Marie Louise looked round the bay that housed him. Someone had pinned up a few cards so you could read the messages. She saw one was from a person called Varrie. And a few, she saw, were signed 'Father Harry'. The parish priest that was, she knew. How sweet of him. They were all depicting bears. Various kinds of fluffy bears. Not what you'd send to an eleven year old boy, really.

The grumpy ward Sister appeared in the bay, pointing primly to her watch, and Marie Louise got up reluctantly to leave. Although she would not be hurried out, and bent to kiss the boy's damp blonde curls before she left.

The young detective seemed to have been waiting for her. He wondered if he might ask her a few questions there and then. He didn't want to leave his post outside the ward, he said, in case any other visitors for the young boy turned up. He said he suspected the boy's injuries might not have been accidental. He asked if she was feeling alright, then, because she had slumped down onto a plastic chair. She was ashen pale and swaying.

The young man chafed her icy hands in his, as she closed her eyes, shivering now.

Marie Louise's large hazel eyes opened again, but she left her hand where it was, in his, as she looked up at him enquiringly.

"You mean he was attacked?" she asked.

"I only suspect that," corrected the detective. "There is not much evidence yet."

He had a nice face, a little squint, with clever grey eyes and a sympathetic expression.

What he meant was that some bastard had done that to Rory. She'd find out who. Then she'd kill him. How to find out? She realised the Detective had pressed a card into her hand.

"Detective Constable Frank Childers" it said, "Mirkshields Police Station, Mirkhill."

"That's handy!" she said. "I'm staying at Saint Jude's, in Mirkhill, with my friend the janitor, Mr Knightley. You can contact me there any time."

Detective Childers took notes as to the complicated family history of her brother. He said he'd already dug something of it up, and then he apologised for his use of words. When a burly police sergeant turned up to relieve him of his supervising duty, he asked Marie Louise if she'd like a coffee in the cafeteria downstairs, and she said she would.

Frank Childers interceded for her with the ward Sister, who had just finished tenderly giving the child a blanket bath, and arranging his thin limbs comfortably beneath the sheets.

So Marie Louise was allowed one more peek before she left, and she thought her brother was looking better. His complexion was a rosier colour, and he seemed to her to be sleeping more easily. She smiled at the young cop as she came out, and took his offered arm as he guided her to the lift. He really was very nice, she thought. And what was that aftershave he was wearing? It reminded her of something.

A holiday she'd had in Rome, it came to her, as she was crushed against him in the lift.

"Will Mrs Childers not worry if you're late?" she asked, when they were settled with basic coffees in the hospital cafeteria.

"Oh, no!" Frank answered, "My mother is used to me being late for meals. Although she's sure I'll give myself a stomach ulcer."

So he still lived with his Mum. Incredible, but nice, in a way.

It looked as if Detective Constable Childers might well give himself a stomach ulcer, Marie Louise thought. He began to fidget after barely tasting his coffee and bun.

"I think, if you'll excuse me," he said standing up "I'll just nip up to the ward again, on the off chance of the boy saying a few words. The staff said he does sometimes."

Marie Louise stood up too, to shake hands in farewell. A little spark of electricity leapt between their two hands, his warm and hers cold, which made them smile. The lady thought that he was perhaps not quite tall enough to suit her style, being so tall herself. Then she couldn't believe she'd had that thought. When the man was so dedicated, obviously, to the welfare of her brother. She put her hand out to him again.

"Thank you!" she said, "from the bottom of my heart!"

Frank looked over his shoulder at her, with one of his sweet off centre smiles.

"It would be a great pleasure to help you in any way, madam!" he said, in the act of leaving, "Apart from it being my bounden duty to find out the truth!"

It was lucky for Liam MacNee that he spotted Marie Louise entering the car park before she picked out the cab parked half way down the hill. He had felt a bit chilly as he waited, and had covered himself with her fur coat, sniffing voluptuously the perfume that impregnated it. A famous, almost hackneyed, Chanel, which she had transmuted by her personal alchemy to a heavenly aphrodisiac. (As far as Liam was concerned.)

Liam flung the coat over the back seat, and jumped out of the cab to wave, and hold the door open for his 'Millionairess'.

As she lay back in the corner of the cab, Marie Louise closed her eyes, to avoid Liam's conversation, and to let her mind sweep over ideas for finding her brother's attacker.

She would go back to the Convent of the Bleeding Heart.

This was quite insightful of Marie Louise. There were plenty of secrets there. But had her psychic powers been greater, she would not have left without the letters and little notes she had glimpsed in the boy's school satchel. And in a certain tin box there were family papers that Renee had entrusted to her son's keeping when she was going on trial for all the funny business she had been up to, with drugs and money laundering...

Marie Louise had glanced at the diaries and letters but had not noticed anything amiss. For all her experience of the world, she had a very innocent mind. And, of course, Reverend Mother Benigna did not approve of anyone going through a child's private papers. Sister Mary of Perpetual Succour had had to sneak the stuff out of his room to have another look at it, which she did in her cell, when she should have been saying her Daily Office.

Liam, driving disconsolately, felt fed up at the treatment he had got from Marie Louise, treating him like any other cab driver, although he played every trick in his book to charm her. He should really stick with Varrie. She needed him. Marie Louise wasn't interested. Then he caught sight of the sweet face in his mirror, her lovely downcast eyes shadowed.

"Tell that to my heart!" he said, as his pulses raced again, and he swerved erratically onto busy Mirkshields Road.

Back at the space age bay of Intensive Care at the Prince's Infirmary, it looked as young Rory was taking a turn for the better. The busy Sister went to tell the cops who were seated outside. The one in the suit had a bunch of hospital bought flowers with him.

"I'm sorry!" the nurse said. "Flowers aren't allowed in Intensive care!"

"Yes, I know that, Sister." the man replied. "These are for you. To thank you for all the help you've given us, in carrying out our investigation."

"What a guy!" the Sister sighed, as she put them in water in the staff room.

In Liam's cab, Marie Louise was dreaming now. Not of becoming a nun. Both her conscious and unconscious mind had given up on that pipe dream. She was dreaming of a little home by the seaside somewhere, for her and her brother, where he could run in and out to the beach to play. Robbie had always loved the seaside. When he recovered.

She woke with a start, as Liam pulled up outside the janitor's house at Saint Jude's, and remembered her dream. When Robbie recovered. If Robbie recovered.

True Confessions

Varrie Valentino was making the most of having her house to herself. She put on a droopy track suit, wiped her elaborate make-up off with cream, and lay down on her second hand sagging sofa to watch her large plasma screen telly. (One of her few luxuries, but it counted in the eyes of Kansas, and of her daughter's telly-mad pals.)

Dakota's daddy had taken Kansas with his family to the ceilidhe at Saint Jude's, where line dancing was on offer. Which was really, really nice of him, Varrie thought, although she was not included in the invitation. Dakota's mummy, jealous bitch, had not wanted Varrie with them. Just because all the guys would have got Varrie up to dance.

Still, it was lovely to be alone. She poured a glass of Merlot and switched on the new TV (which was responsible for a lot of her problems with Kevin, the Tallyman). So she might as well watch the bloody thing, though as usual, among the nine hundred and ninety nine channels there wasn't a single one worth watching.

Varrie switched off the television and instantly heard loud hammering at the front door. She rushed to answer the knocking, thinking it might be Dakota's daddy bringing Kansas back early. Sometimes Kansas got shy and upset, out with other families, and demanded to be taken home. And she could make a racket like that demanding entry. But when she took off the chain and twisted the locks open, Varrie was relieved to see it was Father Harry lounging there against the door jamb, pounding one handed with his mighty fist.

"Where the hell's the fire?" was the family joke that sprang to her lips. Then, "Oh, it's only you, Father," she said, throwing the door open for him to follow her inside. She noticed that he was in mufti, not clerical dress. He wore that to go drinking with a group of old pals, former pupils of Saint Ignatius, the posh Catholic school he had attended. He made a point of not wearing his dog collar on these occasions. Not to scandalise the parish by his wild drinking and womanising, he used to say, keeping his face straight.

And she did detect some whisky fumes on his breath, as he gave her a hurried peck on the cheek, and produced a Co-op bunch of flowers from behind his back.

"Pax?" he offered. "I think somehow I offended you last time we met, mentioning about Confessions. Please accept my apologies. I know the busy life you have, a girl all on her own bringing up a child. The Church has compassion, doesn't expect you to be dancing around Saint Jude's at all hours. Like those Holy Marys at the ceilidhe tonight."

"Not fancy it yourself, Father?" Varrie enquired, to change the subject, and to keep her end up. She wasn't sure she had forgiven him yet. "Not into line dancing?"

"I leave that to my curates. Young Father Tiziano is brilliant at it. He has the cowboy hat and the chaps and everything! Fancy a cup of tea?" he suddenly added, throwing off his raincoat, and dashing into the kitchen. "God, I'd murder a cup of tea, hot and sweet!"

You couldn't really stay mad at Father Harry for long, Varrie thought, when he came back, after an incredibly short time, with a beautifully set tea tray, using all her best things, the ones she hardly ever used, designer teapot and cake-stand and all.

Varrie had a moment of panic about the teapot. She had put Martha's lottery ticket in the good teapot, as a hiding place. She relaxed as she recalled she had fished it out and stuck it down the new under-wired bra she was breaking in at home. Harry had brought the best Co-op cakes money could buy. Varrie couldn't help smiling, as he poured out her tea, the way he knew she liked it, and put her favourite cake, a chocolate éclair, on her plate. He really did know so much about her, the china in her cupboards as well as the peccadilloes she told him at Confession. She hadn't yet put a strain on their relationship by admitting to the real horrors of her life as a part-time, slightly upmarket, tart. Since she didn't enjoy these encounters (who would?), she didn't see why she should be punished for them.

Father Harry himself stuffed his face in silence, washing down a couple of his own cakes with cups of the stewed tea he kept refilling from the large teapot.

"That's better!" he at last said, lying back on the sofa, his face suddenly looking flushed. Then he raised himself. "I could do you a nice quick Confession now, absolution absolutely guaranteed, no questions asked! I can hear it just as well in your home as in a church! Down, down you get on your knees like a true penitent." he said, pushing her off the sofa and down onto the floor, between his own knees. He adopted the pose for hearing Confessions, one big knuckled hand in front of his face, which was turned away.

Varrie saw, with exasperation and embarrassment, that he was serious. She knew people sometimes confessed to priests in open sight, not in the usual darkened booths. Sick people did, or when there was a rush on to perform Easter Duties of soul searching, and the booths were all occupied. But Varrie was not one of those brave souls. And Father Harry wouldn't let her off, even when she wouldn't say how long it was from her last Confession.

"And what have you and your wee pal Martha been getting up to? Not making money from the art department rubbish, to make a nice little nest egg for your business ventures? Fancy yourselves as entrepreuneuses, I hear. Some valuable stuff, I wouldn't be surprised, among that, you know. Did you turn anything up? Never mind", he said, going on, "I'll give you a general absolution anyway. Now make a sincere purpose of amendment!"

"Ego te absolvo..." his voice began to drone in her ears; she was feeling quite spacey.

"And now if you were to die suddenly, sure, you'd go straight to heaven!"

"And if you died now, Father, where would you go?"

"Ah, now, wouldn't you like to know?"

His expression changed suddenly, from his usually bluff vague good humour. It became concentrated, twisted, and malicious. Like a wicked child determined to do some mischief. He moved his tongue around inside his fleshy cheek.

"C'mere." He pulled her up onto his lap. She was as powerless as a rag doll.

But then his face changed again, sentimental and bleary eyed.

"Sure, I remember you as a wee mite. Your first Confession. You in your good school uniform. Butter wouldn't have melted in your sweet little mouth."

He pulled her head down to him, and kissed her longingly, ardently.

She struggled to pull away from him. He grabbed the back of her head and, pulling at her hair, jerked her head backwards, kissing her again, coarsely and slobberingly this time. His face became livid, and he ripped down the new bra to maul her breasts brusquely.

"And don't think I don't know what kind of a creature you've turned into now."

In a second he was out of his jacket and had shrugged off the trousers. Pulling down her track suit pants, horrifically quickly he entered her, clumsily and savagely. He moaned and groaned in satisfaction for a few seconds before realising she was screaming for help. Then he clamped his broad palm over her mouth. She bit one of his stubby fingers, and his groans became a shout. But still he kept engaged with her, plunging fanatically.

"You bitch!" he shouted, as he climaxed. "You bitch! You were asking for it!"

Afterwards, he still lay on top of her. Incredibly, becoming sentimental again, kissing her softly all over her face.

"You won't tell on me, darlin', will you? You're not the kind of a girl to kiss and tell? I'd be finished if you did!" He stood up, struggling into his good corduroys, pulling them over his heavily muscled, wiry hair covered legs. Zipping his cords. Tucking in his checked shirt with what appeared to be satisfaction. Varrie began to realise he considered himself a real stud, as well as some kind of a film star. Oddly, her numbed mouth moved in a sardonic smile.

Misinterpreting it, bizarrely, Father Harry went into his old comedy routine.

"Sure, I'd have to jump off Erskine Bridge. And I hear it's hard to target the water. I'd be more likely to hit a parked car, and that wouldn't be nice!"

"See me to the door, love!" Staggering a little, he leaned heavily on her shoulder.

She guided him to the door, but when they got there, he took her in his arms again.

"I'm sorry, darling." he nuzzled into her neck. "I never meant it to be like this. But, you see, sometimes we men just can't help ourselves. And we priests, however holy we try to be, sometimes our passions are too much for us. But I wish it had been nicer for you. You're special to me, precious. I've loved you from the minute I saw you in your wee First Communion dress, like a little bride, you were. You'll always be that wee lassie to me."

"Would you be my wee sweetheart? Give up your other boyfriends. I'll pay you well when I come into money. It won't be long now." As she still struggled he grasped her more tightly. "You'll like me well enough when I've loads of money! Sure you will, darling? If I won the lottery it would be a different story, then. But you'll not clype anyway, will you? Who'd believe your word against mine? They'd say it was wishful thinking!"

She thought he had sobered up enough to leave, but he hung back again. And again his coarse jocularity shockingly took over. He pressed her against the half open door.

"I hope you won't hold this against me!" he muttered gruffly, pushing himself into her so she felt his retumescent penis through his clothes. He began to grapple with her again, trying to push her back inside, as a footstep was heard on the stairway.

Varrie struggled in the opposite direction, her lips sealed, not wanting to waste her breath. She suddenly realised how stupid this attitude was, and let out a piercing scream.

The person lightly skipping up the stairs was Liam, returning merely to pick up his coat. He had more or less given up on Varrie, since meeting the Millionairess. But a sudden rage of his senses overpowered him as he took in the situation. His pock-marked face became scarlet, and he lunged at the priest and pulled him off Varrie. He punched the priest full in the face, sending him spinning backwards into the house again. Regaining his feet, Father Harry made no attempt to retaliate, but rushed for the door, and made it to the landing.

Varrie leapt into Liam's arms for protection, and also to stop him pursuing the priest.

Father Harry spat foully on the landing floor. "Sorry, I didn't know you were expecting a boyfriend! And don't you be coming back polluting the Church! Bitch! Whore!"

Liam was overcome by his own heroic action. He began to feel protective and possessive. He began suddenly to see a vision of domestic bliss. Varrie could give up her boyfriends, and he would give up his girlfriends too. Not that he happened to have any, just at the moment. They could both drive cabs. They could look after the wee lassie in shifts. A ready-made wee daughter would be nice. It would save going through the nappy thing. And he'd heard that Varrie was only kidding about her partner in Barlinnie. They said Paddy wouldn't hurt a fly.

He swept Varrie off her feet into his embrace, as her teeth chattered and her body shook.

"Varrie, babes," he said, "Do you think we should, you know... For the wean's sake too..."

But Varrie jumped to her feet, squealing. His cuddle had pressed something against her breast, from her new bra. He saw she was screaming with delight, not anguish. As she held up a lottery ticket. Liam was saved from finally spitting out a proposal, which was just as well. He'd have regretted it. And at that moment his cell phone sounded, in his jeans pocket.

Would you believe it! It was the Millionairess again. She wanted to discuss giving him a contract to ferry her about here and there. Grabbing his raincoat, he fled for the door.

At Saint Jude's chapel, Martha knelt in a line of penitents waiting outside the confessional of Father Henry Xavier, Parish Priest. The slats on his door said he'd be available from seven till nine, but there was no sign of him. He was nursing a sore eye and a bloody nose. Martha Dearie was eager to see him. She ached to tell him the news about the lottery win. To ask did she and Jimmy have the right to the cash, or should they share it with Sky?

And she wanted to ask him about Rory. Could he have been deliberately attacked? What could have happened to the crucifix? The police said it had went amissing.

While Liam was waiting for the Millionairess, that is, Marie Louise, outside the Jannie's house, feeling in the pocket of his raincoat for fags, he came across a bulky silver box in a silk cover, containing phials of oil and water, in the poacher's pocket. Liam's coat did not have such a pocket. It was not Liam's coat. It was not even anything like his raincoat, as it was old and unfashionable. And apart from loads of lottery tickets, and note books, it contained a dozen lines of coke, parcelled up like presents for a dolly's party.

At that moment in the Presbytery, Father Harry was wondering why the hell he had six packets of fancy condoms in his raincoat pocket, a tube of spot concealer cream, and a diary for engagements, totally blank. He must have left his own coat at Varrie's. He wondered if he dared go back later that night. He thought maybe he shouldn't. He wondered if Martha would be there, on her way back from Benediction. Maybe he'd better not risk it.

Martha, though, having wasted so much time on Confession, was rushing home to Jimmy. He wanted to know what was the matter with her. He said something was up. He said he could see it. But Martha had learned not to confess anything to Jimmy. Time enough when she knew if the win was right enough. When she saw Father Harry, tonight, at the ceilidhe.

Sister Mary of Perpetual Succour dashed off to see Rory that night. She'd half a mind to tell him off for giving them all such a scare. The nurses were glad to see her. They said they had expected that nice priest to turn up. He'd especially asked to see the boy alone in his bed in Intensive Care. He said he'd wanted to conduct a special service over him. But something must have delayed him. Rory's new nurse thought she might leave the patient for a few moments with her, as there was a new admission who had no visitors. It was sad when some patients had no visitors. People seemed to come round quicker when someone was at their bedside, leaning over, even talking nonsense to them, even if they were unconscious.

Since Rory had no next of kin available, till his mother was bussed in from Cornton Vale, and since the identity of his father was not known, several of his teachers and carers were allowed to visit, strictly one at a time. So Sister Peppy was let in to see him that evening.

In the High Tec ward, his bed space like a space station, the little boy was restless. But he had fewer tubes sticking into him. The monitors were bleeping more regularly. The lines of light rose and fell without interruption. And the attention of the staff was distracted by the new case. It was always on the acutest case, which Rory, it seemed, no longer was.

Rory O'Donnell was moving his arms and legs. He was actually trying to speak. But all that was coming out of his cracked lips was a kind of moan. Peppy bent over him to listen.

"Alright!" came his smothered voice, "Alright, Daddy! It was me! It was all my fault!"

Left alone, friendless, in her scabby flat, Varrie searched her conscience. Had she led Father Harry on? She supposed so. Usually she changed into her 'church helper' garb for him. She shouldn't have kept on her tarty clothes to talk to him and his tramps. She reckoned he'd been a bit embarrassed by that, maybe turned on. People always said you were asking for it if you wore tight clothing. How about the guys in tight jeans? Were they asking for it? Asking women to come and tear their clothes off? Maybe they were at that!

She chucked the clothes she was wearing into the washing machine and went to stand under the shower until the old heater gave up and the water ran cold. Shivering again, she put on a sweat shirt and leggings. The top said Dirty Sweet. She'd never noticed it before. She'd bought it because it was cheap and the colours okay. She took a swig from a bottle of malt whisky a client had left her. It tasted worse than ordinary whisky. She rinsed her mouth with teeth whitening mouthwash. She didn't want Dakota's mother and father thinking she was a lush. She knew she should have reported Father Harry to the police. And her action in getting showered had been, in a way, to save herself doing this. Since she could not present evidence of DNA. She toyed with her phone, but finally put it down. They would never believe her. A tart's word against a priest's. And maybe they'd take Kansas off her, if she confessed to being a part time prostitute. Better shut up. At least she had kept Martha's ticket safe. Harry hadn't got his clumsy paws on that. He'd been in too bloody big a hurry.

Community Ceilidhe

The Community Ceilidhe at Saint Jude's school, although a family affair, went on till midnight. For this, it needed the connivance of the janitors, who had to be kept well oiled with single malts, in doubles.

The party was a great success, if you were not a purist of Scots folk song, fiddle music, or Mid-West line dancing. Because, at Saint Jude's, they had developed their own versions of all three. And, too, the Irish 'come-all-ye's were yodelled rather than sung, in the manner of the back court singers of yesteryear. And the ceilidhe fiddlers in the band were all pupils at Saint Jude's, taught by numbers from a big book by their computer teacher. And the line dancing wasn't exactly in lines, nor was it actually dancing, certainly not in prescribed patterns. If pure line dancing was called vanilla, Saint Jude's Ceilidhe Jiggers offered home-made banana split milk shakes and very sweet crushed strawberry sundaes.

But the good times were rolling for the Royston extended families crowding rowdily round the large square tables in the assembly hall, and hanging over the balconies. The exotic plants, tenderly nurtured by street-wise lab technicians, had been massacred, dried and rolled for the occasion. And joints were being passed merrily round everyone, defying all class barriers. Barriers of age, too, were swept away as elderly grandparents and tender adolescents were offered quick puffs to cheer them up.

Even the distinctions between arts and sports departments were defied. Kirstie Collins, the well muscled highland dance teacher, was flirting with the new guy on the art staff, the very suave Gerry. She ignored his many references to his partner Terry. (Kirstie never let girlfriends put her off. If she had, she would have had a very thin time of it, romantically.) She plied him with the cloudy sweet peach wine she had made in the girls' shower room. She said wine liked a hot steamy atmosphere to ferment in. She asked him if he'd like to see for himself some lunch time. But Kirstie's romance bubble was due to be pricked pretty soon. A big lorry driver appeared at the front door asking for Mr McGee. He was directed to Kirstie's table. Gerry stood up, blushing prettily. He bent forward to kiss the lorry driver's stubbly cheek.

"Kirstie," he said, "this is my partner Terry I was telling you about."

Kirstie's eyes flicked away from the couple as she looked round the room for other fish to fry, and prepared to cast forth her nets again, nothing daunted. Her glance lit on Detective Frank Childers, ensconced at a table of old ladies.

Frank's mother had insisted he escort her to the ceilidhe. She thought he might meet a nice girl, and he had every right to be present, having attended Saint Jude's primary, although he had been promoted (or perhaps banished) to posh Saint Ignatius's secondary. Mrs Childers had afforded the fees for Saint Iggy's from the insurance money she had received when Frank senior died in a fall from faulty scaffolding while helping to finish the pioneering Mirkhill Scheme. Little Frankie had been only a toddler at the time of the traumatic event, and had merely faint recollections of his father singing him lullabies. Although Mrs Childers kept her husband's memory green by threatening Frankie with his father's disapprobation from his paradisal cloud directly overhead.

So Frankie Childers had grown up 'biddable', which in Royston equated with wimpish. And little Frankie had also been sent to elocution classes to ready him for Saint Ignatius. Oddly enough, none of this did the grown up Frank any harm with the Mirkhill lassies, and they eagerly vied with each other to get him up for the dances. They were not so old fashioned as to wait for a boy to dance them, especially if it was the girls who had the good steady jobs. And Frank had a gleam in his eyes that looked far from biddable, although he had obliged his Mammy by wearing the saffron kilt she had hired for him. (He was not entitled to wear a tartan kilt, having only English and Irish blood in his slim, muscular body.) So Frank's chic dun coloured garment, initially designed as a Celtic warrior's camouflage for sword fights across meadow lands, now stood out against the bright tartan kilts and trews, and rendered the cop rather ostentatious. Hardly the plain clothes that his superiors had ordered him to wear to gather what information he could at the ceilidhe.

Kirstie was too late giving him the eye, as two lassies grabbed him for the Dashing White Sergeant. If every dance had likewise needed only one man to two girls, Frank would still not have worked his way through his wishful partners. He himself was on the lookout for just one lady, and until she put in an appearance couldn't have cared less whom he danced with.

That just left the curate, Father Tiziano, tall, elegant and looking like a Risen Christ; he was nevertheless at home in the rowdy throng. He had a large wild gypsy family at home on the outskirts of Milan. And he had been the life and soul of wilder parties than Saint Jude's Ceilidhe. Tiziano was an expert at line dancing, but could also try his hand at Irish dancing, and even the Sword Dance.

Kirstie hastened to him as the music stuttered out, and led him to the bar, where she plied him with home brew beer, made in the art department darkroom, and being dispensed by Miss Wallace, on her pregnancy leave. (Lena Wallace hoped she looked like the barmaid at Manet's Folies-Bergere in her long black dress and apron. She didn't.)

"Beer likes to seethe silently in the dark," Kirstie whispered to a bemused Tiziano, "Like a secret passion!" And she turned her back pointedly on Lena.

But the romantic moment was spoiled when Miss Wallace choked on a large frothing tankard of home brew. (She had concocted it herself, under Kirstie's instructions, from only the purest ingredients, and was sure it would do her nothing but good.) But it brought on an evening attack of morning sickness and, gagging, she threatened to throw up all over Kirstie and Father Tiziano. Luckily, Kirstie managed to run her into the girls' toilets, where Martha Dearie was on duty, although wearing her good silk frock.

Martha managed to guide Lena's head over a chipped washbasin in time. She had volunteered for toilet duty, not wishing to give Donald Knightley the impression she had got a big head since becoming a Polisher. When she and the janitor had managed to push the big lady, weeping quietly like a martyr, into a taxi, Martha thought she really should have a look round for Father Harry. He was conspicuous by his absence, despite having promised, to all the ladies he'd sold tickets, that he'd get them up to dance.

Martha Dearie was relieved the sickness hadn't splashed on the good dress. She sneaked into the assembly hall to get a word with Father Harry, if not a dance. Martha did not want to mention her win to anyone till she spoke to the priest about it. He would keep her right, before she worried Big Jimmy with the possibility of a win. Martha retired to sit down sadly at the back of the hall like a wallflower. But she was rescued right away by Big Josie, who, because of her power as Head Polisher, could be counted an honorary man when, as usually happened, the numbers were uneven. And because the dance was a set dance, Martha progressed from Big Josie to real men, till returned to her neatly at the end.

As she was making for her hiding place at the back, behind a potted palm, nice Father Seamas jumped up to intercept her and ask her for the next dance. It was Seamas's last night at Saint Jude's, before he exchanged places with Father Tiziano in Milan. No-one in the parish had seen fit to mark the occasion, and he was at the Ceilidhe simply to do his duty dancing with stranded females. He also chatted to grannies and let the Saint Jude's school kids tell him rude jokes, letting them pull and push and nudge him with their elbows when he didn't get the point.

But for charm, he was no match for Father Tiziano. And certainly not for Father Harry, whom he adored, and of whom he was a pale imitation. Father Seamas had not wished to leave Saint Jude's. He worried how Father Harry would get on when he was no longer there to take the early masses for him. And there were a few ill parishioners who were always delighted to see him when he struggled out to the dangerous distant schemes to visit them. Because nondescript, sandy-haired Father Seamas, not having charisma, still had a true vocation for the priesthood. Seamas delighted in sneaking in extra chores for himself. And every act of self-abnegation gave him a secret thrill. In a way, he felt he held the whole parish together by the power of his concern.

"Ciao! Martha!" he said as the dance came to an end. "I'll have to go now. Off to sunny Italy. I'm taking my Italian for Dummies with me. Catch you later." Father

Seamas had a soft spot for wee hardworking Martha. "If you ever need me, there's my cell phone number. I hope you're Okay. You and Big Jimmy."

He turned to wave goodbye at the door.

But Martha was already peering over the crowd to see if Father Harry had come in.

Apart from Frank Childers, who was fanatically good at Scottish country dance, and whose pas de basques were perfect, if not too perfect, the school kids were the only ones to get the set dances right. In spite of Gerry McGee's running up and down the ragged lines calling out instructions through a mouth mike, and poking at the dancers with a pointer.

Saint Jude's school kids, though, had been well trained by Kirstie, and took it all very seriously. None more so than Kansas and Dakota, who made it their business to lead off the sets, disdaining all offers of partners from sweaty little boy kilties from their own class. A group of big fourth year kilted boys, though, were uber cool, and earned every girl's admiration by their barbershop close harmony version of 'I Belong to Glasgow', which they completed by twirling their straw boaters on their canes.

The concert part of the show was brought to the end by the Primary Sixes singing *Bonnie Wee Thing* and *Kimming throo the Raie*, to vomiting mimes by the other kids.

Father Tiziano got a nearly swooning Martha up for a dainty waltz country dance, and then he danced with all the other Polishing ladies too. He held each of them thrillingly in turn for a brief moment in his embrace, straining their buxom figures to his slim torso.

More modestly endowed dinner ladies grumbled. "He must like great big weemen!"

But he did dance with one other lady. Marie Louise appeared like a will o' the wisp at the far end of the hall.

Slender, mysterious and untouchable. All the single guys in the crowd wished they could summon up the courage to ask her to dance. So did the married guys, and a couple of the gay guys too. But Father Tiziano did not lack courage. He happened to be standing near the door when she materialised, as he was gulping a pint of home brew beer.

It was just Frank Childers' luck that he had allowed Kirstie Collins to sweep him off his feet onto the dance floor for Strip the Willow as Marie Louise appeared.

"You're a terrific dancer, Kirstie!" he said politely but through gritted teeth, as she whirled him round in the bone crushing four hand turn that ended the dance.

Marie Louise was dressed in the same simple chic shift that she had worn on her visit to the Convent, and on her subsequent visit to the Prince's Infirmary. She had only come into the hall to deliver a message to the janitor. She had just been sent by his wife to instruct Mr Knightley to shut down the noisy party and get back home. (Mrs Knightley could sometimes be a bit of a spoilsport.)

Tiziano put his glass down on the makeshift bar. He thought his eyes were playing tricks on him. Where had this vision of loveliness come from? She looked like an Etruscan tomb engraving. Or maybe a Modigliani, or most of all, like a portrait by Titian, his namesake.

"Scusi Signora!" he addressed her. "Sono Tiziano. Maurizio Tiziano. Wanna dance?"

"I'm Marie Louise, Father." she replied, acknowledging the dog collar he wore along with his spangly shirt and velvet waistcoat. "Yes, I wanna dance! Perche non?"

She knew perfectly well why not, but it didn't stop her. She had never seen anything like Tiziano before. Even the male models she worked with habitually would look coarse beside his ethereal masculine beauty. He looked like an angel, or an ikon, or maybe a Titian.

"I love Titian!" she confided as they glided round. "Especially his Madonnas!"

"Anche Io, Signora!" Tiziano replied. "Anche Io!"

He slid Marie Louise effortlessly into a tango, to a pop tune that didn't sound anything like a tango, to her ears.

The squiffy dancers drew back to give the elegant couple room. Tiziano and Marie Louise danced on, lost to the world. Meanwhile, the other dancing couples were being touched on the shoulder by organisers, and withdrew. Spotlights bounced off the unsuspecting couple. There was a fanfare and a drum roll from the stage. They remained trapped in the spotlight.

Head jannie Knightley approached with sashes and crowns, which they were hustled into.

"I'm sorry, Father," he said "but youse two are Tango King and Queen! Yuvtae kiss!"

"Aye, yuvtae!" the crowd encouraged. "The sooner yiz dae it, the sooner ye'll get hame!"

Reluctantly, Father Tiziano and Marie Louise put their lips together in a gentle kiss. Then Marie Louise pulled his head down to her again, and kissed him expertly, lovingly, and for rather a long time under the circumstances, as even her friend Donald Knightley had to admit.

The crowd cheered, and under that cover Tiziano whispered in her ear,

"Tu me gusta, Marie Louise!" and gave a sigh.

"Me too! Tu me gusta!" whispered Marie Louise. "Anche Io, Maurizio!"

"Scusi, Signora?"

"Signorina!"

"Scusi Signorina! May I see you home?"

"E perche non?" agreed Marie Louise.

They slipped out of the door, and Marie Louise led him by the hand towards the jannie's house across the playground. So it wasn't very far. But much later, when Donald Knightley got home after doing the locking up, they still hadn't reached it.

Meanwhile the rabble of parents, grannies and grandads, teachers, and amateur and professional thieves, who flocked to such events, were singing *Old Lang Syne* with crossed arms and following that with the Hokey Cokey. The ceilidhe ended with a bang, as bad boys let off fire crackers across the polished wood floors, when Mr Knightley was distracted, exercising his 'droit de seigneur', kissing all the dinner ladies goodnight.

Outside, on the pavement, the crowd enjoyed shouted leave-takings, the voices ringing in the night air. Waking up neighbours who had been too wimpish to attend the wild ceilidhe.

Splinter groups formed to sing the Red Flag, as their parents before them had done, at the end of get-togethers, knowing all the verses. From the same atavistic reasons, some sang *Faith of our Fathers*. And others, greatly daring, sang *The Soldier's Song*.

Frank Childers, standing impatiently with his mother, as she bid a fond adieu to the members of her Women's Guild, hoped none of the neighbours would phone the police, out of badness.

The kids rushed around, their steamy bodies cooling pleasantly in their sticky dance clothes, in the frosty night air. Till they were called by their parents for a nice walk home, their footsteps resounding thrillingly.

Dakota's parents escorted Kansas right home, up her close, after the ceilidhe. But Varrie didn't even ask them in for a cup of tea.

"Jealous, snidey bitch!" said Dakota's mum as they clattered downstairs again.

Father Harry turned up at the nearly deserted assembly hall right at the end, drank some home brew, and grabbed a couple of ham sandwiches.

Martha was waiting for him, and managed to catch up with him as he was sneaking off.

He had no desire to stop and listen to her potty wee stories. Earlier, he had been up at the Prince's Infirmary to check on Rory. The bed the boy had occupied in Intensive Care was being stripped as he peered through the glass. He hadn't hung around to ask questions. He didn't think he could control his face. He didn't know what signals his expression was giving. So he'd gone to a pub, a shebeen, where you could stay really late. (He didn't want to get back till the ceilidhe was over.) He'd bought himself several whiskies, whether in relief or grief, he hardly knew. He'd been both amused and annoyed when an old guy had tried to pick him up. He'd tried to cover up his facial bruises with the concealer cream he'd found in his pocket. Maybe that had given the wrong impression. Anyway, he'd been trapped by Martha Dearie after all.

"Father Harry!" she was gabbling, hanging on to his arm. He could hardly bear to listen.

"What would you say if I told you I'd come across a lost lottery ticket? In Jimmy's coat! Should I give half to Sky? He's the one that warned me Jimmy might have a win. And I think he might have paid half of the stake money. I'm so worried about doing the right thing. I wouldn't want to cheat anybody that had a claim! Will you come and talk to me about it?"

"Yeah, yeah, sure hen!" the slightly fuddled priest said, turning on his heel, not quite hearing. Then he did a double take, and turned back. "Have you got the ticket on you, pet? What was it for, a tenner?" he asked, kidding he was daft.

"I don't right know. That's what I want you to find out."

"Would you like me to take it for safe keeping? And I'd advise you to tell no-one!"

"No, that's alright, Father Harry. Varrie took it to look after. I've got so absent minded! But, about my moral dilemma, will you come and advise me tomorrow, Father Harry?"

Harry reeled. Varrie Valentino had had the ticket all the time. The sleekit wee bitch! And never bloody mentioned it! You could never trust a dame! But what got to him most of all was the betrayal by Sky. Whom he'd let into some of his business deals. Sky had given Martha the wire about the lost ticket. It was clear to Harry now, what had been in Sky's mind. And the old tramp had nearly managed it. Stupid wee Martha Dearie, at one word from Sky, would have shared her winnings with him. Well, over his dead body would that happen! He didn't have wee Rory to worry about now. He reckoned it wouldn't take long to sort out Sky, who would be waiting for him at the camp for news of Rory. Though what business that was of Sky's, Father Harry would really like to know. So that just left Martha.

"Martha, pet!" he cuddled up against the little lady, leaned over to give her a saintly kiss on her lined forehead, and then quickly released her, as his loose tooth wobbled.

"Martha, hen! Worry no longer! You just get the ticket back from Varrie, and I'll handle it for you! You'll not have another day's anxiety about it! You can take my word for that!"

Harry sloped off then, desperate to get at the whisky stowed behind the Good News Testament on his bookshelves. And the silver crucifix hidden behind it.

But that wasn't the end of the interviews Father Harry had to give. There was no peace for him even in his study. His curate, Father Tiziano, was waiting there to speak to him. The young man looked very nervous, Harry thought. Typically wimpish curate. White and shaky at the prospect of owning up something or other to his Parish Priest. Probably some stupid crisis of conscience, or spiritual problem.

The Parish House housekeeper, plump Mrs Mulvey, was there too, circling Tiziano and growling insults under her breath. She had tried to stop him annoying poor Father Harry, who had been out all evening, administering to the sick. But the curate wouldn't be stopped, even though he was white as May blossom, and shaking like a leaf.

Father Tiziano came to the point at once.

"I wish to renounce my vows and marry with lady."

"And which lady would that be, Father?" Harry asked, leering. "Any one in particular?"

"She is named Marie Louise. I not knowing her last name."

"Believe me, Father, that is no lady! She is the daughter of a whore, and probably a tart herself! Let's talk it over tomor..."

Before he could get the word out of his mouth, Father Tiziano socked him on the jaw and stormed out.

Father Harry picked himself off the floor and felt his face. The tooth that Varrie's client's punch had loosened had come right out. That was all he bloody needed. He spat the tooth into his large hanky. But Harry was no wimp. He rinsed his mouth with whisky.

"Mrs Mulvey, has Father Seamas left yet?"

"Indeed no, Father. He's just dragging his luggage out to the taxi for the airport."

"Tell him to drag it back. Pay the cab off, and tell it to wait. I've a sick call to make."

Liam MacNee was crushed. He had thought the cab would be for Marie Louise. He responded to every call for Saint Jude's, hoping it would be his Millionairess. But Marie Louise and Father Tiziano were walking round the football pitch hand in hand for the second time that night, talking and talking, in the shadow of the trees that bordered it.

The girl's mobile sounded. A number she didn't recognise. It was Sister Mary of Perpetual Succour, interrupting their *tête a tête*, But not before Marie Louise and Father Tiziano, on the basis of one tango and a talk in fractured English and halting Italian, had plighted their troths, each to the other.

"Oh, Peppy!" Marie Louise gasped. "If it's about my late vocation, I'm afraid it's too late! I've just met a wonderful guy, and we've got engaged. You are the first to know! Can nuns be bridesmaids?"

But it turned out that hadn't been why Peppy was phoning. It was about Marie Louise's wee brother. Peppy had found some papers in the little boy's school bag, which she thought Marie Louise should read. Peppy said all the nuns were asleep, and she would be waiting to let them in, Marie Louise and her fiancée.

"You wanna ride my motocycletto? Mi raccomando!" begged Tiziano.

"Sure!" said Marie Louise, in the mood for taking risks, "Perche non?"

When Varrie Valentino was trying to get her daughter Kansas into bed, it wasn't easy. Kansas was high as a kite, telling her about Father Tiziano and a big tall lady dancing the tango and kissing. On the mouth! For ages! Then she noticed that her mother was crying. Probably out of disappointment at not getting to the ceilidhe.

"Bloody priests!" Varrie muttered under her breath. "They're supposed to be bloody holy!"

Father Harry, the cause of Varrie's tears, was business-like as he stepped into Liam's cab, without recognising his erstwhile antagonist.

"Old Royston cemetery!" he barked. "The Gatehouse!"

Darkness

Shivering among the overgrown ornamental bushes behind the Gatehouse of Old Royston Necropolis, Father Harry fished in the back pocket of his moss and lichen stained trousers, for his silver hip flask of whisky. The old guy had put up a tremendous fight. They'd been crashing and rolling over those marble shards of gravestones for what seemed like hours. You'd almost have thought that Sky had had something worthwhile left to live for, the way he tried to defend himself. He must have known the game was up, when he saw Harry coming for him, his trusty crucifix raised in benediction, he must have known he wasn't going to get away with clyping to that wee wifie about her husband's windfall. The money was his, morally, after all the time he had spent pandering to smelly down and outs. The lottery ticket must come to him. He would use it for good works. After compensating himself just a bit for his life of genteel poverty and monstrous frustration. And if wee Martha Dearie had somehow got hold of it, well, so much the worse for wee Martha.

He had changed his mind what he would do, directly Camelot received his claim. He'd go public. The papers would love pictures of him in the graveyard, with the remaining derelicts, distributing charity.

"This win will help me keep up the good work for the homeless. No, I think I'll continue to live in the priests' house. Might put in some decent central heating, though." He smiled slyly, in spite of himself, as he imagined the headlines in the newspapers, but froze as he saw a fox's luminous eyes staring out from the undergrowth. In a russet blur, the half tamed big dog fox, contemptuous of his presence, made a dart for the remains of the priest's discarded ham sandwich, lying nearby. Harry hadn't been able to get a morsel over his tight throat, though he was stupidly hungry. His nerves, probably.

Father Harry had started chittering and shaking again. He raised the flask once more to his hot chapped lips, but spilled the grog down that other guy's raincoat that he still wore. In a sweat, he grasped the flask in both hands; forcing it against his chattering teeth, he got a swig down. He felt better right away.

"Here, fella! Here, boy!" he called to the savvy urban fox, holding out a remaining bit of the old sandwich. But the fox skedaddled in a blink, turning his head just once, in a scornful glare. And Harry found tears standing in his red-rimmed eyes. The fox was just like that gang of derelicts, the Wanderers as they called themselves. They took what they wanted, trashed the rest, and despised the giver, usually himself. Well, the derelicts would have a nasty surprise when they returned at dawn. The sight of Sky's body, nude, dirty, grey and misshapen, beneath his old musquash coat, would put the wind up them. He'd be surprised if their campsite wasn't deserted by noon. Harry reflected that, in a nice touch, he had left some rolled up bundles of Sky's poetic works over the body, under his crossed arms.

Father Harry jerked alert, suddenly. He hoped it was a body! He had detected a slight movement of the tatty fur coat. He didn't think it was the breeze. But he needn't have worried, he saw, with a gasp of relief. Two pointed ears appeared above the hummock of tall grass that concealed the body. The old battered fox was nosing at Sky. He looked a bit like the old tramp's alter ego, ragged, thin, and battered looking. Must have been in a fight, or been pelted with stones by the bands of wild boys who came there playing hunters. Harry had to laugh as a sheaf of Sky's poems, disturbed by the animal, scattered in the wind.

Well, he had tried to keep them together for posterity, he grinned. If Sky's spirit was floating above the tombstones, he couldn't blame him for that. He should blame the scrofulous fox!

Below the graveyard, the last lights were going out. The take-away shops were putting up their shutters. The signs over garages and laundrettes were going out. But still the dawn did not break, and Father Harry felt a darkness closing about him. It was closing about Father Henry Xavier, of the Society of Jesus, too. He should be in his soutane with his collar for protection. What was he doing out here in messed up good civvies? Soon he'd look like a tramp himself. He'd have to find somewhere to wash this stinky muck off. Putting his hands up to his nose he realised it was Sky's minging blood, black in the odd light.

He emerged from his hiding place in the bushes, and twisted round and round on the sunken platform of a gravestone, trying to work out which direction he could take. He couldn't go back to the priest's house. In case Varrie had complained to the Police. In case they were insensitive enough to believe her. So where now? He'd get funny looks at the Drop In centres if he turned up covered in blood. Suddenly he panicked, the blood draining from his brain so that he nearly fell down.

And then the darkness overwhelmed Wee Harry too. Wee Harry Brown, who had loved his Mammy. Whom his Mammy had loved so dearly. Who had encouraged him when she heard his prayers, and he had shyly told her of his dreams to be holy. To be a saint, looking after the poor and the unfortunate. And then when he had torn himself away, as a laddie, to go to Junior Seminary, she'd up and died on him. From something nasty she'd kept hidden from her boy, not to distress him. And somehow or other, his big bullying lout of a father had seemed to blame him for that.

"Oh, Christ, Mammy! Where the hell will I go?" He fell down on his knees under a stained and chipped Madonna, who kept her eyes steadfastly downcast.

But Harry's Mammy wasted no time in sending her poor son his answer. A scatter of lights twinkled in the far distance, from the chapel of the Convent of the Bleeding Heart, setting hope flaring in his sad heart. And, as the cell lights, too, came on one by one there, he knew the Sisters who ministered to the homeless and the hopeless would be yawning and getting up, and going for their first service without a bite of breakfast. The good nuns would take him. The little nuns loved him, in spite of, or even because of his scarcely concealed boyish contempt for the manless women. He could trudge across country from the cemetery, and reach the picturesque place before their first service was over. He could gain access to Rory's old room by the balcony and fire escape they had both used many times in the past. When everything between them had been so nice.

A thought struck him, and he reeled under it. He had sent Rory a few little notes, inviting him on innocent outings. Maybe those letters hadn't been quite discreet enough. And if Rory had kept them! Their tone would fool the affectionate sentimental nuns, but maybe not world-weary police officers. Harry hastened his steps through the mud of last night's rain and the mounds of lifeless leaves that clogged the paths, unseen in the dark, making him stumble. His mind whirled with memories.

Back to the beginning, when he loved Rory and he thought Rory had loved him. When he had stopped the big boys bullying him. Even going so far as to twist a few ears, and punch a few well filled school jerseys painfully, if playfully. He had kept a few of the pathetic, carefully copied out letters Rory had sent him at that time, thanking him. Even drawing little hearts on the inside of the envelope, with their two initials entwined. His heart swelled with pride to think of the little unspoken love letters nestling still in his breast pocket, where he always kept them, no matter what clothes he wore. Wee Rory should have known how much he loved him. He would never have let anyone hurt him. He would never have handed him back to his slut of a mother when she got out of women's prison. He would have made it up to him that he had no daddy to pick him up even occasionally for holidays, as the other boys sometimes had. And at first it had been lovely for both Rory and himself, he believed in his heart and soul. He remembered on one little holiday, when he was taking him to visit the mother at Cornton Vale, (where, by the way, she was happy as Larry, with her girlfriends and her gardening), on the way back they'd stopped at a Bed and Breakfast, as daddy and son on an away day. For a little prank Rory had filled the bath tub with bubble bath, nearly suffocating Harry, but making up by tenderly washing his back. Harry still dreamed of that, one of his sweetest dreams.

And he had offered to be Rory's Daddy. And in return had only kissed and caressed him as a loving Daddy might have done. And even if, later, in his tenderness, he had got carried away sometimes, he was never brutal, never uncaring. Rory should have known that. If Rory had grown up, he would have understood. They would have lived and loved as equals. And what a shining future would have stretched out for them both! With the money, once he got hold of the winning ticket, they could have lived as Gods, with everything to make an unorthodox life style easy and accepted. And they would have performed secret saintly acts of charity, never revealing their identity.

So why in the name of all that was holy, had Rory set out to spoil it all? Leaving a trail of faeces wherever he went, out of badness. Almost as if he was intent on drawing attention to himself. And then shitting all over the store room floor as if he was scared, terrified, of Father Harry, his own Daddy. He was just giving him a wee spanking over his knee, as an angry father, losing his temper with a wee rogue, might have done. And no wonder he had lost his temper! Rory had taken to avoiding him, running away from him. Maybe just to lead him on, so Father Harry would increase the allowance he paid the wee scoundrel and take him on more treats again. He hated that attitude. Almost as if he was one of the rent boys that hung around the Tollbooth at Glasgow Cross. And God knows, you couldn't love a rent boy. They didn't want loved. They wanted to take the money and run. Some of them even had girlfriends. And babies too, that they were proud of. One young guy he'd been fond of, and who had made out to like him back, had actually brought his smelly brat to see him, thinking he'd be pleased!

But that was all over; even without Rory he'd never go to a rent boy again. With cash he'd be able to pick and choose. Maybe pick up an artistic type, or a poet. But his poor heart still cried out for Rory, now gone forever. To a better place. To paradise. Where maybe Mammy would care for him. He'd have to explain to Mammy, when he knelt down to pray to her tonight, what had happened when he'd found himself lathering Rory with the crucifix. What did Rory think he was going to do with it? He was only giving his backside a few light taps with it. To hear him screaming you'd think he'd been going to stick it up his arse. The way he started screaming hysterically, and wouldn't bloody stop. And the darkness had come over Harry's brain, as it had again now, just thinking about it.

He remembered now why he'd got so annoyed with his wee Rory in the first place. When he'd admitted spying on him as he went through the pockets of all the old jackets in the store room. He told him he knew he was looking for Big Jimmy's jacket, that Sky said the ticket was bound to be in. He boasted that he'd wormed the secret out of sly Sky High. He said him and Sky were going to get the ticket. He said he'd found out that Sky was his real Daddy, and when they got the ticket, they'd run away together and take to the open road in a big jeep, where he would never find him. He said Sky never hurt him either, the way Father Harry did, when he was in a bad mood. And when he was in a good mood.

And that's when, Father Harry explained to Mammy in his mind, it had all got too much for him, and the darkness had come down on the right side of his head, and his left eye had gone blind, and the black rage had overpowered him. When Rory wouldn't confess that he had deserved the spanking, that he had been in the wrong going to Sky behind his back.

And even then Harry would have forgiven him. They might have finished by kissing and cuddling and making up, as they had done many times before. But Rory wouldn't confess. Just because Harry had torn up Rory's stupid fluffy chick, his mother's gift. Wouldn't admit he was wrong. Although Harry had found himself, standing over the boy, only too ready to kiss him and absolve him if he gave in. Then they'd both heard the inner door to the class clank open, and boys' shouts echoing through the complex of classrooms. Then Rory gave one loud shout too, before Harry brought the crucifix down on his head, and he collapsed silently to the ground. The daft wee cleaner hadn't heard a thing, as her big sons rampaged around. Still, she was a good mammy to those two cheeky blond boys. Father Harry would try to deal with her gently if he could.

He remembered uttering one silent prayer to his Mammy in heaven to get him out of this, and sure enough, his mind went calm, and the lights stopped flashing in the darkness of his brain. And he'd got Rory quickly bundled up in the old jumble sale clothes. He'd slipped out the door to the corridor, no bother, and made his jolly way to the drama department, smiling at everyone he met. And he'd been brilliant rehearsing his part as the Whizz in The Magical Whizz of Oz. At first frightening the cast members with his ferocity, then calming them down with his gentleness and his meekness.

"Thanks, Mammy!" He muttered a silent prayer, in honour of his escape.

When Father Harry got to the convent, and to the fire escape round the back, he'd almost completely recovered. Dawn was breaking, and he loved the dawn. Mammy and him used to go walks in the dawn, before Da got up. He wondered if he might have pleased her more by chatting to one of the girls that had hung around him, on his holidays from the seminary. His well-tailored uniforms and holiness had made him a popular figure. He might have had a pack of kids by now. But by that time he had got in too deep, and chosen another path.

He glugged down half of one of the cartons of milk he found at the back door. His mind ran on to what might have been. He might have got a young girl like Varrie. He had to admit, she was the one he would have chosen. But she hadn't appreciated him either. He'd poured himself into her. Anointed her with grace, and she had acted angry. Maybe just to save face, but it had hurt him all the same. Many a girl would have loved to go with him, a fine, still young guy, a man of God. Considering she advertised in the papers for any scumbag with fifty quid and a cock.

Father Harry, now mumbling to himself in annoyance, climbed the fire escape and got to the balcony outside the room where Rory used to live. Where his toy trains would be, that Harry had bought him. The teddy would maybe be on his bed, whom the priest had arranged to be delivered by post last Valentine's Day, with an anonymous 'Love Ya Rory' embroidered within a heart on his fluffy chest. He peered through the light net curtains at the window.

No teddy bear. Instead, two figures lay stretched out on top of Rory's duvet. Two slim figures, equally tall and equally elegant. Lying side by side like effigies. But not armoured and clothed like effigies. They lay stark naked and vulnerable to the priest's outraged gaze, only the tips of their long fingers touching.

Father Tiziano and that annoying girl from London. That big stookie and erstwhile tart, Marie Louise, on innocent Rory's blue duvet.

Father Harry felt a growl rise in his throat, as his hairy fist tightened round the crucifix stuck into the belt of his stained and bloody party trousers.

Life And Death

Two trolleys just managed to pass each other in the glassed over corridor of the Prince's Infirmary. They contained a seriously ill patient each, and the two unlucky ones could hardly have been less alike. And their fates, too, were opposite, although they were linked in two all-encompassing manners, and could hardly have been closer.

Rory O'Donnell, eleven years old, looking even younger, male, blonde and angelically pretty, immaculately clean, with hardly any sign of injury, was escaping from the Intensive Care Unit, on his way down to the High Dependency Unit. So he was going up in the world.

Charles Lavery, sixty-seven years old, male, grotesquely ugly, old-looking for his age, and with blood still escaping from raw, gashed wounds, was entering Intensive Care. So he was on a downward spiral, shortly to go out of control. His name tag, though, said Sky High.

But Charles still had some life in him. When the park ranger who had found his nude, moribund body had identified him as Sky High for the ambulance men (It was the only name he knew, and all the Wanderers in the part of the graveyard he patrolled used nicknames.), Charles had not wanted to demur. Even if he could have got his blackening lips to work, and a glimmer of a smile had touched them. Being prepared to be fitted out with tubes in the bay just vacated by Rory, Charles was still able to give the nurses a run for their money.

The two nurses, one milky-white and frothy from County Cork, one cafe au lait and sweet from Sudan, were struggling to wash him, trying to get all the blood and mud off, so that the harassed doctors could ascertain the extent of his injuries. They were attempting to wash him while trying not to disturb the lines already fitted in. The part of Sky's brain that was still functioning didn't like that. He fought desperately against the intrusive washing of parts of his body hardly ever seen by woman.

Katey was glad she had Nubia to help her. She was good with the elderly, the dying, the brain damaged, and the cussed, all of which their patient was.

"Now, Mr High," Nubia coaxed him, "just let us make you nice and clean. We're only doing this for your own good, you know, just getting the gravel out of this wound, Mr High!"

But when Katey attempted to wash the grime from Sky's nether regions, his limbs convulsed again, trying to fight her off. Katey leaned forward, to kiss his seamed forehead. Suddenly he gave in, and lay back quietly. As the nurse moved across him to wash his poor grey head, he reached up to kiss her bare white arm with his gumsy lips. (His gluey dentures were now in Steradent on his locker.) He managed to mouth what looked like 'Angel' and Katey blushed delightedly to the roots of her brown curls.

"Sky!" Nubia whispered to him, as she prepared the injection that would put him to sleep, "That's a lovely name, one of the nicest I've heard in this country!"

Sky was trying to say something. He was acting out rocking a baby in his arms, and pointing to himself. Mouthing a word. Nubia thought it was 'father' he was saying.

"Oh, look, Katey. He says he's a father. So you're a father, Mr High?"

That wasn't what Sky had meant, but he zonked out suddenly as Nubia's syringe scratched the skin of his stick-like wrist, and his hand relaxed and lay still on the coverlet.

But the clerk for the ward had already found out Sky's real name. The medic was a clever young guy, and resourceful. When he heard that Sky had been picked up at the cemetery, he remembered that one of the chaplains, the Catholic one, often ran services there, and brought food and comforts to the tramps. On a hunch, he rang a number he had on his phone. So, amazingly, Father Harry got a call on his mobile just as he was about to climb in a window at the Convent of the Bleeding Heart with the irrational purpose of murdering Marie Louise and Father Tiziano. The buzz of his phone brought him to his senses, and he withdrew down the fire escape to answer it.

"Father Harry here!" he replied, "You don't say! Poor old Sky! Yes, I can give you his proper name. I'd like to administer the last sacrament, sir, if that's all right. Shall I enter by the after-hour ambulance gateway as usual? Charles Lavery, his real name is. A lovely fellow, a Wanderer and a poet! Yes, it is sad. Is he still alive! I'm surprised! I mean I'm surprised he didn't give his right name, the rogue. Did he say anything else? You think he was trying to? I'll see you soon. Take care!"

This odd piece of luck cheered Harry up. He would go and spread some DNA around Sky's person and possessions in case they traced something. And if it looked as if he was about to make a miracle recovery, unlikely as that seemed, considering how many times, he'd heard the crucifix crunch into bone; well, he could handle that too.

Enlivened, and calmer, Father Harry looked about him. He should have noticed the downstairs bathroom window open before, left for Mother Agnes's big cat to get in and out. He reached his hand in and, undoing the latch, pulling the sash window up, swung in. He enjoyed a good wash with the nunish white carbolic soap, and then, thinking again that nothing could go wrong, ventured into the hall, where the hall stand gave him a long waterproof anorak that would do for male or female. Mother Agnes's massive wellies lay where she'd abandoned them on the inside doormat. Gagging a little he also put on the manky tracky bottoms she wore when she went to feed the animals in the morning. Nipping into the kitchen, he shoved all the clothes he had taken off into the huge, old fashioned solid fuel furnace that still managed to heat the converted mansion. He knew all about the vagaries of that boiler having often got it going for the nuns on winter days. As the furnace flared, he rammed the crucifix in. He retraced his steps to the bathroom, and escaped outside, buttoning up the coat, to cover his blood-stained shirt.

Outside, on the roadway, he was lucky enough to flag down a passing cab. In minutes they were on a slip road to the motorway, which took him right onto the High Street where the Prince's Infirmary had its main ambulance entrance. The cab driver had really speeded up when he heard father Harry was taking the Sacrament to a poor dying parishioner.

"No charge, Father!" He said, "Say a wee prayer for me!" and went off smiling sadly.

Which was just as well, Father Harry thought, with an amused smirk, as it turned out that Mother Agnes had not a five pence piece in any pocket of her garments.

"Talk about vows of poverty." Father Harry said to himself. "Sometimes I think those Sisters take their vows a bit too seriously."

No-one stopped Father Harry as he made his way to Intensive Care. He reeled when he saw Sky in what had been Rory's bed space, whether from grief or relief, he wasn't sure.

"So the wee guy's had it?" he enquired of Nubia.

She not being up in Glesca dialect, thought he meant Sky. "I'm afraid that's true!" she said. She made the sign of the cross as she passed him on her way out.

"Dies irae, Dies illa!" the priest intoned, to give Nubia her money's worth. Then, as if taking in for the first time the full horror of Sky's injuries, he let out a sob, and threw himself on the hardly breathing body, shouting out the victim's name and broken words of affection, and rocking it in his arms. The nurse paused, shocked but impressed by the priest's emotion.

A strange reaction came from Sky; his body went completely rigid, shuddered, and then, in a cough and a gasp, a torrent of brackish blood erupted from his throat, and poured over Sister Agnes's anorak.

"Help, nurse!" Harry shouted, in good earnest, actually. "What have I done?"

All the monitors showing Sky's vital signs flickered and flatlined.

"I'm so sorry, Father." Nubia said. "I'm afraid he's gone!"

She tried to get the blood off Harry's jacket, but couldn't. And she noticed his shirt was heavily bloodstained too. She offered to get them laundered for him. (By this, she meant take them home and wash them herself.) She wanted to help the poor cleric, so strangely dressed in the middle of the night. He looked as if he'd been mugged, or had had some sort of an accident. That's what came of trying to assist drug addicts. The only thing she could get to cover him was a doctor's white coat hanging on the peg.

Father Harry swaggered along the corridors, playing doctor.

At that moment, Rory's life hung in the balance too, as Harry passed the High Dependency Room where Rory lay; his dedicated nurse, hearing the alarm bleepers go off upstairs in Sky's room, swithered if she should go and lend a hand, since Rory looked quite settled. But just then, exactly as Father Harry was about to pass his door, Rory began to moan. He sat up, clutched his tummy and asked to go to the bathroom, which was en-suite.

"What a good boy!" said the nurse. He was really coming on. How much easier nursing him would be now. Although unable to form sentences, he was able to make certain signs to show what his needs were. The nurse dashed to help him into the en-suite.

Harry popped his head in the door, hesitating on the threshold. Hearing revolting noises in the loo, he stood there transfixed. "What a disgusting job to do!" Harry thought, making a wry face, as he dodged away.

Harry passed, and slipped into a staff cloakroom. He chose a nice shirt, jacket and trousers. And a nice coat containing a well filled wallet, then walked out of the hospital, his head bowed and his hands clasped together, as if in prayer.

On Rory's innocent bed in the Convent of the Bleeding heart, his big sister, Marie Louise, woke up next to her lover, Father Tiziano. She spread her long hands over her slim naked abdomen, seized by a sudden thought. That new life might be taking root there already. She didn't feel like getting up when Mary of Perpetual Succour knocked quietly on the door. Peppy, an unlikely Cupid, had locked them in the night before, when they had come to claim the shocking documents she had unearthed for them. To give them time to read the copy of a birth certificate they found, and the two bundles of letters. Afterwards, she had been kept busy when Philomena had taken one of her turns, refusing to stop riddling out the old boiler. And she had thought it best to leave them to themselves.

To be honest, Peppy had looked in once, but had been overcome with a strange emotion when she had seen the lovers lying in a moonlit embrace. She had gone, but locked the door quietly behind her. Now was their opportunity to get out by the fire escape.

"Quick, quick," she pleaded, "I've let Sister Philomena into the basement, to keep her out of the way, but Mother Agnes will be coming back from feeding the animals soon."

The young lovers dressed quickly, but Tiziano would not go without enveloping dumpy Peppy in an embrace which left her usually apple cheeks the colour of Mother Benigna's geraniums in the window boxes. She sighed, watching them zoom off on the motorcycle. They were a lovely couple. Wrapped up in themselves just now, of course. Neither of them had seemed to pick up on her own suspicions. Peppy reluctantly made her way to the kitchen.

When Imelda turned up to put the kettle on, Sister Peppy asked her to sort out Philomena, who seemed to be working herself up into hysterics next door. She was crying and shouting. Something about the ancient boiler was really upsetting her. The old nun was trying to pluck something from the flames with tongs. Imelda snatched up an oven glove and prised it out. A piece of the crucified silver figure of Christ, separated from the copper base plate.

Father Harry's crucifix, although purged of its blood, had not disintegrated yet when brave Imelda had peered into the flames, and snatched it from the burning.

"Sacrilege! Pure sacrilege!" Sister Philomena moaned to Imelda, her partner in crime. "I can't let the others find it. Help me hide it. We'll pray to Saint Philomena to fix it for us!"

Father Tiziano and Marie Louise went off with the precious documents in his saddlebag. Both had such innocent minds they hadn't picked up on Harry's unseemly notes to the little boy. Anyway, he used some code. D.B. meant Darling Boy. L.Y. meant Love Ya. They thought Father Harry's notes were rather sweet, always planning outings and giving blessings.

Tiziano began to wish he had not punched Father Harry so hard.

Rory's little scribbles starting 'Dear Daddy' (afterwards copied out by him painstakingly), they thought had been written by him to his birth father (Charles Lavery, university lecturer retired, on the birth certificate, next to Renee O'Donnell, model and actress.)

So Sky, subsiding into the shadow, and Rory, emerging into the light, were brought together in the documents held in Marie Louise's slender hands, and in her tender hopes.

And in Father Harry's dark and demented musings.

At that moment some other innocents hung between life and death in Father Harry's plans. He had a savage grievance against Varrie for not letting on she had that lottery ticket of her pal's about her person. He wondered where she'd hidden it. He cast back in his mind, to their encounter.

And then he remembered, or thought he did, a kind of rustling that had come from Varrie's black lace bra, as he had pulled it down contemptuously, eager to get on with the main event. He remembered thinking maybe she'd kept money down her bra. Money some other punter had given her. He'd always noticed the similarity of texture of a lottery ticket and a banknote. Thinking she had some hope of getting any from him! Right, in her dreams, he'd thought. He deserved some freebies, in his hard sad life. And he'd lent her cash before, and never got any back. So he was due anything he could get, Harry thought, crudely.

Now he wished he hadn't been in such a hurry. If he'd taken his time, with a bit more foreplay, he would have identified what that rustling was, where the ticket was hidden, and maybe he would have turned Varrie on to his manly charms.

Father Harry began to regret, quite genuinely, the coarseness of his sexual behaviour. He reckoned it was all down to the years he'd consorted with rent boys. They left no room for delicacy. If you tried to cuddle one of them, they'd soon put it about that you were nothing but a big cissy. What was a guy to do? And Varrie had been sweet, he couldn't deny, in spite of everything. She'd tried to pull that big plooky guy off him. He thought he'd leave Varrie alone. A quick vision of her lovely breasts swam before him, and he felt dizzy, overcome with belated tenderness for her, as he strode home.

But as for wee scrawny Martha, she'd had it!

Slip Up

The Polishing did not go quite as well, after such eager anticipation, as we would have wished for brave little Martha. It did not go well at all, right from the bleak morning start. Almost as if someone had it in for Martha, and had set out to queer the new Polisher's pitch. First there was a mix up over the tea. Since she had not had time to put her share into the kitty, you would have expected she would have been given a day's grace and found a cup of steaming tea left for her on the Polishers' tray. No such luck! As the last tea was snatched up grimly by Big Lorna, Martha saw she was not included. Rather than start the new work minus the stimulus of the caffeine and tannin in the strong, masked tea, Martha slipped out from her new abode and flew along the corridor to the art base, to brew a solitary cup. Varrie was always late, so she'd be alone, and it would take her only minutes.

But the unofficial staff room was not empty. The light was blazing, and the room smelled of percolating coffee, which the art staff only used for parties and high holidays, say the kids' outside toilets had frozen, and they had all been sent home. And it was not any of the motley band of art teachers who were ensconced there, sighing and whispering. It was Tiziano and Marie Louise, reading over the bundles of papers they had scooped up from Rory's desk.

Martha paused on the threshold. The conversation sounded somehow romantic. Then she identified the sound of mixed Italian and English masculine rumblings, like in the 'Godfather'. Father Tiziano! Martha identified the voice with relief. He would be giving some poor lassie counselling, some poor girl in trouble. But fair's fair, Martha needed her tea. She knocked and bustled in.

Father Tiziano and Marie Louise jumped to their feet, from adjacent battered armchairs.

Martha wasn't all that surprised. It had looked to her that Marie Louise had something on her mind since she'd returned. And Father Tiziano was such a nice priest, he must have made time for her in his busy schedule. They both started talking very fast, offering coffee. Martha refused, but gave up all hope of tea, and opening an old filing cabinet, she took out her own Irn Bru and gulped some down, along with a tea biscuit. Skipping back down the corridor, she unluckily, as it seemed to Martha, collided with her best friend, Varrie. The last person in the world she wanted to meet at that point.

But Varrie, for once in her life, had managed to be early for work. She had got a bunch of white heather for Martha, for her first day Polishing, to show she was not jealous of the promotion. And to congratulate her on her winning ticket, which Martha had asked her to take charge of, till she got her head sorted. Martha began to worry if she should get it back, as Father Harry had advised her. She stood there swithering, jumping from foot to foot uneasily, as the sounds of the big Polishers' cries began to ring down the corridors, and the wheezing of their machines revving up began to be heard.

"Gonnae give us back our ticket, Varrie?" she finally blurted out.

"But how?" Varrie exploded, meaning why, "Do you not trust me?"

"It's just that Father Harry says I've to give it to him, and he'll sort out Camelot!"

"Sort out is right, you wee nutter!"

"That's not very nice, Varrie! He's a holy priest of God!"

"Aye, and I'm Mother Theresa!" Varrie pulled a blue checked duster over her head.

"No, I'm not giving it to you. Useless wee idiot!"

"I'll remind you, I'm not so useless or such an idiot now! I'm a Polisher, and you're not!"

Martha and Varrie were having their first quarrel, in all the eight years they'd cleaned together, from when Martha had let Varrie bring the baby with her to work. Varrie stood back, stunned at the insult, and her jaw clenched. She fumbled in her purse for the ticket.

"There you are, then. Give it to Father friggin' Harry, and much good may it do you!"

Martha was lucky to catch Father Harry just as he was leaving the Polishers' bay. She wordlessly pressed the ticket into his hand, and he wasted no time in shoving it into his wallet. He made the sign of the cross over her.

"Bless you!" he grunted, and made himself scarce, only just managing to stop himself breaking into a run, and slowed down into a stiff legged swagger, making a strange figure, dishevelled and oil-stained, battered and bruised, in his posh looking borrowed clothes.

Only Big Josie was left, and she trundled her machine out snootily past Martha, pointing at her watch. She paused, though, for a Parthian shot, rocking the heavy equipment lightly with one hand, as casually and proudly as a mother might rock a pramful of babies.

"Punctuality, missus, is the politeness of princes. Or, in our case, princesses. What the hell kept you, woman! Me, giving you a chance, and Father Harry even lubricating your machine for you, so it'll not be too much for your wee skinny arms!"

But Big Josie, apart from looking as if she could go twelve rounds with Mike Tyson, had after all, a heart of gold. She looked closely at Martha's flushed screwed up face, and her trembling lips. Then she took a close look at Martha's machine that Father Harry had fixed.

"Just one wee minute!" she advised Martha, swatting her back into the bay again, as she was having a pathetic go at jiggling out the huge old fashioned machine. "I believe I left strict instructions for Lorna to give up her new wee machine to you, in view of your heroine status, and skinniness. That big brute would kill you!"

"Lornaa! Big Lornaa!" Josie yodelled like a Valkyrie, "C'mere! You're wanted!"

Even the good new machine, when huffy Lorna had returned it, proved almost too much for a distracted Martha. Her court shoes slipped after the machine, which made its own way down Martha's allotted bit of the corridor once it had been switched on. The Polishers stopped for a moment, switching off their machines to watch and laugh, as Martha was dragged this way and that, on the slippy, newly waxed surface. But, taking their cue from Big Josie, their leader, they switched to sentimental smirks, as though watching a child's first steps.

In spite of their quarrel, Varrie peeked out of the art room to see how Martha was doing. She was relieved to see her friend getting control of the machine, at last, and gallusly working the new gears that she had swotted up on, from the manual, before dawn.

Varrie had retired to the art store room to puff miserably at her fag, as tears spotted her elaborate make-up. She had got through the horrors of last night without breaking down, and had got Kansas to bed at last, even watching a video with her, to calm her down after the School Ceilidhe. And now a few wee words with her pal had laid her low. She turned over the contents of her purse, counting out if she had enough cash for a quarter bottle of vodka. She still had some ancient worthless lottery tickets of Martha's. She might as well give those back to her too. She glanced at the familiar numbers, based on Martha's birthday, Jimmy's birthday, and the twins separate birthdays, born on either side of midnight on Midsummer Night. And her lucky number, thirteen.

Varrie's cigarette, smouldering on her glossy lip, seared through the lipstick, as she leapt off the counter she was perched on. She had caught sight of the date on a crumpled up ticket. The winning date, May 28th. Kansas's birthday! She had given Martha back the wrong ticket! Varrie shoved her purse in her lab coat pocket. Because the art store room door was opening slowly and silently, without its usual warning squeak.

Father Harry entered and stamped over to hold Varrie at arm's length, speaking to her in the mock stern manner he used, his twinkling blue eyes staring into her shadowed dark ones.

"Well, have you got over your huff, honey?" Then he grabbed her fiercely in his arms to growl in her ear, "You women, you're all the same! You'll never admit you enjoy sex! You have to make up wee reasons for going in the huff!"

Then, at last, he noticed her tear-stained face. Sentimentally, he traced the course of the tears with his stubby nicotine stained forefinger.

"You mustn't worry about what I shouted at you, Varrie! I wouldn't inform on you to the Social because you've turned a few tricks and done a wee bit grass and charlie. I'd never get Kansas taken off you. We'll all be so happy together. Now I've got my ticket. I'll have to hide out for a while, to avoid the publicity, but I'll come back for you, pet. You know I will!"

"But Martha!" she managed to gasp, "What about wee Martha?"

"Don't you worry about wee Martha! I've got her fixed!" Harry punched himself in the chest just where his wallet containing the ticket made a slight bulge. "Just you wait and see!"

And he leant over and kissed Varrie gallantly and tenderly. She leant away from him, backwards over the hard formica shelf, paralysed with terror. Then he groaned at his sore mouth.

What made Big Lorna decide to batter her lumbering machine into that particular store room, which wasn't even on her route, was a mystery. Maybe she had a suspicious mind, and had been tracking Varrie and Father Harry. Afterwards, she couldn't remember anything about it, except for the big bang and the smoke, and the burning pain between her thumbs.

And if Big Lorna had not had her nail extensions newly done, and had not been wearing her outsize red polisher's gloves, for once, she might not have had any thumbs left at all. And if Father Tiziano had not kicked off the power supply switch, bravely, with a sandal, Lorna's new perm might have been even more annoyingly curly. And if the jolt with which the polishing machine had rebounded against the door sill had not thrown the big woman down on her back, outside the door, sports-sock-lined wellington boots sticking up in the air, Lorna would have been the second of mad Father Harry's innocent victims in that very room.

As for Father Harry, he disappeared by the other door, in a puff of burnt rubber smoke. Father Tiziano took charge, dismantling the machine.

"Scusi Signore, scusi! Allow me! Permesso! Degree in electro engineering from Milan University before seminary. Something in works. Something smelly! Like rat!"

It was not a rat but a little medal to Saint Philomena which had caused the trouble and short circuited the huge machine. That and some frayed cables.

"My God!" Big Josie crossed herself. "That's two mechanics in holy orders have tried to fix that poor machine! We're never going to get back on schedule!"

But the Polishers and their newest recruit were not easily put off. And once Lorna had gone home in a taxi, and the others had cups of tea and fags, they got down to business.

"You could keep that wee violet patterned mug as yours, sunshine!" Josie told Martha.

Martha blushed with pleasure, and then got stuck into her new duties so hard that the Polishers gave her sidewise looks.

"Allow her!" they said to each other. "You'd never have thought that Martha had it in her! Give the poor soul her due, she gets pure beasted in!"

And when the cavalcade made it back to their base eventually, mission accomplished, composition floors gleaming but not sticky or slippy, Martha joined in the singing too. As the sounds of their anthem echoed and re-echoed through all the interconnecting doors, Martha's high quavering genteel tones soared an octave above the big lassies' booming contraltos. And Varrie risked slipping in an alto descant of her own.

In his dingy bedroom in the parish house, Father Harry had to lie down on his bed, biting his pillow, thrashing about, when he discovered he had been given the wrong lottery ticket. Then he suddenly fell into a leaden sleep, spark out till the sun set over the big black Victorian church and his depressing dwelling next to it.

On Harry's pillow, Rory's torn apart fluffy chick shed more feathers.

Mrs Mulvey woke him with a message.

"It's that daft Sister Philomena, again, about their boiler! She says it's not going again. She says the devil has been in the furnace, and will you come and exorcise it? She says something about a crucifix!" Mrs Mulvey said, wincing as Harry leapt to his feet, cursing.

"I'm away out, Mrs Mulvey. Don't worry about dinner. I may be some time!"

As he pushed past her in the narrow hallway, Mrs Mulvey saw he had his big travel bag with him, stuffed. He must be planning on an overnight at one of the hostels he helped in, for the homeless. And she'd had a nice stew all ready for his dinner.

Outside, Harry stepped into Liam's taxi, again. The second time he'd hired him, and he still didn't recognise the pimply neck in front of him. Liam, though, recognised Harry's big beefy mug right away. He cast his mind back to his classical studies. The guy looked like a gladiator about to get the 'thumbs down'.

Poor Philomena

Poor Philomena had begun to get on peoples' nerves. She had started wandering about like Ophelia, with bits of her habit loose, or missing, and garlands of wild flowers trailing about her. She had little to do all day, since she had lost interest in the central heating system of the Bleeding Heart convent now the old boiler had been scrapped. She had plenty of time now to prepare for eternity and annoy all the other nuns while she did so.

Mother Mary Agnes, who had been a novice with Philomena, was all for keeping her at the convent, although her behaviour had become bizarre, even dangerous. For such a big plain woman, Agnes had a very tender heart. She could not bear to see any injured creature turned away from the convent's oaken, brass studded door. She it was who cared for the animals in the sanctuary, getting up first on frosty mornings to feed and groom the old donkeys, to let the dogs out to play and then entice them back to their kennels. She fed the little wild tiger-striped mother cat in the secret garden, who had delivered such a large litter of kittens she was quite worn out. And of course the one-legged robin who fed from her hand. Philomena hadn't managed to feed him, frightening the bird off with her high-pitched childish laughter. In her second childhood, though still in her fifties, just five years older than Agnes.

But Mother Mary Agnes, although manager of the estate, was but one nun among many. And it was

One Nun One Vote in the Democratic Convent of the Bleeding Heart, their official charity nomenclature. Many of the younger nuns would have been glad to hand over Philomena to another religious house better suited to her needs. One not so much in the public eye, or even, to be brutal, to an ordinary care home.

"But how would she know when it was time to read her Office?" Mother Agnes asked.

"How would she know when it was time to go to the toilet, even?" a postulant whispered to a novice, when they were taking their exercise in the garden. On their little half hour of leisure before going back to look after the bad boys in the west wing. It was alright for the estate nuns to talk. They didn't have to wipe up after Philomena in the kitchen.

At that time Mother Benigna had stood her ground and not agreed to send poor Sister Philomena away. But Agnes had heard that it was just a matter of time till the younger nuns got their way, and got rid her for good.

Mother Mary Agnes, some mornings as she did her rounds, had made plans to spirit Philomena away and hide her in one of the stables. The donkeys would keep her warm enough. The Christ Child had been born in a stable breathed on by an ox and an ass. Agnes fell down on her knees at the thought, and gasped a little prayer for her old friend, the apple of her eye, even now. Now that Philly looked and acted so much older than Mother Agnes.

The apple of everyone's eye earlier, when she was young, slight and girlish looking, first to do the worst of the chores. And in the evening, after Benediction, laughing quietly, trying to make jokes in sign language, when they were supposed to be under silence.

Agnes had tried to interest Philomena in the gardens and the animals, but Phil was just not an outdoor girl. If she had stayed on in the world, she once confided to Mother Agnes, she would liked to have been on TV.

A presenter or something. And she had always had a lovely soprano voice. Even better than Agnes's mezzo. She might have become an opera star. Agnes could always picture her on stage, in Traviata, in a fancy ball gown, curtseying.

Poor Sister Philomena had taken to getting up in the middle of the night and going downstairs. To listen for the doorbell, Agnes thought. Phil had given the game away that she was waiting for her daddy to come and fetch her home, when he got back from the East. She thought she was still a little schoolgirl, sent to an army kids' boarding school. Not that she didn't like it, she had explained to Mother Agnes. And everyone was so kind to her. But after all, home was home, be it ever so humble. Even just a little tenement flat. With Mummy and Daddy and baby Freddy, who needed a mansion like this? And she didn't want to miss Freddy growing up, she had explained.

Agnes had caught her unlocking the door and leaving it ajar at night. After all the trouble they'd had in the grounds with poachers and vagrants. She had some sort of secret, too, that she shared with Imelda the kitchen maid. Fancy her trusting Imelda, and acting funny with her best friend. Who had looked after her all these years. Done her chores when her health was breaking down. Stood up for her when the nuns had got offended by her strange ways.

So Imelda and Sister Philomena had started whispering together. They made secret visits to the chapel. Said many strange prayers, mere mumbo jumbo, that they had made up between the two of them.

Even Tam, the rag man, knew more about Sister Philomena's doings than her old and faithful friend. Things had been shifted about in the kitchen and scullery, that had required the strength of a man to move.

Agnes had just not been able to figure out the world she lived in any more. People were saying terrible things about priests. Rumours were even starting about poor Father Harry, since he had run away from the chapel house, and grumpy old Ma Mulvey, his stern but devoted housekeeper. Agnes didn't blame him. Man does not live by Irish stew alone. And the house was dusty, if you looked in the corners. And still had sixties wallpaper. And the furnishings! You could sell them on eBay now as antiques. Harry's problem was that he had spent all his stipend on those down and outs. And borrowed, too, for them, she'd heard, from the tallymen. No wonder he was in hiding, if those wild thugs were after him.

Beforehand, Agnes had used to look forward to his visits. He fancied himself as an expert on animal husbandry, since his family had a share in that wee farm in Ireland. And he would often do the rounds with her, looking at the poor beasts, suggesting remedies. Shedding a few tears, furtively, over the sickest, the ones they'd have to send the vet to deal with.

But stolid practical Mother Mary Agnes had her share of secrets too, like all of us. Harry had once said to her "See if I'd met a fine big girl like you at the right time. Sure I wouldn't be lonely as I am today. Nor you neither, Alanna!" He always put on an Irish accent speaking to her, as a joke, because she'd never lost her own Galway brogue.

And, a thing that sometimes troubled her conscience, Father Harry still came to visit her. He usually came at sunset, when she was bedding down the animals, and gave her a hand with them. He was worried about Philomena too. He said she had phoned him to come and fix the old boiler, and exorcise the demons from it. She'd found an old bit of trash in it, he'd said, and that was upsetting her. Maybe a bit of an old gas poker or something. He wondered if Mother Agnes had found anything out about it.

Well, she hadn't then. But she had made Imelda own up. And found out it was an old bit of a crucifix, probably fallen in by accident when Philomena, in her dementia, was poking about in the furnace. She almost wished she hadn't told Father Harry about that, the state he had got into. She had almost been afraid of him, as he punched his fists into the old whitewashed lathe and plaster walls of the stable, frightening the animals.

But the two of them had made it up later, right enough. Father Harry had put his chilly fists inside the wide sleeves of her brown working habit, to warm himself. Just as little Philomena used to do, when they slept in the cold attics, among the russet apples, as young postulants. Home sick and heart sick, sometimes, as every girl is, who has left her home behind her.

That night Father Harry had asked if he could spend the night in the stables, which he had never done before. In order not to compromise her, he said. That had made her blush, although she had joshed that you couldn't compromise a battleship. Which she was now. Ironclad. She saw that when she couldn't avoid looking in a mirror. And she hadn't wanted him to have the long walk home, to wherever home was at the time, upset as he had been.

So Agnes had brought him some food. Good lentil soup, her specialty, that always reminded him of his Mammy's cooking. With some bread and cheese, and pickles. A ploughman's supper. He said he'd have liked to be a ploughboy. He liked horses. And dogs, he said. Father Harry was always petting the rackety guard dogs.

She'd got him a sleeping bag too, and some blankets, and he'd settled down in the truckle bed in the tack room. He'd said that, somehow, he was worried about Philomena that night.

"I've devil a weapon about me!" he'd said, in that comical way he had, "But sure I've a good strong right arm! Not a man nor a brute will get past me this night!"

So Mother Agnes had waved farewell from the doorway. Though he had called out to her sweetly,

"Mammy! Mammy! Won't you be tucking me up?" and she hadn't known if he was serious or not, the great card that he was. She had been laughing when she went back into the big silent house. The sisters were used to her going out and in, tending to the sick beasts.

But in spite of Father Harry's protection, and no doubt the prayers he had offered up too, seeing he had his rosary within reach, and despite Agnes keeping an ear open, that was the very night it happened. Why had nobody heard a thing? The hour Philomena was tortured before she gave up the ghost. There was thunder that night, she remembered. Agnes was used to thunder, it never frightened her. Not like some of the young ones, who enjoyed being scared, and hid their silly heads under their pillows, with cotton wool in their ears, or ran in and out of each other's rooms screaming.

Anyway, if screaming there had been, if Sister Philomena had managed to open her poor mouth and force the air through her lungs and out her little drooping lips to scream, none of her Sisters in Christ heard it that night. A really young detective from Mirkshields, the local police station, had told her that Philomena would probably have gone into shock after the first deep blow to the cranium. She might not even have felt the assaults on her poor chaste body that ensued.

But it was clear from the bloody drag marks in and out of the kitchen rooms, that she had been manhandled through them. As though her assailant was searching for something. It had been Sister Peppy who had found poor Philomena's body, and she had been sensible enough to stop anyone disturbing the 'scene of the crime', as they had learned to call their downstairs kitchen and pantries. Agnes had only seen the taped out shape where her friend had been (angular twisted lines suggesting a broken dolly). She had little Sister Mary of Perpetual Succour to thank for that.

But someone in the police department must have leaked details of Sister Philomena's martyrdom to the avid paparazzi. Maybe to gain sympathy for the case, and persuade the public to come forward with information. The investigators had not received very much information. They said just one phone call could blow the case wide open, and beseeched people to try to recall anything odd they'd witnessed that day. The young detective appeared on Crimewatch, begging the public to co-operate. He said the killer might strike again, and that someone must be protecting the psychopath. Someone was bound to have noticed a friend or member of the family who was acting suspiciously. Mother Mary Agnes began to worry about Father Harry, if he had got home safely that night. He wasn't a young man anymore, who could fight off an assailant. And who would notice if he went missing? Except, of course, Mother Agnes herself. At least he had one friend, poor man, in these terrible times.

One tabloid had actually printed a reconstruction of what poor Philomena's body must have looked like, marking where each of her many injuries had been. With a description of how they had been made, whether stabbed or slashed or twisted or screwed or battered. The nun's guimpe and wimple had been torn off, and tufts of cropped grey hair had been pulled out. Blood pouring down from her scalp must have nearly blinded her. Her own rosary beads were biting into the flesh round her neck. But the blow that finished poor little Sister Philomena off was deep and straight to the heart, with one of the stainless kitchen knives.

It came out that she must have opened the door to her murderer, dressed up in the middle of the night in her best white ceremonial habit. The forensic medics thought that Philomena had probably known him. And that she had not attempted to defend herself.

Mother Mary Agnes took it badly. She said she wished it had been herself that had been attacked, in front of the embers of the kitchen fire, with old Moggy purring round her feet. He might at least have left old Moggy alone. But Moggy had survived after all, she comforted herself. And Philomena would be singing with choirs of angels now. If there were any angels. Mother Agnes couldn't help doubting it.

Where had Sister Philomena's guardian angel been, then? And what of Saint Philomena? She hadn't stepped up to the plate either. Although maybe, Mother Agnes thought, the saint considered that her namesake would have preferred the martyrdom to the old folk's Home.

In the aftermath, the worst thing had been when the press had insinuated the killer might be one of the Sisters. But it had been proved that the attack would be beyond the strength of any woman. And the copious DNA left was male.

Agnes sometimes thought of asking to be sent home, back to beautiful Galway, but she knew no-one there now. And sometimes in the very early morning, she couldn't help looking at the old flax pool longingly, as it glittered in the mist. There were plenty of reeds in it, to stop a hopeful suicide from floating unwillingly to the surface. But despair, the Church taught, was the worst sin of all. Also what would the poor little animals do without her?

And young Sister Mary of the Angels was being very nice. Very good to the old nun. She always kept her breakfast hot for her when she got back from the stables. And Sister Mary of Perpetual Succour had an idea for a TV programme based on the rescued animals. She said she'd had a few nibbles already from interested directors. She said she was sure it would be a hit.

"You'll be famous, Mother Agnes," Sister Peppy had said. "While you're still young and feisty enough to enjoy it!"

Tam Tam

Tam Tam sat nervously on the edge of his plastic chair in an out of the way interview room on the second floor of Mirkhill Police Station. He had been nearly run over several times as he had tried to gain access to the building, which squatted like a nuclear bunker on an atoll surrounded by seas of whirling traffic. Not just ordinary traffic, but lorries and heavy goods vehicles. None of which took any pains to avoid a five-foot-minus ex-Jaikie-and-Grass.

He was also unnerved by a large mirror on the wall opposite to him. He kept catching glimpses of his own round worried face, a bit lower than normal people's faces would be. And his simple ball face was a kind of funny colour too. Although Tam Tam (Thomas Piper, as he was known to officialdom) had at last painfully given up the booze, the damage it had done to his liver was evident in his odd complexion. He almost looked as if he had a healthy tan. In a way he did, spending many hours out of doors on the tramp, and getting a bit wind-blown and weather-beaten. He had done what he could about his appearance. A nice girl helper at his hostel had cut his hair that very morning. And at first he had thought it looked quite nice. He wasn't so sure now, though. His fringe seemed to fall over his face in a kind of a girlish way.

Tam was well dressed in the best of the clothes he took in on his ragman round. They were of the very best

materials, but the sleeves when shortened had left their elbow bumps down near his wrists, and the trousers' knee hummocks were midway to his ankles. The charity shop lady he supplied to said the clothes would even out in time, but they hadn't yet, so Tam kept his arms under the desk in front of him.

What was really annoying Tam Tam was that the smart detective guy, who was supposed to be interviewing him, kept walking about the room as if he wasn't listening to one word. And every time the guy landed in front of the big mirror, he paused for a moment, sucking in his stomach and squaring his shoulders.

"Sir!" Tam Tam interrupted, "Can I shift my chair? Sun's in my eyes off that big mirror."

The Detective gathered himself together. He took off his sharp jacket and hung it over one of the chairs. He was revealed in a blue striped shirt and red braces over hipster pants. His hands strayed to his abdomen, satisfyingly slim and ridged under his tanned spatulate fingers.

Tam wondered if the guy had a stomach ulcer or something. But the cop would have said the opposite was true. He was bouncing with health. And it was getting on for the time when he had his fix of exercise at a posh gym downtown. Detective Constable Childers liked to keep fit. In fact he was quite obsessive about it. His musculature was just this side of scary. He could almost have entered a body building contest for fly weights.

Frank Childers had been so pleased when he'd passed his police exams and had been fast tracked to Detective Constable. It was great getting out of uniform. But Frank hadn't grasped the dress code expected of an officer of his grade. He would have been better off going to Marks and Spencers like everybody else. He had opted for a far too stylish cut. And people mistook his olive skin for a Man Tan. Which wasn't exactly the case. He came from

that special breed, the dark skinned Irish, who traced their ancestors to the mariners of the Spanish Armada galleons wrecked off the Irish coast. Though Glasgow born and bred, that was Frankie's story, anyway, the one he handed out to the girls at wine bars and bistros, and he was sticking to it.

Frank felt he was simply cut out from a different cloth from his colleagues, and that made it inevitable that he would have a hard time fitting in. And somehow his workmates got the impression that he fancied himself rotten. Which he didn't. He was just nervous that he might be losing his good looks early. He ruffled the loose dark curls on the top of his head, above the macho shaved bits, his face anxious in the two way spy mirror. Could his hairline be receding at only twenty three?

Tam coughed. Frank remembered the question.

"Sure Tam Tam," he said. "Sure you can move. You've come in here on your own account, remember. Without being asked. To give me some vital information."

"Could you not call me Tam Tam, mister? I don't like it."

"I thought your friends called you that!"

"Yes, but they only do it to annoy me. Sky never called me that."

"Tam? Tom? Thomas?"

"Tam's fine. My girlfriend calls me that."

"Your girlfriend? You were telling me ..."

"My girlfriend Imelda's pure terrified. Since the murder."

"Which murder?"

"The one that's in all the papers. "Sister at Convent of Bleeding Heart Slaughtered."

"Oh, yes, the convent. Your girlfriend's a nun?"

"Not exactly, but she could have been. There was nothing to stop her, Mother Benigna said, if she'd wanted to. Turned it down but. No vocation. You really have to have a vocation, Imelda says. She works in the kitchen now. Sort of cooks if it's not too complicated. Washes the dishes when the dishwasher's full."

"And Imelda's terrified?"

"That's what I came to tell you!"

"Look here, Tam Tam. I mean Tam." Frank had gone white under his olive skin. "I'm afraid I'm absolutely starving. I'm going to have to have a banana." He dived into a drawer and, peeling a banana with one deft flick, wolfed it down. "I wasn't expecting to have to work overtime. Sorry!" He held out a banana to Tam. "Would you like one?"

"No, thanks, sir, but do you mind if I smoke?"

"I do, a bit. Sorry, I mean a lot. I mean it's against the rules."

"Sergeant Black does!"

"Yes, but he's a law unto himself!"

Detective Constable Childers began to muse disconsolately how the uniformed staff hated him almost as much as his colleagues, the detectives. He was sure they'd put this tramp in his interview room out of badness. Sergeant Black had caught Frank just as he was about to leave the building, sixty seconds early, from his shift, and sent him back for some really unwanted overtime. Said the informant had asked for him by name.

"Listen!" Frank leaned forward to rivet Tam with his light grey stare. "Did you ask for me by name? How come? How come you knew me?"

"My girlfriend's friend is a millionairess. She knows you. She gave us your name."

Tam produced a card and handed it over. It had Frank's office number and mobile on it, and also his home landline number scribbled in. He recognised the card right away. The one he'd given to the terrific looking girl at the hospital. The boy victim's sister, she'd said. And Tam's kitchen maid girlfriend wasn't too wide of the mark. The girl had looked like a million dollars. Not girl, lady. Millionairess, the wee guy was right. He looked at Tam with new eyes.

"How can I get in touch with the Millionairess, do you know?"

"Through the convent. The big lassie told Imelda she was wanting to become a nun. Imelda, my girlfriend, advised against it, and I think the big lassie changed her mind. But you could ask for her at the convent."

"Tried it, no joy. No luck at the jannie's house either. About your girlfriend."

The banana was beginning to make Frank feel funny. He snapped the top off a bottle of water and took a glug, then gestured invitingly with it to Tam.

Tam looked at him in contempt. Offering a man a sip of gassy water! He shook his head.

"Listen, son!" Tam, in his turn, sat forward. "I mean, listen sir. I've got urgent news for you. You better listen. I mean it! You could get promotion through this, you really could!"

Frank had been doing little push-ups aslant on his desk. He stopped. His brain cleared.

"Got you, Tam!" he said, sitting down and frowning. "Speak up! I'm listening!"

"I've got something to show you, sir!"

Tam undid a large zipped shopping bag and carefully took out an object wrapped in many layers of newspapers. He unwrapped it and carefully passed it over the desk to Childers.

"That's the murder weapon. The weapon that done in my pal Sky. Can you make it out?"

At first the Detective couldn't. It looked like a piece of modern sculpture. He quite liked the flowing metal outlines of it. Almost like a crucifixion. Then he got it, it was a crucifix, but melted down and burned. Only part of the Christ figure remained, welded to a burnt part of the cross, which had leaked some kind of reddish resin over the ivory and silver figurine.

"Note the bloodstains!" said Tam, leaning over to stab at them with his twisted blackened fingers, his stubby nails ragged and split.

Frank jerked it away from him, but let it slip to the desk top. It gave him a horrible feeling. He got a plastic bag from a drawer, and sealed the melted object into it. Then he slipped over to lock the outside door, and was about to press his intercom for assistance, when he all at once changed his mind.

It was all looking a bit too easy.

No, he thought, maybe he'd been set up for this by one of his 'pals' on the force. They all knew how it had become an obsession with him, finding the crucifix. The bit that matched the INRI plaque that he'd found among the tombstones. He couldn't match it with this lump. They could have mocked up the object easy, and sent the down and out informer in with it.

"Did someone put you up to this?" he asked Tam suspiciously.

"Yes, sir! My girlfriend Imelda. I told you, she's scared stiff. She's sure that's how Sister Philomena got done in. Philomena found this when she was raking out the furnace below the big rusty boiler. She was always raking out the furnace, even when it was still flaming and white hot. She'd went a wee bit gaga. In a really nice way but, the poor wee soul."

"Sister Philomena got all worried by it. She said it was sacrilege. And it had also jiggered the central heating just as the cold nights were coming on. And then, Imelda said, the wee nun went to the chapel to pray to Saint Philomena to sort out the problem. And she got inspired. She said she'd just phoned an old friend to come and repair the boiler and to bless the furnace from the stain of desecrating an image of Christ. Then, Imelda said, she was just as happy as though she was in her right mind. And she asked Imelda to help her hide the melted bit somewhere fly. She wanted to try if Saint Philomena could put it back together again. She said we'd not to tell Mother Benigna or anyone or it wouldn't work. Not that me or Imelda really thought it would work. But you never know."

Tam looked all round the room as if expecting someone to disagree with him.

"So now we've decided to give it to you, you can find out the murderer from it. And Imelda and I would like police protection, please."

"Tell me, Mr Piper," Frank was suddenly smooth and ingratiating. "The furnace, is it working now?"

"That heap of rust, no it's not!"

"So I could come and examine it? At the convent? Maybe find something else?"

"Not really, sir." Tam hung his head. He was beginning to think something was up. "Mother Superior called in British Gas, and they done a deal with her for scrappage. The nuns have a brand new boiler now. Imelda said it's lovely. They're all taking baths all the time now, not that they didn't before, only coldish."

Frank sighed deeply. "So no chance of forensics there!"

What had he expected anyway? That the solution to a murder investigation would fall into his lap? It was sounding more and more like a set up.

He slammed the 'evidence' in its bag into his sports bag below his desk. Then he opened his desk drawer and took out a cash box, which he unlocked and counted out some notes.

"For your fares and your trouble, Mr Piper", he said. "Thanks for the information."

"No, no, sir! No need for that. I'm doing this to protect Imelda. And suppose I was asked to give evidence, and

I'd taken your money? I watch television, you know, like everybody else. Anyway, I got my giro yesterday. And I make a wee bob or two on the side."

Suddenly, the Detective Constable's ferocious hunger pains came on again, and with it his desire for violent exercise. He felt a vein in his forehead begin to throb. He unlocked the outer door as if in a dream

"Thank you Tam Tam. I'll be in touch."

"And what about our protection, sir?" Tam turned back at the door to ask earnestly.

The Detective was usually quite a courteous young man. He was kind to animals and never forgot his Mum's birthday. But Frank Childers had had enough for one stressful day.

"Have you thought of praying to Saint Philomena? I hear she's pure dead brilliant! You and Imelda should try making a novena."

Working Out

Tam Piper was trapped, marooned on a traffic island amid the surging currents of heavy traffic that thundered round the interchange. How he had made it even that far across the six lanes of traffic was a miracle, perhaps only explained by the special Saint Philomena medals that jangled in his stained raincoat pocket. (Imelda had access to all the latest types that were traded on the Bleeding Heart internet site. She helped to package them and had absolute faith in their amazing powers.) He had been helped to his precarious refuge by a bus driver, who had finally lost it when Tam kept diving out nearly under his wheels at the taxi and bus lane, and then leaping backwards to the pavement again. When the bus driver lost his turn at the lights because of Tam, he had jumped out of his cab, foaming at the mouth in rage. Mindful of the overhead cameras, though, instead of battering the wee guy, he had run out into the remaining traffic, stopping it with widespread arms, and then gone back to conduct Tam across to the traffic island, bowing before he climbed back into his cab. Now Tam was stuck there. He might have been there still, if his new found friend, Frank Childers, had not got into the wrong lane in a temper. He had been halted at the manned barrier to the police car park by a Jack-in-office attendant who had asked for proof of his Detective status. Frank scorned to give it and the guy scorned to open up till he did.

Frank scraped the inky black wing of his BMW on the island's iron clad edge, and cursed. He cursed louder as he made out the small figure leaning on a bollard, a tartan shopping bag at his feet. D.C. Childers would have been right to ignore him. No-one would have blamed him. Except maybe his mum, who had brought him up with very nice manners. She worried that the police job was making him a bit rough. She wished he had stuck in at his violin instead. And every night she said a wee prayer for him. Sometimes asking that he would be let go from his job (that's what they called it now, not sacked) so he could join an orchestra. And she often asked all the saints in the litany, including Philomena, to find him a nice artistic girl. (Maybe Philomena wasn't such a good choice, considering her views on marriage.) Her neighbours were beginning to hint things about Frankie, since he was still only a bachelor and girlfriend-less at twenty-three. Frank knew all about her evening prayers, since he was still living at home, while his new flat was being done up. Fatherless Frank would have liked to make his widowed mother proud, but he couldn't bear all the practice, and especially those weird scales in thirds. But anyway, his good nature outweighing his rotten temper, he shoved open his passenger door.

"Get in!" He grunted at Tam, who did instantly, as if the big glamorous car had been some minicab he'd ordered.

"Thanks, son!" Tam replied, settling his shopping bag on his knee."Y'alright? You seemed a wee bit upset earlier."

Frank's face twisted as he tried to control his rage. So now the old tramp was expecting him to apologise for being, well, he supposed, kind of rude to him earlier.

"Sorry!" Frank managed to squeeze out from whitened lips. "I didn't mean..."

"No, you're alright, son. Just let me off at Saint Jude's. Just over there."

The trouble was that Saint Jude's school, though so near that the lights of its further education wing shone like a lighthouse over the damp wilderness around it, was almost inaccessible from the Police Station's exit roads. It would have been easier and it might have taken less time to zoom up the main road and out to one of those picturesque little villages to the north. Little commuter hamlets with nice little pubs where you could get a decent bouillabaisse. Although a nice steak and chips would have been okay too. Frank's mind was really beginning to wander. He felt kind of spaced out, the traffic lights dazzled his screwed up eyes. His stomach was rumbling with hunger. He shouldn't have skipped lunch again, planning an early evening exercise class. His abdomen and thighs were cramping after last night's class, and he really wanted to work off the fatigue.

Luckily Frank knew the district well, and managed to get off the main drag, and onto the secret rat runs that led finally to the back doors of the school. He stopped to let Tam off, and waited in silence when the older man didn't go. Tam obviously had something on his mind. Frank closed his eyes. He felt like crashing out then and there.

"I've been thinking." Tam finally announced. "You know how you're not supposed to speak ill of the dead, and you're not supposed to speak ill of the clergy either?"

Sensing a reply was needed, Frank nodded wearily, though keeping his eyes closed.

"But see Sky?" Tam began again. "See my pal Sky? And see Father Harry? Him that looks after us vagabonds? Well, I think they were up to something. Drugs and stuff. Maybe other stuff too!" Tam's speech had speeded up with indignation, and his face had become flushed. "And see this!" Tam rooted in his bag, and brought out a plastic bag of burnt scraps of clothing. "That's bits of Father Harry's good party clothes. His checked shirt. His cords, and that's a bit of his good tweed jacket. I'd know them anywhere. Father Harry told me he'd give them to me when he gave up partying. So why were they in the furnace? With the crucifix. That Imelda helped Sister Philomena wrastle out of the fire. And see the crucifix? I think that was Father Harry's, too. That he used for his last rites, that he kept in Saint Jude's."

Detective Inspector Childers woke up suddenly. The cramps had gone. No headache. His mind was working overtime now. The brain that had made him top of the sixth form at Saint Iggies, and that would have got him through Uni if he could have stuck it, crashed into gear.

"How come you never told me this back at the station?"

"I don't like most Polis. You're not like them. Here you are, son." He passed over the bag to Frank Childers. "Anyway, cars are safest for informing in. I'll need to away to my flower arranging class at the FE wing. I'm supposed to enhance my practical skills to keep on drawing my dole. One other thing, er..."

"Frankie!" the Detective broke in eagerly, "You can call me Frankie!"

"Frankie, sir." Tam compromised with the familiarity. "There's a lassie works at Saint Jude's. She could tell you about Father Harry, I heard. Varrie, she's called. Varrie Valentino!"

"Do you have any idea of her address?" Frank smiled at Tam, showing his especially charming dimples and flashing his cutest porcelain smile. "At all?"

He needn't have bothered; once Tam had got going, he could hardly have been stopped.

"Don't bother with that. She's working here tonight. Aerobics instructor. An awful nice lassie, too, never mind what anybody says about her. Come in and I'll show you around."

Frank's mind went into overdrive. He could see it all. The crucifix used to batter the wee boy had been Father Harry's. Sky had been about to clype so Sky was crucified too. It was Harry that the nun had called to bless and repair the Boiler. Now all he needed was proof of the guy's other wrongdoings. Maybe Varrie would oblige. Then Frank would move! He wondered if he could remember all of his reasoning. He wished he could write it down. He didn't want someone at the cop shop taking the credit. His head was spinning again.

Inside, the hallway was like a conservatory, with troughs and baskets of indoor plants. Orchids and palms and yuccas were stacked there in profusion, under special lighting. Tam led him past a side room where the plants were growing in regimented lines. Hardly artistic, thought Frank. You could almost have thought they looked like cannabis. Probably some scientific project the biology department was doing. But the whole hallway smelled fragrant.

The smell of rancid sweat, though, led to the boys' Gym where the aerobics class was already taking place. A poster announced that the class was taken by Varrie, and there was a flattering shot of her gesturing in invitation, with the mottos below,

'LET VARRIE GIVE YOU A WORKOUT!
BEGINNERS AND EXPERTS ALL WELCOME!
DON'T PAY IF NOT FULLY SATISFIED!'

Brilliant, thought Frank, what a brilliant excuse for grabbing an hour's exercise! He dashed back to his car and got out his exercise bag, full of his trendy black exercise gear. So Detective Constable Childers made quite an entrance in his tight lycra, that showed off his defined and honed musculature. His chic gear contrasted with the weird stuff most of the class were wearing. Two grannies on their way back from bingo in the dinner school were just wearing their usual stuff, crimplene trouser suits. Several girls were wearing short shorts and Tee-shirts with different obscene invitations printed on them. Slobby fat guys back from the pub showed shaming contours through sweaty vests. Wayne and Darren had both turned up in full karate gear, hoping to impress Varrie, whom they fancied. And at the very front Kansas and Dakota, in pale blue leotards, were taking the aerobics class very seriously. One correctly sports dressed old guy accompanied by his carer was doing very well from his gleaming new sports wheel chair. There were also two plump girls doing training for a charity walk up Machu Picchu for the Duke of Edinburgh.

But at the very back row some guys gave Frank a run for his money. These were a couple of P.E. teachers incognito to keep order if too many fly guys turned up, and he also saw Kirstie Collins, the highland dance teacher, getting really stuck in. Kirstie somehow got locked in competition with Frank over press-ups and tried jealously to manoeuvre him out of the best place in front of the mirror.

Varrie handled the lot of them with amazing skill, devising extra bits for the fittest, and letting the weakest off with all the hard bits.

"Sit this one out, Isa, till you get your breath back!"

"Got your Volvic, Mr Smith? We must keep hydrated!"

"Youse two! Darren and Wayne! Leave those lassies alone, or I'll tell your mammy!"

"Feet, Dakota! Feet!"

"Hands, Kansas! Hands!"

She caught sight of Frankie at the back, strutting his stuff, and gave him an alluring wink.

"Keep it up! Keep it up!" she encouraged him, smiling salaciously.

One big guy was a real show off. Frank nearly killed himself trying to keep up with him. Frank thought, personally, that his biceps were too chunky.

Varrie brought the proceedings to a close with a rather childish relaxation session, where those present were expected to lie down and close their eyes, like nursery school children.

"Imagine the scene!" she advised, standing over their various recumbent forms. "You are on a mountain top. White clouds go scudding by. And little rabbits are playing near a stream. Your eyes are closing, closing. You are completely relaxed." Varrie said, losing the place.

Her round of the now docile class had brought her to Frank's mat, where she paused, background muzak taking over from her. She thought the new young guy looked really hot. And it seemed as if he was really asleep. Her relaxation programme must be working.

Frank, on his mat, looked sideways at her through his half closed eyes, masked by his black eyelashes. Varrie bent over him, intrigued. Was he really sleeping? Was he kidding on? She leant a little further over and discovered. Frank raised himself from the hips, reaching up to clasp her in his arms. She struggled very demurely as he kissed her lipsticked lips with a sudden frantic passion. He'd never felt this way before, certainly not with an instructor. He remembered, too, that she was part of his investigation. Somehow, he didn't care.

"Can I see you later?" he whispered in her ear. "I'm Frank. Frankie to you."

Before she could reply he collapsed back, feeling suddenly dizzy. Feeling stupid too. Not in a million years would he do something so crass. He cringed with embarrassment. That girl must really be doing things to him. He was boiling hot, sweating, in a real fever. Could he be falling in love? He'd heard some of the guys say it sometimes happened like that. She was certainly a lovely looking girl, with her dark hair tumbling damply round her head. Frank began to sweat, and then to shake, shivering with cold. To his horror, suddenly he felt awful. He shouldn't have done those extra push ups. He rolled over, and, leaning on both hands, got up on his knees, before the pain got so bad he collapsed again, curling up in a foetal position.

When Frank Childers began to groan and scream, the exercise class decamped in a few seconds, leaving Varrie to deal with the emergency with only her pal Kirstie to help her. Varrie pulled rank (it was after all, her aerobics class) and got rid of Kirstie Collins once the handsome newcomer, now half conscious, had been stowed away safely by the paramedics.

Varrie went with him in the ambulance. She took charge of all his gear, when he wasn't allowed to take it into Emergency. She took it back to her flat, in his car, when she found all his keys among the half eaten lettuce sandwiches in his briefcase. And the bag of scorched rags. Some of them, she saw with horror, were blood stained. And the half melted crucifix.

"And he looked such a nice normal young guy, too." she said to herself sadly. "He looked really really nice."

She should drop the stuff off at Mirkshields Police Station, she thought, but it was against her religion to grass anyone up to the cops, even a Detective Constable. But the stuff looked so horrible. She swithered. Then she remembered that kiss he had given her, before he started to scream with pain. She delved deeper into his bag, and came across stuff in a side pocket.

And she came across the Saint Philomena medals that Tam Tam had slipped in the bag, for luck. And an elegant birthday card to The Best Mum in the World all ready to be posted.

Varrie thought she wouldn't give up on the guy yet. And she'd post the card to his mum.

In the anaesthetic room, when they were getting Detective Constable Frank Childers ready for his emergency appendectomy, he amused the staff there by calling out for help.

"Police Protection!" he shouted, "I have to get Police Protection!"

Through his clouding senses, Frank couldn't believe they were laughing. He had only just realised how right Tam Tam had been to demand protection for him and his girlfriend Imelda. With the last bit of consciousness left after his pre-op medication, he thought of the lovely girl. Of Varrie. She had taken his stuff. She would be at risk too.

"Varrie!" he shouted as the anaesthetist fed the knock out drug to his veins. "Varrie!"

"Must be his girlfriend." one nurse mumbled through her mask. "Lucky girl!"

Ghosts

There were rumours that Sky's ghost was floating about Old Royston. A figure in a lady's fur coat had been seen peeping out from behind the gravestones and monuments at Royston cemetery. A big rusty-bearded figure wrapped in the fur coat, with the knapsack Sky had carried. Father Seamas, tramping the district out looking for Harry, had had several sightings.

The enthusiasts who were always trying to film the Mirkhill foxes by night thought they had captured a Royston yeti, as a big furry creature fought the foxes off for enticing scraps. The night time cameras didn't film colour, but the beard, when close-ups had distinguished the creature as fully human, was the same shape as Sky's. The figure was not chunky, as had been reported, but quite gaunt, and seemed to be dragging the left leg, as poor Sky had.

But of course it wasn't Sky. Sky was in his grave. Rather a nice grave, in the Old Ossuary cemetery the nuns still kept up, in the grounds of the Convent of the Bleeding Heart. Mother Benigna had professed herself delighted to receive the earthly remains of a poet into the convent demesne. And Marie Louise had endowed the grounds with some of her Page Three savings, so there were gardeners always on hand to restore the site and maintain it. Apart from a bouquet that was delivered on Sky's birthday, from Marie Louise, there were often little posies found there. The nuns thought they were gathered from the convent's kitchen gardens, because as well as flowers like michaelmas daisies and wild poppies, there were always some rosemary and thyme, as well as nettles and brambles. And the odd lettuce. Mother Benigna suspected the kitchen maid, Imelda, of these depredations, but the posies were so pretty, she never accused Imelda, the former Wanderer, and Sky's last girlfriend.

In Old Royston burial ground there was no space at all, even for a Wanderer, who had chosen to live there, and wandered his last in the precincts. It was absolutely choc-a-bloc, and protected by conservation orders and by-laws, and European Union regulations. And if anyone had attempted an interment there, there would have been a scene like the Last Judgement, with ancient cadavers rising to protest. And the fine mist of bones left from prehistoric buryings would have heaved, crackling, to the surface.

But Sky had a lovely headstone amid peaceful convent gardens, with a few lines of his own engraved on it as an epitaph. Marie Louise had gathered pages and pages of his work scattered amongst the gravestones, or spiked like blossom on the bare hawthorn bushes.

CHARLES LAVERY
LAID TO REST
BY HIS LOVING SON AND DAUGHTER
HERE LIES SKY HIGH
HE TRIED HIS BEST
NOW HE'S AT REST
BENEATH THIS STONE
DON'T CRITICIZE THE GUY
LEAVE HIM ALONE

Marie Louise had traced birth certificates for both Marie Louise O'Donnell Lavery and for Rory Robert

O'Donnell Lavery on a research programme you can buy into on the internet. Most people would not have been delighted to discover their father was a Wanderer, but for her, his being a poet and Oxford graduate outweighed that. She was only sad not to have seen him before the end. And at least he had not been an anonymous punter of her mother's. Sky had hung about as a down and out in Royston, hoping to catch a glimpse of his kids sometimes. He had had the insane idea that he would suddenly win fame and fortune by his poetry, and be reunited with his family. With Renee, too. He always remembered her as a goddess who had brought sensual delights to his lonely academic existence. But once he had started experimenting with Father Harry's heroin, and his front teeth disintegrated, he gave up on even that pathetic dream.

When Marie Louise and Tiziano had raided Rory's little bedroom at the convent, with the connivance of Sister Peppy, and despite Mother Benigna's embargo, they had discovered several little notes that the boy had written, but not posted, to Sky, they thought. "Dear Daddy", one of them went, Why have I not to get calling you Daddy? You said you were my Daddy and I was your boy. I am part of you and you are part of me. You said so. So why can I not come and live with you, Daddy? Your loving son, Rory p.s. I am trying to write you a poem."

The postscript had been proof positive for Marie Louise that the letter had been meant for Sky, Rory's father, Charles Lavery. But in fact they had happened upon the boy's letter to Father Harry, in his first flush of a crush on the priest, when he had been saved by him from the Saint Jude's school bullies. Harry was also of a poetic mind, and in the early days had read poems to Rory, ballads and sonnets.

So neither Marie Louise nor Tiziano had picked up on Father Harry's guilty secret, then, and the ghost of the strange perverted love affair lingered on unsuspected. Marie Louise had even brought the letter for Rory to keep in his locker, so she could show it to him when he was well enough.

Marie Louise also wrote to Renee, their mother, in open prison, and asked her to drop a line to Rory. She received back an odd scrawl half printed and half cursive on lined paper, with the expletives deleted in red ink. The gist of it was that she had never in her life had anything to do with Sky, whoever he was. And if Marie Louise would take over the upbringing of Rory, she, Renee would be relieved. She had the chance to make a new start with a lovely lassie she had been banged up with. And she had come to the conclusion that being on the game was a mug's game.

Marie Louise had written back insisting that Renee at least came to see her son in hospital, before taking off to a job in a fish processing factory with her girlfriend. Renee had reluctantly agreed

One person who did remember Sky, and was proud of having been his girlfriend, was the little kitchen maid at the Convent, Imelda Reilly. She always put sandwiches out on the doorstep, in case the ghost that had been seen was the real Sky, and another Wanderer had been buried in his place, by mistake. The sandwiches vanished, anyway, and so did a lot of other stuff.

Once, when the nuns were having a reception for overseas patrons, an intruder had ruined the party by raiding the convent fridge the night before, and scoffing the nicest things, including all the cream cakes. Imelda admitted, in tears, that it was the ghost of her former lover who had done it, and offered to make it up out of her wages.

But Mother Benigna had been spooked, anyway, and posted gardeners at the kitchen doors. With shotguns, legally held for shooting vermin. The fridges were not raided again, but one game-keeper and gardener had been lucky to escape with his life. He was found at his post, unconscious, his shotgun gone. A holy picture of Saint Philomena had been placed in his hands. Mother Agnes thought that had probably saved his life.

Poor Sister Philomena's ghost was pretty active too. Although no-one knew if, like her namesake, her hair continued to grow in the grave. (If it had, it would have been lank and grey.) But the relics of her holy existence had had wonderful effects on sick kids. And many a special wish had been granted through her intercession. Although no-one had won the lottery yet, through her means. Martha Dearie refused to acknowledge her novenas to Saint Philomena. Because she said she had made novenas to lots of other saints too. And she said it would not be the right image for a modern business woman to create. She said it would make people superstitious, and anyway, she didn't believe in gambling. But that didn't stop Mirkhill folk from asking her to bless their Saint Philomena medals they had bought at the Convent of the Bleeding Heart. Some of them actually crossed themselves when they caught sight of Martha stepping into her chauffeur-driven limos on the way to her Polisher's job at Saint Jude's, in a posh designer trouser suit and non-slip Ugg boots.

Martha would never discuss the extent of her win. She had got a bit snidey and uppity, people thought. If anyone harassed her, say in the queue at the chippy, as to the exact sum, Martha replied that it was vulgar to discuss money. And that it was not as much as some people made out. She was telling the truth there. Varrie had benefited, if not to quite the 'halfers' degree of her wildest dreams, but perhaps to a reasonable dream of security. Martha had other things she wanted to do with the money. She gave some to the Convent of the Bleeding heart, and they sang a high mass for her every week, so it must have been quite a lot.

And money would never bring poor Martha back what she had lost. Returning, the week after her win, from a happy overtime Saturday Polishing, Tabby had met her at the door with a horrible caterwauling, and clawed at Jimmy's armchair. She had found Big Jimmy slumped in his chair, betting slip in hand, the television blaring. The twins had just made his very last wager for him, and he had seen his accumulator come up, the only one of his that ever had. Martha was glad, afterwards, that the horses had run for him that day.

Not only that, but her boys, Darren and Wayne, had been sent off to a young offenders' unit, for stealing cigarettes from a corner shop. Their defence was that they didn't smoke, and they'd robbed the fags for their poor dad. They hadn't known their mother had won a fortune when they burst the gaff. It was all their Mammy's fault, really. She hadn't let on to them.

And Martha, alone in her flat with only Tabby for company, kept having nightmares about Father Harry. She dreamed he was after her for her lottery ticket, and that Jimmy was trying to get back from purgatory to save her. She told her GP about them and he put her on tranquilisers. Which she gave up, because it made her dizzy on Polishing duty. She just sipped a little champagne when she got home, toasting the absent Jimmy.

"You, see, I've taken to the booze at last, pet!" she used to whisper to him.

It turned out that Jimmy hadn't needed the tranquilisers either. What had done for him was a blood condition. And so he hadn't been a malingerer either. She wrote to the DSS to tell them so. They ignored her complaint, countering that she had been a week late providing his certificate, and an officer would call to collect his last week's benefit, issued in error.

Martha had wanted Jimmy's funeral to be a wee quiet affair, but folk crowded to gawp at her. Fancy a lottery winner not giving up her job as a cleaner! Money was wasted on Martha! But the word had got round about a high sung mass for the repose of Jimmy's soul, and folk began to ask the nuns to say masses for their dead too. It couldn't hurt to keep on the right side of Saint Philomena.

Devotion to Little Sister Philomena of the Bleeding Heart (as Sister Mary of the Angels named the dedicated website, to distinguish her from the numberless other Holy Philomenas) had become so profitable for the convent that a scholarship had been set up in her name. A scholarship in heating engineering, which had been one of Philomena's last interests.

Detective Constable Frank Childers had already proved, in his methodical way, that Father Harry had been guilty of all the murders he had been suspected of, including that of poor Philomena. He had the evidence. The weapons. The DNA. The sworn testament of various witnesses. The wee scraps of burnt but still blood-stained clothing. The horrific diaries. The pathetic love letters. The lot. All undeniably incriminating, and if his superiors were slow to act on it, it wasn't his fault. He had given them the case, all sorted out and tied up in a bow. All he needed now was Father Harry. Not even Father now. Excommunicated in absentia. Bell, book, and candle. But Doubleday, his superior, wanted hard and fast evidence. He had a theory of his own he was hoping to prove. About a taxi driver seen near the crime scenes.

When Mother Agnes called the police to complain that someone had tunnelled into the chicken coops and massacred several of her best layers, D.C. Childers had to persuade Sergeant Black to drive him there. Frank's appendectomy scar, though tiny, was still giving him pain. Frank limped round to the wilderness behind the coops where the bonfires for rubbish were built. There were chicken bones and feathers there, and blood and hen guts. Imelda thought it might have been a very large angry fox, but Mother Benigna pointed out the fag ends scattered around the embers.

Frank was furious. The embers were still warm, but foxy Father Harry had disappeared.

While the Sisters went off to make the cops a cup of tea, and Sergeant Black waited impassively but unhelpfully in the squad car, DC Childers gave vent to his annoyance. He stamped up and down through the ashes of the bonfires. He even picked up a white feather, and sniffed it, as if that would give him a clue. Then he shook his fist at the sky, to complain about his rotten luck.

Then, from the corner of his eye, he caught sight of a large dark figure peering out of the open door of the stable. Mother Agnes, motionless there, had witnessed his undetective-like histrionics. But the expression in her brown glowing eyes was sympathetic, even admiring, she came out, her hand outstretched to shake his.

"I'm Mother Agnes!" she said, "Mother Mary Agnes of the Holy Child. We've met before. And spoken on the telephone. The robber has murdered my best layers. What a waste!"

Her voice was mellow and cultured, with a slight Irish brogue. He recognised her voice right away, but not her appearance. Though he must have seen her in the crowd of frantic nuns in the immediate aftermath of the murder of Sister Philomena.

"I'm Frank! Frank Childers. Detective Constable. Happy to see you again, even if I'm a little too late." He sat down suddenly on a boulder by the extinct fire, probably the one Harry had sat on to roast Mother Agnes's prize fowl. "Too late again!" he grimaced, putting his head between his knees as he clutched his abdomen. Feeling really rotten now. Not just because of the disappointment. His hand went to his scar. The dressing seemed to be coming off. They'd said not to worry about that.

He felt his head swimming, and the next thing he knew, he was lying on a truckle bed, in a little sweet smelling room. A room full of fodder and tackle. Through the open door Frank could see into the stable block, and heard the neighing of the ponies there. Frank could see Mother Agnes's bulk over by the window, energetically scrubbing her hands at a square sink. She came over to him quietly.

"I didn't hurt you, officer, I hope, getting you inside here, did I?"

So that meant that this big soft-voiced woman had actually carried his limp body indoors. Frank felt like fainting again with humiliation. It got worse. He felt his waistband being opened and his patterned Gucci underpants being rolled down to reveal his scar. He felt Mother Agnes's large hand being laid gently across it, and then palpating the tissue around it. Under the gentle hands he relaxed.

Then he squealed in an unmanly treble, as Agnes ripped the dressing off.

"Sorry! I didn't hurt you, did I?" She spoke again sweetly.

The dark lambent eyes he stared into were innocent of mischief, he thought, and coolly sympathetic. They reminded him of the liquid eyes of a large mare he had sometimes ridden at Saint Ignatius, before the compensation money had dried up, and riding lessons had had to be abandoned (along with elocution). He had doted on that mare, a big strong powerful animal, but sensitive and intelligent. He thought she must have missed him.

"I'd take a swift run in to the Infirmary, young fellow." Mother Agnes advised him. "You may have got a small infection in your scar. Does it hurt like hell? Wait now, and I'll spray it and replace the dressing."

As Mother Agnes's fingers were busy about his groin, she too began to feel embarrassed. His cool looking olive skin was hot to the touch. And the ridiculous attitude of despair he'd adopted made him look like a piece of Greek statuary. Not a God, but a fawn. She could hardly restrain herself from running her hands through his sweat dampened brown curls. But instead, she left him to recover, and busied herself making him a cup of camomile tea, which she handed to him with two paracetamol tablets in the saucer.

"You'll feel better almost right away, so you will!" she predicted, and sure enough, he began to feel the pain drain away. And his wound cooled down under the light weight dressing she'd applied.

Mother Agnes's voice reminded him of someone. Of course, his elocution tutor, Brother Ambrose, whose Galway accent was rather more pronounced than Agnes's.

And Frank, in his turn, had sparked off memories for Agnes. She had always dealt with her brothers' small cuts and abrasions they got round the farm. And despite all of them being bold boys, strong and brave as lions usually, they hated having plasters ripped off. They used to close their eyes in terror, and turn their heads away, as Frank had done. It was a good job men didn't give birth, she'd always thought.

Frank Childers got up from the camp bed, and rebuttoned his shirt over his ridged abdomen, tucking it into his stylish trousers over his flat belly, and clasping his belt buckle about his narrow waist. He endeavoured to adopt his official persona again.

"You'll let me know, Mother Agnes," he said, "if you have any information, or even suspicions, however far-fetched you may think them. Any insights you have to offer, I'll be glad to listen to. I'll give you my card."

When Frank had gone back to the truculent Sergeant Black in the car, (still sipping the nuns' tea and chomping their cherry cake), Mother Agnes stared at the nicely printed card before tucking it away in the pocket of her habit. What a taking young man he was, she thought. A bit like a very mischievous altar boy she had known as a girl. Or like the last cheeky young foal the old mare had unexpectedly dropped last year. And in a different corner of her brain, he brought to mind the Strauss waltz, *A Dashing Young Blade*. The tune started to ring in her head, and she set to tossing around the bales of straw with gusto.

As he left the stable blocks Frank Childers began to feel rejuvenated and hopeful about the investigation, with a confidence he had not felt since his agonised community aerobics.

And his phone rang just as he was scrambling into the police car. It was brilliant news he got. A taxi driver with information of a fare taken to the crime scenes. At just the right times. Identifying Father Harry. The downer was the guy wouldn't give his name. And he said he was going to London. Not that he was a coward, but he had a business trip there. While Frank was trying to persuade him, the guy rang off. Hadn't left his number.

The informant, Liam MacNee, that is, didn't fancy hanging around with a murderer on the loose. And he had a brilliant job on. The ultimate business trip. He had been booked to taxi Marie Louise to London, for the weekend, and ferry her about there, then drive her back. He secretly thought it was possible that neither of them would ever return to Mirkhill. Once he had a good long run at her. When he drove his valeted cab to fetch her, though, exactly on time, he nearly cried when he saw she had turned up with Tiziano in tow.

Imelda, on her day off, doing a round of visits to her old haunts and drop-in centres that afternoon, heard someone playing the fiddle up Roystonhill. Strange and eerie, like how Sky used to play. Only faster, and a bit less out of tune. And Sky's old fiddle had disappeared, spookily, from beneath his bunk, she saw, when she reached the hut at the Cemetery gates.

Driving past the Prince's Infirmary on the way back to Mirkshields Station as the sun set, after an exhausting series of calls, Frank Childers felt like asking his Sergeant to stop so that he could nip in and have his scar seen to. It was getting sore again. But snidey Sergeant Black didn't look in the mood for delays in going off duty. And he'd have it all over the Mirkshields Station that Frank Childers was the ultimate wimp. Black would maybe put it about that Frank could no longer run the one and a half miles an active police officer must be fit for.

Frank sighed. Maybe Varrie Valentino would help him recover his strength, He was really looking forward to seeing her again.

Unhallowed Ground

Father Harry. (We'll have to get used to calling him Harry.) Harry had done a Houdini. In Tam the Ragman's pony and trap. While the Ex Wanderer Tam had been in the kitchen with his now, at last, girlfriend Imelda. He had only become a self-employed ragman to impress Imelda. And it was really working. He stood at the huge open kitchen fire, bolting down Imelda's cheese sandwiches and gagging down Mother Benigna's dandelion wine. While Harry exited in style. In a nice new outfit from Tam's newly collected bundles of second hand clothing. With balloons flying from the trap, and toys stacked for any kid who would trade in his father's second best suit.

Harry flicked his whip, and tipped his hat at Sister Evangeline, who was about to lock the convent gates for curfew, as the pony trotted past her. He kept by country paths till he got to the bleak hinterland that surrounded the Mirkhill scheme. Then he whipped the pony up, standing up in the trap, and headed at a clip down the asphalted road that led to the derelict railway bridges. He made a gallus entry, shouting out encouragement to the tired pony, as he rattled through the open gates into the travellers' encampment there.

With his usual scary luck, Harry had found cash in the good twill trousers that poor Tam had not had time to go through. Tying up the pony, he bought beer at the nearby garage, and treated the tinkers who gathered round him. He still had to exercise all his charm before they would agree to let him stay. He told jokes and sang songs, and promised unpaid help with their labouring jobs, from himself and 'his' pony and trap, hoping desperately to fit in.

In time he did. His beard grew and grew. And his hair grew and grew. He tied it up gypsy fashion. And he plaited the pony's mane and tail, and brushed its coat. And the pony got used to him, and didn't shy away any more when Harry came near her. And he kept his hands off his neighbours' wives, and talked to them very respectfully. He even began to look after some vagabonds in the outer areas who were trying to live rough without the tinkers' skills and resources. The local garages gave him their stale sandwiches, and he distributed them from his trap. He may have been too cavalier doing this, but Harry really liked doing good works.

Tam, taken on as handyman at the convent, had no intention of letting Father Harry get away with his good trap and his nice pony, whom he was sure was missing him.

"Over my dead body!" he said to Imelda one night.

Imelda had the sense to shudder and tell him to shut up.

Harry began to make a life for himself. He took up (Sky's) fiddle again, playing jigs and reels for the travelling folk to dance to in the evenings. He got hold of a little grass, and gave it judiciously to the guys. He lent a little cash, and didn't take interest. The whole camp admired him when he told them of his hard life. An orphan boy, with nowhere to go when he left care. Unjustly accused by the Brass of thievery. His step brother taking over his lawful inheritance, a fine farm in county Cork. The women shed a few tears, and the guys came up and slapped him on the shoulders, and took him to their special pubs, although somehow they never asked him into their vans and trailers.

But they asked him to their dos in hotels and he did them proud, making speeches to the bride and groom, sometimes in a hired suit. And afterwards singing his mother's songs. Or in a community hall, celebrating First Holy Communions, he would tell jokes and give out some of the holy pictures he always seemed to have on him.

"He's like a spoiled priest." one of the flyest of the guys remarked. "A real Holy Willie".

"Nothing of the sort!" his wife had disagreed. "He's got a quiet eye for the lassies. I do know one of his dearest hopes was to have a nice family of his own. Like our two sweet wee ones, he told me the other day He said if he'd a son like Jack and a girl like Molly, he'd be in seventh heaven,"

And the wife, overcome, had had to bury her face in the shoulder of her husband's rough jacket, to hide her tears of pity.

"Ah, you have too soft a heart, woman!" her husband countered, stern but pleased.

Then one evening Harry began singing a come-all-ye round the fire.

> "Oh come all ye lads and lassies, now
> And listen to me a while
> I'll sing to you a verse or two
> Will cause ye all to smile
> It's all about a young man and I'm going to tell ye how
> He recently went a courting at
> The foot of the sweet brown knowe."

If a few of the young gypsy guys were jealous as their girlfriends wiped their eyes, they tried to hide it, and brought Harry another beer.

Maybe Harry had been given a few too many beers that night, but somehow or other, he grabbed the wee

Molly child up on his knee, and started tickling her, making her nearly choke with laughter and her rosy cheeks blaze crimson.

"And I have another song for you, Molly Maloney, Molly my Ownie." He called her that for a laugh. "This is a song about a Molly, my Gran's favourite." he said, making it up as he went along. "Sure you have to get up on my shoulders, as if I were a pony you were riding!"

He hoisted the little girl aloft, 'Donkey Derby' fashion, and cantered around the outside of the circle singing winningly,

> *"Trotting to the Fair*
> *Me and Moll Maloney*
> *Seated I declare*
> *On a single pony*
> *How was I to know that*
> *Molly's safe behind*
> *With her head in oh that aw aw aw aw aw*
> *   awkward way inclined."*

Packy, Molly's father, rose abruptly to his feet, and started stamping out the embers. Some of the other men rose too, and went over to talk to Packy. Harry should have taken the hint. But he was feeling great, happier than he'd felt in ages. He sat down again on his oil drum seat, took the girl on his knee once more, for the last verse. The women at least were hoping for that, he thought. He bounced the little one wildly, comically, up and down on his lap, as he sang, tenderly, in a sweet ringing voice.

> *"By her gentle breathing*
> *Whispering past my ear*
> *By her sweet arms wreathing close around me here"*

He clasped the girl in his arms.

> *"When I asked her may I*
> *Steal a kiss or so."*

He kissed the little face staring up at him with light funny kisses.

"Then my darling Molly-grey-eye
didn't answer No-oh-oh oh!"

He jumped up again for the last bit, a reprise of the first, and dashed round again with the girl on his shoulder.

"Trotting to the fair
Me and Moll Maloney!"

Harry had the sense to gallop with her to her caravan and toss her into her father's arms.

The women laughed and clapped, but Harry retired almost at once to his dingy van.

So he'd got away with it, more or less, with his usual uncanny luck.

And it's possible Harry might have lived there forever. Or for long enough to get too ambitious about helping down and outs. He was already wishing he could give travellers little services behind the hedgerows, like old time pastors. Or the police dogs he had foiled during his escape, by splashing through the many streams from the boggy lands, might have been brought back to track him down. Or he might have got too bold at going into local pubs and been caught on CCTV.

But the reality of the end of his rural idyll was more shaming. He began to help the kids making their little dolls to sell round the doors. He was a dab hand at it, and had plenty of rags to spare. But he began to be sentimentally attached to the little Molly one. And to give her extra sweets and to sing her wee songs, and to play wee games with her. When he was with her he sometimes felt like crying over his wasted life. He might have had kids like her. Sometimes he felt the kids' parents worked them too hard. If he had been her daddy, he would have treated her like a little princess, he told himself.

Then once when he was by himself in the old caravan he had rented, he was totally overcome with tears. And the little one, peeping through the door, and hearing him sobbing had gone over to his battered bed, and put her little frail arms around him.

"Never mind! Never mind, Harry!" she had said.

And that was the moment when the guys had burst in on them, with their dogs barking and snarling. Throwing him out of bed and out of the caravan. Snatching away the crying wee one. If he'd had the sense to shut up, maybe laugh it off, it would have been better for him.

But it was so damned unfair, he thought, he had a right to fight his corner.

"Do you really believe I would have hurt her?" he shouted, rounding on his accusers. "What kind of men are you, to believe that? Me! An ordained priest!" he blurted out, in fury.

He suddenly thought he shouldn't have said that. He'd gone too far, as the men stopped shouting and looked at each other, drawing back. He got the last of his beer out of the trap and went round offering it to the men. None of them would touch it. The women went into the caravan and shoved his goods into bundles and loaded them into the trap. He got into the trap and took up the reins. Then he thought. The trap was a give-away. He gathered some bits and pieces, among them Rory's nicest letter, and put them in his knapsack. He went round and stroked the pony's head. He'd never given her a name. Horse, he'd called her, or when he was in a good mood, Wee Horse.

Throwing down the reins he walked away, struggled with unlatching the iron gate as he went. Suddenly, around his head, the full cans of lager he'd left for the guys came thumping past his ears. One caught him on the shoulder, one on the forehead. And one on his sore leg, that he'd ripped open long ago on a rusty railing. Roaring with pain and anger, Harry rushed for the shelter of the bridges, turning now and then to shout abuse at his tormentors.

Resting at last under the farthest bridge, he began to calm down. Only turning round from time to time to call in the direction of the camp in broken words and phrases.

"Lovely wee lassie! What did you think? You should've. You should've. Looked after her! Her! Me, I love kids. Ask anybody! Ask my Mammy! Mammy, you tell them."

Finally, in spite of being too near the camp for safety, he fell asleep where he lay, under the bridge, clutching his knapsack, amid the moss and puddles.

The tinker guys let him be, though, and didn't come after him. And when he woke to the chill of dawn, he felt well enough to clamber over the undergrowth to the cattle tracks that would lead eventually to the wastelands surrounding the Old Royston cemetery. Where the typhoid victims had been buried in mass graves. And later, executed murderers (when relatives had paid to retrieve their corpses) had been buried in the unhallowed ground. He would be like one of their ghosts, he swore to himself. One of their ghosts, risen from his unmarked grave.

Once more the nice Harry had been rejected. Let them see how they liked the nasty Harry! The one who kept up spite. And paid back old scores. He began to count on his fingers the people he would settle up with. Father Seamas, hoping for his job, would be one.

There was snidey wee Martha, who'd done him out of his winning ticket. Varrie, her pal, he knew how to get her back. Those stupid nuns, setting the police on him. Even Rory hadn't died when he was supposed to. Now he wouldn't make an innocent cherub in heaven. And that crazy spotty guy, who'd battered him. And Father Tiziano, who'd broken his sacred vows with that big tart from London. And even the two Wanderers he'd looked after. Imelda, called herself Sky's girlfriend. Now he'd heard she was running after Tam. And Tam. He'd heard it had been Tam, wee short arsed Tam, who'd gone grassing to the police.

Harry felt the blinding rage sweeping over him again, and nobody near to vent it on. Oily scalding tears stung the cuts and scratches on his face. He was reduced to punching the empty air, short jabs with his ringed right hand. He concentrated on the image of Tam. Tam's round face, contorted with terror, as it would be.

"You're not so cheeky now! Are you, wee man?"

Jab jab went his fist against his huge back pack, his imaginary victim.

"Are you? Are you?"

He felt the release in his body that he usually did when he had exerted the stressful force of his malignity. He had already stopped shaking. He rubbed the fist that had 'punched' the wee derelict he was spiritually targeting, grinning again. He had noticed something else. He wouldn't give up the game just yet.

The traveller women had shoved his violin case into his hands as he left.

Obliging of them, Harry thought with a sneer. Since alongside the battered old fiddle was the spanking new shotgun. The gun he had taken off the sleeping guard at the Convent of the Bleeding Heart. That guy had had a lucky escape. He had spared him because he had wanted to see his face when he woke up, with his gun gone and a holy picture and medal of Saint Philomena's lying on his knee. (Harry had boldly hung around, he recalled, the gun trained on the man. Who had saved his own life by falling to his knees and making the sign of the cross, in gratitude to the saint. Harry had laughed so much he'd nearly given away his hiding place, when a startled thrush flew up out of Harry's chosen laurel bush.

He grinned again, as he took the shotgun out. He had skilfully pared down the stock with one of his saw toothed knives, till the gun fitted snugly into the old velvet-lined case.

Father Harry knew exactly what he would do when it got to the stage that he could not see any reasonable life ahead of him. Maybe soon now. He'd tried with the tinkers, but they wouldn't come and go with him at all. Just because he'd had a wee cuddle with one of the kids. They were totally unreasonable. So if he was going, he was going to take plenty of them with him. And other traitors. His luck was due to turn soon. It always did. At the end he'd walk into Mirkshields Police Station and start shooting. They'd have to finish him off.

'Death by Cop' they called it. It sounded dead glamorous.

However, the unhallowed ground he'd liked in theory was bleak and unsheltered in fact. He'd have to find somewhere a bit cosier, to spend his last days on earth. Before he rejoined his poor Mammy. She must have grown tired waiting for her martyred son to come to her again. And lie upon her breast. And cover her with the purest of pure kisses.

The Betrothed

Tam Piper's intended, Imelda, was not very pleased with him. He was wanting to have Father Seamas call the bans the very next Sunday, although it was getting on for Advent, and Benigna would not be pleased. Tam had forgotten himself so much as to say he wasn't marrying Mother Benigna, so stuff her. After she let him kip in the convent attics from time to time! And the one thing Imelda had really liked about Tam, apart from the extreme cleanliness of his personal habits, under sometimes trying conditions, was his genteel mode of speech. Not like some of the gardeners and handymen about the place, when the nuns weren't around.

And Tam had said they'd have to get a place of their own once they got hitched, to party in at weekends. Imelda thought that sounded coarse. She was really beginning to wonder if Tam was the right guy for her after all. Sky would never have said such things, never in all their long courtship. And Imelda had fallen heir to Philomena's room. All the nuns who had a claim to it were too spooked out to take it over. It was the prettiest room of all, Imelda thought, with its sprigged wallpaper, and antique furniture. It had got damaged by soot when Imelda had found the crucifix stuck half way up the chimney. And that was after the technicians had powdered over the looking glasses and panelled doors, trying to find any fingerprints. After the ... After the horrible thing that had happened.

Imelda thought separate rooms would be fine and dandy anyway. She liked reading the books Sister Peppy gave her, before she fell asleep. Books of the martyrs. It made you glad you hadn't been born in olden days, when such awful things happened. Being fried on a gridiron (a huge frying pan, it meant), or fed to lions. Tam might want to put the light out early. Or it would be embarrassing if he wouldn't, when she was getting undressed.

Tam had sprung out at her from behind the hen coops the other morning, when she went to gather eggs. He had kissed her on the mouth, hot and strong, in a way they had never kissed before, and Imelda hoped she would not get pregnant. She hoped she would fit into the wedding dress Sister Peppy was making for her out of an old First Communion dress of a very large little schoolgirl. Some lassies said if you kissed like that before you did 'It' you might get pregnant.

And now Tam was looking for someplace for them to stay together. Couples weren't allowed in the hostel he was in. And it was no place, anyway, for a lady, Tam said. And Imelda didn't want to leave the convent. It was lovely and cosy with the new central heating system. And Mother Benigna had offered her, as a special favour, the chance to take minor orders. You could take some, even if you were lucky enough to be married too. As long as you were chaste within marriage. Imelda wasn't quite sure how that worked.

Tam had got very funny, since he had got back from visiting his new friend, the detective, in hospital. Sort of frightened and edgy. He had bought Imelda a mobile phone, pink and glittery, but she couldn't use it. Although she carried it around with her at all times, just to please him. She'd thought of getting one of the young nuns to help her to phone him, because she'd some good news to cheer him up.

Early that morning, Sister Evangeline, who looked after the gatehouse and its electronic alarm system, had run in and wakened her up. She said a big handsome guy who looked like something out of The Lord of the Rings had driven up to the gates in Tam's pony and trap, but without the balloons. He'd said he knew about the animal rescue centre. Did they want to take them in? While Evangeline was swithering, the guy had jumped off. Blossom, allow her, took the law into her own hooves and cantered up the driveway, by her own self, towards the stables, where she used to be billeted.

Evangeline said the guy didn't stay to explain. His mate, not quite so handsome but not bad, had driven up behind him in a truck, and picked him up. They both drove off without a backward glance, Evangeline had said. A wee bit rude of them, maybe. Anyway, Tam Tam would be delighted. What mother Agnes would say she didn't know.

Imelda stood at the kitchen sink in a dream, washing the best crystal glasses that weren't allowed in a dishwasher. From the party for Sister Columbkill's golden jubilee the day before. 'Fifty years in Christ' iced on a great big cake. Some of the old nuns got to their feet to dance the Dashing White Sergeant. It had all been very funny and a lot of fun. Pushy Sister Peppy and pretty Sister Angel had got Imelda up to dance, and she had got through all of it, with Mother Benigna on the piano. Imelda blushed happily at the memory, her face rosy with the steam from the hot water gushing gallusly over the crystal glasses. She was plucking them out adroitly from the soapy water and sliding them neatly onto the draining board, just as the in her apron pocket rang. She made to grab it, and a precious goblet from Mother Columbkill's dowry smashed into smithereens in the stone sink.

Peppy and Angel stopped larking about, playing chases round the big kitchen table, and rushed to sweep up the pieces. So Mother Mary Agnes wouldn't clock it when she came by, hungry as a hunter, for afternoon tea, after being out all day with the animals. Naturally, Imelda hadn't been able to pick up the phone in time to speak, but Angel had got the message left for her. From Tam Tam, of course.

"Baby," she heard, "I really really need you. Now. Get here quick, the old place. It's him."

Because Tam had thought of the perfect place for the two of them. The old hut the Wanderers had crammed into at night, in Old Royston cemetery, was now deserted. The Wanderers had dispersed, having been frightened off by Sky's fate. But Tam reckoned Old Roystonhill was the last spot on earth the murderer was likely to return to.

And so many other people had agreed with him on this. The verger from Saint Eustace's Episcopalian Church nearby had taken to walking his dog there again, taking notes of some of the more historic gravestones. (As Sky had started his decline by doing.) And some of the young Junkie tarts at the lower end of the market haunted it too, slipping out at dawn to take their babies to nursery school. Mirkshields constabulary, who had staked it out for quite a while, merely drove past in Panda cars, shaking their heads as they glanced towards it, maybe thinking of poor old Sky. Even the mounted police, who made light work of the embanked terraces, had given up patrolling majestically, helmeted like demi-gods, at dusk.

So there was no-one to stop Tam on his foolhardy mission. There were no police barriers with officers asking nosey questions, and giving people funny looks. There was nothing to stop Tam trudging up the gravel paths that zigzagged steeply from the outer gates. Except the jackdaws ensconced in the turrets and chimneys of the Gatehouse. Were the birds warning him, or warning someone of him? Tam sat down on the baby's monument, Sky's special seat. None of the half wild roe deer poked their noses out, though. Because since the mounties had vamoosed from the graveyard, someone had been picking off the shy little creatures one by one.

Even the paparazzi had given up. Since Harry had disappeared they were hunting another story, like a pack of hounds on a wrong scent, always disappointed but refusing to give up, following their tails, skirmishing in ever diminishing circles.

The Press was intrigued by the sudden disappearance of Father Harry, just as Marie Louise scooted off to London. He had been re-instated by the press to his former name, to furnish headlines such as 'Father Harry hunted by Drugs Barons' and 'Father Harry Escorts Model' and finally 'Hunky Father Harry elopes with Page Three Girl'. They'd found plenty of people to gossip, especially his housekeeper, Mrs Mulvey, who was a pal of the janitor's wife. In an exclusive interview, she had given sworn testimony that the model who had been staying at Saint Jude's had told friends she had fallen in love with a priest and was planning to elope with him. And the model, a famous page three girl, was pregnant! How did she know that?

Marie Louise had gone back to London, that bit was true. She had to sort out her contracts and sell her flat so she would be free to marry Tiziano and care for her little brother. Tiziano had dreamed that he and Marie Louise were standing in the sunset surrounded by children. They had made a good start, and to prepare for his early nuptials, he had written to his uncle in Rome, who was a Cardinal, asking him to bend the Pope's ear, and get a dispensation for him. And also to ask him to name him as his heir, since he was wealthy, even by Roman standards.

Marie Louise had asked Liam to be their driver, so as to give them freedom in London. And she'd offered to introduce him to some nice women, only a little bit desperate.

Father Harry, as we shall resume calling him, had come to the same conclusions as Tam and the young tarts, and the mounties, and the Panda car drivers and many others. But he decided to implement a process of double bluff. So he had sneaked back to the very place where Sky had been murdered, and bedded down in the old hut, actually on Sky's bed. Roystonhill Gatehouse was the most convenient place to operate from, for his vendettas.

Father Harry was cosier and dryer in the hut than he had been in the leaking van at the tinkers' encampment. He'd actually found some booze planked under Sky's bunk. And he was growing plump on the venison he poached. Murdered was a better word, because the little deer were half tamed, nearly pets. He'd bagged a few pigeons too, and some rabbits. But he really longed for vinegary fish and chips.

That was what woke Harry from his dreams, the odour of fish and chips. Tam had bought a fish supper at a van parked below, and was scoffing it on his cold marble seat. He was putting off looking into the hut, but setting the half-eaten snack aside he went and tried the door of the hut. It was locked, but Tam had a key. The lock groaned, the damp swollen door complained. But then it gave way, and Tam, stumbling over the threshold, was inside the warm, paraffin-scented hut. He detected no light, till he became conscious of two spots of light, red eyes glowing furiously in the dark, and a figure huddled in a fur coat, rising from the bunk growling in rage.

Father Harry recovered himself before Tam. His eyes even took on an amused look. His prey had tracked him down, to save him the trouble.

"Come in, wee man, come in." he invited. "Never expected to see you again. Take a pew."

Hypnotised, Tam sat down on the opposite bunk, the one that used to be Imelda's.

"Hold on a wee minute, son!" Harry grinned down at him, "Must just go for a leak!" And Harry made for the door. "There's whisky under Sky's bunk. Be back in a minute, old pal! Have a dram!" said Father Harry, exiting, turning Tam's key in the lock after him.

But Tam didn't. He'd taken the pledge to give up drink, for Imelda. He didn't want to be seen staggering up the aisle with a red nose. That's if he got out of the hut alive, Tam thought.

Because Tam wasn't such a fool as not to have noticed the fury on Harry's face when he first clapped eyes on himself. He would know about Tam's visit to the cop shop. And Tam Tam had a good idea what was in store for him.

It was at that moment that Tam managed to ring Imelda up, and ask her to come right away. To come over to the old hut, at the cemetery gates, and save him.

Except that that wasn't exactly the message he had actually recorded.

The Last Stand

"Baby, I really really need you. Now. Get here quick. The old place. It's him."

That was the message that Tam actually left, and it was open to different interpretations. It took Imelda ages to get it. At first she thought Tam was being uncouthly romantic, asking her to join him at some old haunt of his. Peppy and Angel took a similar view. Peppy's eyes twinkled and Angel's baby blue eyes widened with shock. It didn't take much to shock Angel.

But that wasn't the kind of wee guy Tam was, Imelda knew. He would never come right out with it and ask a girl to join him for a wee carry on, or a wee lie down. He was too polite. Imelda thought she would try her luck with Mother Agnes. She might be more understanding.

She waited till Agnes had had her tea, and was polishing off the last scone. Then she clutched the senior nun's sleeve, and pushed the phone towards her, for her to listen to the message from Tam.

At first Mother Agnes smiled too, the way the others had done. Imelda pushed it silently towards her again. Sometimes Imelda wasn't good at talking. Agnes thought some of her cats and dogs and donkeys and sheep had more highly developed communications skills than Imelda. But, listening to the message again, Mother Agnes began to get it.

"Do you think he's not asking you to ... er ... Do you think it's a cry for help? What can he want you to do? I think the key is the 'he'. It's not Tam. Who do you think 'he' is, girl?"

Imelda had now worked it out. But she hardly dared say to Mother Agnes. But Mother Agnes was psychic, and could read people's minds. Any of the postulants could tell you that. She was always able to tell who had a vocation and who had just liked that black and white film, 'The Song of Bernadette' and had practiced bits of it in front of the mirror.

Mother Agnes could see that Imelda was getting more and more agitated.

"Speak up, Imelda! Come on, spit it out!" Mother Agnes used the tone of voice that worked when she had to get the animals to take pills, or get their hair or wool or fluff combed out. And it now worked on Imelda, too.

"Tam's saying Father Harry's got him. He thinks Father Harry done it!"

"Done what, my child?"

Mother Agnes was feeling a bit distracted. And surprised by the mention of Harry's name. She had been thinking of him all day, worried about him, now the press was pushing that new scurrilous story about that lady who had come to the convent, with a pretend vocation. She'd only to take one look at her to discover she was up to no good. Now why was she getting so cross about the big lassie, Agnes wondered. She knew it was rubbish. Why should she care?

Imelda was still staring at her. And holding out the stupid pink mobile again, for her to listen to it once more. She did. All at once the truth flooded her mind in a scalding torrent. Of course! What Imelda had just said was the gospel truth. Harry had done it. Killed Philly! Little Sister Philomena whom she had vowed to protect. Who'd been like a little sister to her, although Philly was the elder, watching their shaven locks landing on their bridal gowns. And lying prostrate on the floor to take their first vows. Both crying afterwards, then giggling. And why had she not been able to admit that obvious truth to herself before. Agnes closed her eyes and swayed back in her dining chair, her head banging against the high oaken back. Of course, she knew why. And it was no use her kidding herself any more. She had allowed herself, one of Christ's anointed, to develop a kind of liking for Harry. An affection. She shilly-shallied round the point.

But Mother Agnes had cauterised wounds when she had to. And she did so now with her own sad heavy heart. The truth was, she loved Father Harry. And must have loved him for so long! He had practically, mischievously, confessed his crimes to her, and she could not, would not understand. What a fool. What an old fool. And this simple little lady beside her must have sussed it out, must have known, and not liked to put her right. Till now, when she had to, out of desperation.

And, hanging her head in shame, Mother Agnes realised that, if she had not been stung by a kind of jealous rage at the thought of the Page Three girl, she might not have admitted his guilt even now. When she thought of that young detective's passionate plea to the public for information, just suspicions even, she could not forgive herself.

"Tam is quite right, Imelda. I am sure Father Harry done it. Did it. I'll phone the police!"

The young detective, Frank Childers had given her his card, and she dialled his cell phone.

Frank was staying over at Varrie Valentino's place. His mum thought he was supervising stripping in his own apartment. Kansas was away for a sleepover with Dakota, and the coast was clear. It had been the intention of both Frankie and Varrie to have, at last, a day of love and lust. And the love bit went okay. The lust, however, was interrupted by Frank yelping in pain, if he moved six inches from a propped up position on his back.

They had both fallen asleep at last, worn out from frustration, and had subconsciously adopted the positions of mother and child, rather than lover and lover. Varrie coiled round him, supporting his body, and Frankie curled up like a child, uncaring elbows jolting her body if she moved, his sprawling legs cutting off the circulation of hers.

Varrie was almost relieved when his phone rang. She answered it for him, out of badness, hoping it was his mum.

"Mother Mary Agnes here." a smooth Irish voice announced. Varrie nearly dropped the phone, then shoved it towards Frank.

"I've got Imelda Reilly on the line. She has an urgent request to make."

A squeaky voice took over. "He's got Tam. Come quick! The old place!"

Frank would have come quick, too. Although he hadn't managed to do that all day, even with Varrie's expert guidance. But suddenly a pink splash appeared on his grey silk pyjamas, as he reached over for the phone. The pink deepened into crimson and spread over the Japanese patterned bed covers. Frank's wound was haemorrhaging, and as Varrie pushed a pillow against his abdomen with one hand, she disconnected Imelda's squawks to ring the emergency services.

When Mother Agnes phoned the Mirkshields Station she had no luck. The line was bad, and stress had exaggerated her Galway brogue. Also, it was hard to sum up the problem, based on psychic insights regarding a garbled phone message.

Agnes shouted distractedly, "Officer, I've a funny feelin' somethin's the matter with one of my friens!"

"Blast!" Sergeant Black, at the desk, hissed to a fellow officer. "One of her hens, again!"

"Listen, Reverent Mother," He raised his voice and spoke clearly, "You're having trouble with your hens? I suggest you contact the S.S.P.C.A. Although by this time I'd have thought you'd have known how to wring a hen's neck!"

"Oh, Mother Agnes, who's gonnae help us?" Imelda covered her head with her apron.

"Why, the two of us will help each other, you silly thing, and then we'll help Tam! Help me get the pony between the shafts, and we'll go in the trap."

Mother Agnes had never learned to drive a car properly. She was alright with tractors, but no-one would trust her with the keys of a car. Anyway, Blossom would take them through the hinterlands and over the little pathways over the marshy ground. Shortcuts not many cars could negotiate. And Agnes was brilliant with horse-drawn vehicles.

"We're coming, Tam!" Imelda shouted as they rattled along. "Me and mother Agnes are coming for you. Don't give up!"

And Tam certainly needed all the encouragement he could get. Father Harry was taking his time with Tam, who had always annoyed him. Tam never admitted he found reading hard. Father Harry was questioning him about his catechism. When Tam got a question wrong, he was given a thwack with an old fashioned tawse (a thick leather belt, used in the past to punish schoolchildren for minor misdemeanours). Harry loved playing at schools like that. He had pinched the tawse when he was a boy. He'd been expelled from school for it.

"Who made you, Tam Tam?"

Tam knew that one. "God made me."

"And why did God make you, Tam Tam? Tell me now. I've often wondered."

"God made me to know him, love him and... and ..."

"Why don't you just read it off the book, Tam Tam? Start again."

"To know him and be happy with him."

Father Harry got up from his seat on Sky's bunk, towering over Tam. He had his mock stern expression on. "I am going to have to give you the belt, Tam Tam. Hold out your hand!"

Tam held out his small broad hand and Father Harry, raising the tawse above his head, brought it down in a stinging slap on the other man's hand. Tam doubled up in pain. He sobbed in spite of himself. Father Harry lay back on the bunk, helpless with laughter.

"God, you make me laugh! You were brave enough to grass me up to the cops, though. Look, enough of this play acting, let's get down to business. We'll go outside. I don't want to mess up the hut." He dragged the wee guy to his feet, so he could whisper into his ear, "With blood and other messy fluids."

Father Harry was looking around for something. Then he got his eye on it. His shotgun leaning in the corner. He picked it up, and checked that it was loaded. Tam kicked himself. Why had he not seen that?

It was at this point that Tam gave himself up for dead. If he got the chance, he would jump off the vertiginous edge of the terrace, and finish it off. He'd never been very good with pain. Had a carer to go with him to have a tooth out. But suddenly he got a bit of courage.

"Harry?" he said, "Father Harry? Why do you hate people?"

Harry looked amazed. "But I love people. I would even have loved you if you'd let me! Never mind how ugly and smelly you are! Saint Theresa kissed the lepers!"

"But I always loved you, Harry. Your fine voice, and your height. I always loved you. All of us Wanderers did! Especially the hymns. God, we loved the hymns!"

Harry sat down at the edge of the hillside, looking shyly and sheepishly down at his hands.

"You're not making that up?"

"Christ, no, Father Harry. As God is my witness!"

Plucking up his courage, Tam started singing one of Father Harry's favourite hymns, in his gruff cracked out of tune voice. Harry couldn't resist. He started striding to and fro, a kitchen knife in one hand, the shotgun shouldered carelessly, and gave full vent to his fulsome high pitched voice.

The jackdaws in the deserted chimney heads complained at the human uproar.

"Mother most pure
Star of the sea
Pray for the Wanderer
Pray for me"

Tam was watching his chance to dive over the edge of the hillside. But before he could, another voice joined in the hymn, rather like Father Harry's, the pitch identical, filling in harmonies, while Harry kept to the melody. Mother Agnes had never been in better voice.

He raised the shotgun, but kept on singing as a point of honour. Agnes didn't stop either. Tam could see why. She too held a shotgun, braced against her wimpled cheek, her brown habit flapping round her, her legs underneath braced strongly, her feet in their heavy ridged work boots getting plenty of purchase on the mossy ground.

"Send Tam over to me, and I'll let you go. You know I'm a better shot than you, Harry. I'm a better shot than anybody. Sure I should have been born a boy!"

She looked as if she meant business, and Father Harry could see that although she had cracked a joke, her usually calm and mild expression was somehow different.

Father Harry put up his hand in a 'Pax' sign, and then, turning his back, walked away casually down the slope, elegant in the camouflage ex-army fatigues he now wore, and limping only slightly. He changed his tune, though, as he did, to "The last rose of summer", his Mammy's all-time favourite song. And Mother Agnes had loved it too. He had often sung it to her when she was sad, and he in sentimental mood.

" 'Tis the last rose of summer
Left blooming alone
All her lovely companions are faded and gone ..."

Father Harry's voice echoed in the golden sunset, as he made his way carefully along the pathways down the steep hill, the shotgun always aimed upwards. And occasionally Harry presented a perfect target, his back turned, his gun useless. But Mother Agnes was unable to shoot. And when she thought of it afterwards she blamed herself bitterly for this weakness. She would have shot a mad dog. But somehow she could not shoot this worse than mad man. And as he swung out beyond range, Harry gave out a scornful guffaw, that she knew was meant for her. Because he knew her weakness, that had let him escape into the dusk.

Trotting down Roystonhill Road, the traffic rushing in the opposite direction, Agnes dwelt on the past, insensible to her surroundings. A ridiculously early full moon hung in the sky over Mirkhill reminded her of her one-sided love affair with Harry. His ascendancy over her, she realised, had begun with the decline of Philomena, her pure and till then, her only love. When her friend had changed from being clever, funny and admired, to being the object of rueful amusement and reluctant sympathy. Had she been unconsciously complicit in little Sister Philomena's horrific death?

Shaking herself, and slackening the pony's pace, she began to be conscious of crowds of chattering parents and kids streaming past, as she neared Saint Jude's School. Of course, how could she have forgotten? It was the last night of 'The Whizz of Oz', at the school, and Harry had been the Wizard. That's where Harry was heading to so brazenly, in his best army fatigues, and with a loaded shotgun!

Pulling sharply at poor Blossom's docile head, she turned into Mirkhill street, and, drawing up near the brilliantly lit, bannered and ballooned front entrance to Saint Jude's, she flung the reins to Tam.

Some wit had scrawled a poster "Standing Room Only, and you're not allowed to stand."

Gathering up her stuff, Mother Agnes jumped heavily down from the driver's seat heavily.

"See ya, kids!" she shouted back gallusly to Tam and Imelda, who stayed huddled together in the back, just where she had left them, till, after a bit of an argument with the gate keepers, Mother Agnes disappeared in the front doors.

Then the trap jolted forward, Tam Tam and Imelda clinging to each other in the driver's seat, Blossom trotting off at a clip, glad to get going.

Curtains

Saint Jude's was abuzz with excitement. The final night of the run of three nights of the fabulous 'Magical Whizz of Oz' production. The school assembly hall was stowed out. Many people who had drawn a ticket for a first or second night performance were sneakily pushing in at the back, to spoil the enjoyment of the lucky ones who had drawn a last night ticket. The show was so popular that lots were drawn for paid tickets.

Everything was forgotten but the glittering spectacle (made from the cheapest of cheap materials, merely thin fabrics, sticky paper, glitter and crude poster paint). And all on a tiny school stage, with only a couple of small changing rooms behind it. All the recent scares from homicidal maniacs at home and abroad were pushed to the back of everyone's mind.

The front row was occupied by baillies and town councillors. As well as by ridiculously high-powered diplomats, who wanted to see life in the rough on a sleazy old Glasgow housing scheme. That night the Japanese proconsul was there together with an American lady ex-senator. Both were determined to put Pearl Harbour securely out of their minds. Even the device of a pretend hot air balloon made them jumpy.

Headmaster Jon Goodly was toadying like mad, hoping for funds. (Some hopes!) Martha sat in the second row (with the better view), surrounded by

Polishers. Kansas and her pal Dakota had got parts as munchkins in the new dystopian interpretation of the classic Wizard of Oz. The show now featured poignant early American folk songs and interludes of illegally downloaded Punk Rock and Heavy Metal.

Kansas would, of course, have preferred the lead role. She had treated her mother to many hours of pretend rehearsal, singing 'Home Sweet Home' with wistful flashing glances over Mirkhill towards the distant Campsie Fells, where she had an imaginary cottage, an imaginary garden and an imaginary dog.

Lena, the ex-art teacher, sat demurely at the back, hugely pregnant. Looking larger than Auntie Magg's house. She wished now she'd been able to stay on longer. The show would have been a channel for her creativity. And it all looked so much fun. Although at the time of leaving she had wept tears of pure gratitude to her unborn child for having delivered her from her hell hole of a stinky art classroom.

But it was good luck for the drama club that Lena had fallen pregnant when she did. Gerry, her replacement, also replaced the play's director, a lugubrious English teacher, who had finally given in and gone on the Sick with depression. Not the easiest disability to handle while doing musical comedy (with a load of shitty kids and rank amateurs, as he had put it to his doctor, weeping, while he was getting his sick lines signed.)

Gerry, on the other hand, was always upbeat, flitting about the stage effortlessly, giving precise orders in a light persuasive voice. Petting the nervous bit players, he could be stern with stroppy stars. Making all sorts of people make things, for nothing, from nothing. Cutting the script, writing in new scenes in defiance of copyright. In fact he was a bit of a genius. In another sphere of life, where his talents might have been given full rein, he could have become an Oscar winner and a millionaire, easy! That's what the kids at Saint Jude's thought, anyway.

Gerry had one small worry. Since Father Harry had mysteriously disappeared, there was a vacancy for the Whizz that no-one seemed to be able to fill. It was hard to live up to Father Harry on the top of his form. The headmaster himself, stage struck, would have liked to fill it. But it turned out that, although good at readings, on the actual tiny stage he froze into a cataleptic trance, and had to be helped off, his eyes rolling in his head.

"Let's face it, Goodley!" his wife had commented abrasively, "On stage you're nothing but a bloody embarrassment!"

His lady assistant head teacher, though, was more tactful.

"You just can't spread yourself this thin, boss!" she soothed him.

Gerry was reluctant to take the role himself. He had ordered flowers for himself and wanted to make sure they were presented at just the right moment, when he had rehearsed his Dorothy to lead him, protesting, from the wings.

But it turned out that modest Father Seamas was a brilliant actor, had been in amateur dramatics before, and could even apply his own make-up. He was skilful at the Whizz's stage business, and Father Harry's costumes fitted him, too.

Another brilliant actor took the role of Toto. Pinkie Paws Knightley, it was, the head janitor's talented white bulldog. Though he never learned to answer to 'Toto' for the play.

But on the last night, at the last act, the nervous animal was blotting his copy book in more ways than one. He was growling and dashing up to the curtained booth that contained the Wizard. Actually lifting his leg against it, as the crowd tittered. In this case, it was no use giving Gerry the director's advice when something went wrong.

"Simply react in character!"

However, the good natured audience seemed to think it was part of the show.

Gerry had devised a sound system for enhancing and garbling the Whizz's speech at first. It came on, loud and strong, and the audience were all properly spooked by it. When it came to unmasking the Whizz, a hidden line pulled the booth apart, as Pinkie was supposed to do, as he pawed the booth's curtains. A hush fell on the audience as the Whizz was revealed. Dressed in a fancy costume, with large specs and a wild red beard, Gerry had excelled himself in designing the costume.

The wild, unkempt figure strode forward to centre stage. In his hands there appeared to be a shotgun, which he pointed at the audience. At first the crowd responded with amusement cowering in assumed fear, and guffawing at the ludicrous implied danger. The strange figure did not move, and the laughter died away. The Whizz approached the front of stage microphone. He spoke into it, judging the volume just right. Still pointing the gun.

"Yeah! That's better! You're none of you laughing now!"

The footlights made Pagliacci shadows across his broad face.

Varrie was the first to suss it. She still had her phone in her hand, having just checked on Frank. She had been sorry to abandon him, but watching Kansas perform came first.

"And the first one to move for their mobile gets it! Any heroes?" the Whizz asked, smiling. "And you are goin' no place!" He'd seen the child principal characters attempt to shuffle off.

"C'm'ere!" he commanded, and gathered the kids in front of him, still pointing the gun at the audience over their heads.

The diplomats on the first row looked puzzled, then gratified. A happening! They were being treated to some cutting edge drama, along with the slightly hackneyed show.

"Obviously a protest against violence and militarism," the ex-senator lady whispered into Jon Goodley's bald ear. "I hope to God they're not going to dig up Afghanistan again!"

Father Harry, throwing off the fancy silk costume, did look a bit like a desert warrior, in his combat boots and camouflage clothing, which he always wore now. They disguised him when he was in hiding, living rough among the tomb stones.

Mother Mary Agnes, too, was in disguise. Her brown habit was the exact colour and texture and degree of shabbiness as the curtains masking the sides of the balcony, which had been closed off for use. It was thought the press of people stamping, yelling and cheering would be too much for the jerry built structure. No-one else had been allowed up there, but who could argue with a nun, especially a massive one like Mother Agnes?

And Agnes had a camera and tripod with her for cover. Well, it looked like a camera and tripod. In reality, the objects wrapped up in waterproof covers were a bible, and her trusty shotgun. Stepping into the shadows, Agnes took aim.

But Father Harry seemed to have eyes in the back of his head. As the munchkins, shaking with terror, slid away from him, Harry reached out a long arm and caught hold of Kansas. He lifted her up in one arm, smiling at her, cuddling her, but always, it seemed to Agnes, keeping the child between himself and the trajectory of her gun.

"You traitors!" He threw the other kids out of his way, but kept hold of Kansas, taking time to fire a malicious glance at Varrie, who was trying to hide the phone in her hand. "Have you no consciences? You've tried to hunt me down like a wild animal. After all I've done for you." He took a Shakespearian pose suddenly.

"You blocks! You stones! You worse than senseless things!" Then he was biblical, pulling at his beard. "When you were hungry I fed you! When you were thirsty I gave you to drink! And which of you has done the same for me, when I lay starving up yon hill?"

Father Harry cast his eyes upwards to heaven to witness his plight, and his eyes were screwed up, trying to resist tears. Agnes, hoping she was well concealed upstairs, wondered if he had glimpsed her shotgun. This would have been a good time for somebody to get a cell phone out and phone the cops. But somehow no-one did. Not just because they were terrified the wild man would see them. No, they were bizarrely beginning to feel guilty, as he harangued them. They hung their heads, squinting up at him in fear, and only the smallest kids, who shouldn't have been there anyway, had the courage to cry.

Father Harry had descended into total mania. Most of his ramblings were completely inaudible. Most of them concerned his Mammy. But as the audience, terrified yet enthralled, hung on his every word, he began to relish the limelight. He became more coherent, giving accounts of his holidays in Ireland with his Mammy. And of the farm the family had there.

Finally he sat down, show-biz style, on the edge of the stage, his legs sprawled over it. He took Kansas on his knee, toying with her munchkin ringlets.

Terrified, Dorothy, Lion, Scarecrow and Tin Man sneaked off sideways into the wings, as Harry turned his attention to the little school band which had faltered to silence under the ashen pale music teacher's trembling baton. Now, at a curt gesture from the mad priest, he raised it again, and the interrupted strains of *Home,*

Sweet Home came from the cowering band, mostly from the teachers that had been planted there to swell it.

Kneeling, with his arms wrapped round Kansas, Father Harry took on the part of Dorothy, and gave a charming rendition of the traditional song.

And for a stage struck middle aged ex priest and psychopathic murderer, Father Harry had a pretty good lyric tenor voice. High, sweet, a little eerie, like the late John McCormack on speed. He belted the song full out, then, by gesture, invited first Kansas to join in, and then, the mass of the petrified, stricken dumb, audience. At first only a few rasping notes were heard. Then, as Kansas sang out, angrily, it seemed, the kids in the audience sang too.

"Mid pleasures and palaces, though we may roam,
Be it ever so humble, there's no place like home."

And fat little Mrs Mulvey trilled along. Among all the people who Father Harry hated, seated in terror of him (all of whom he considered had let him down), there was Mrs Mulvey, his devoted, doting housekeeper. Who had put food out for him. Who had slipped into the army surplus stores in the Briggait, to get him his camouflage fatigues. And who had passed on the gossip from other priests' houses, and kept the tabloids for him. And fed the gossip he wished back to the newspapers. Who had gifted him a large proportion of the wages he had paid her. (Some had not even touched the sides of her bank account.) In fact, who would have laid down her life for him. And who had been the one to turn the lock on Father Seamas when he was searching for his missing costume in his tiny dressing room (the mop cupboard), so Harry could realise his desire of playing 'The Whizz'. Small plump Mrs Mulvey, as she sang loyally and obediently for Harry, began to shudder too. As she realised that the shotgun casually and indiscriminately pointing over the audience at large, might well spray her with shot, as much as her pal, thin Mrs Knightley, the janitor's nosey wife, sitting beside her. A tiny lady who had always detested him, and who was making only a low moaning hum.

But during the odd wistful, choked, swelling sound, Harry had caught sight of Varrie.

"And you? You grass! I know what you're up to with that cop! You're a common tart!" The band faltered to a stop again, and the crowd, silent, cowered in their seats as Father Harry pressed Kansas against his jacket, caressing her. Kansas stared at him, steely eyed. "Your mammy's not fit to clean my boots, darlin'! Will you come with me? Let's run away!"

Then he saw Marie Louise. She was sitting in the middle of the hall with Father Tiziano, now father Tiziano, since Marie Louise was now noticeably pregnant.

"And you, ya hoor! You think you're great! I could tell you a thing or two about that mother of yours. That tart! She taught you young enough!" Warming to his theme, sweat was beginning to pour off him, making channels on his grimy face. "I could have had you then! But I've never fancied big stookies!" He had begun striding up and down, dragging Kansas. "What was your mother's name again? Rena! Calls herself Renee now! Renee!" He made voluptuous shrugs supposed to be seductive, looking over his shoulder and pouting, "Well, if Renee had the brass to show herself here today!" He scowled into the audience, then into the wings, as if searching for her there. Gerry McGee, hiding in the wings, trembled.

The door at the back clanged open. When he saw it wasn't the cops, Gerry fainted.

"And who the fuck do ye think you're talking about? What would you do, if Renee had the brass to show her face? Come on, you big poofter. Renee'll give you a square go!"

Marie Louise's mother, newly glamorised on rehabilitation outings, strode up the central gangway, hefty and muscular; you wouldn't have wanted to get on her wrong side, especially on a dark night. Being short sighted, she did not see the gun till she was nearly upon him, as she was poised to leap up onto the stage, her face purple with rage, her eyes bulging. Whereupon, she shrieked loud and long. Harry took deliberate aim, and a shot rang out.

Some people later swore they had heard two shots, fired simultaneously. Then several things happened at the same time. Renee collapsed, bleeding, and the audience shrieked too. Brave 'Toto', maddened, dashed out from the wings, and got a grip on the crazy man's left ankle. Harry spun round, bent double. He lashed out with his right foot, but couldn't connect. At such close quarters his shotgun was useless.

"Toto! Toto!" screamed Kansas, as she leapt for the cover of the wings.

Backstage, in the Medical Room, three janitors detailed to shove Auntie Em's house on stage at the end, were still playing pontoon, unaware of the real life drama onstage. With a start, they realised they were late, and hurried round to the wings. Just in time to hear the words "Toto! Toto" and leap forward. The words were their cue for action. They pushed with all the might of three strong, hardworking janitors, used to stoking furnaces and moving unwieldy furniture. But earlier, Gerry the director had had the big castors oiled one last time.

The house, or really, the projecting corner of a house, whirled onto the stage on its huge, now heavily oiled, castors, and battered into Father Harry, who slipped and fell underneath, squashed by the entire weight of the construction. The gun in his hand went off, the report muffled by the massive carpentry work above him.

Only his feet in the muddy combat boots stuck out from below the crude 'house'.

And at that moment, Lena shrieked, stood up, her waters broke and she went into labour.

A medic in the audience ran to Renee. One, running backstage, rushed to Lena instead.

When the janitors managed to move the ton of splintered wood off Harry, he looked as dead as mutton, his own bullet in his groin. But as the last spar was eased off him, an odd grimace, almost a grin, contorted his face as Mother Agnes rushed to help raise him up.

"There's a spark of life!" she told the janitors laying him down on the medical room couch. "Leave him with me! I can help him! He needs my expert care."

Father Seamas, released from his mop cupboard, had dashed round, in tears, to see if he could help his old friend Harry, that they were saying such terrible things about. But as he reached the room, and struggled to open the door, he heard an inner bolt jammed home.

Mother Agnes had just managed to secure the door in time. And Agnes did not attempt resuscitation. Although, if you had been peeping through the keyhole you'd have thought so.

Agnes bent her statuesque bulk carefully over his battered body, and holding his wounded and crushed body between her two large hands, pressed her mouth tenderly on his. As Harry felt her strong hands on his diaphragm, some vital force lifted his ribcage. So he was alive!

"Then this was my first kiss for you, Harry!" she said, raising her head.

Then, fixing her lips violently on his mouth, she exerted her full force against his bruised and wounded torso. And felt his already damaged bones snap in her muscular arms. The mouth beneath hers struggled uselessly to open and take in a last breath. A rattle came from his throat, and foul air pushed Agnes's mouth at last away from him. One last spurt of air was expelled from his crushed lungs, in a sigh. As his body contorted in agony, the gasp seemed to Mother Agnes to sound like "Mammy!"

"And that was my last kiss for you, Harry, my love!"

Onstage, to keep the surging hysterical crowd back, the janitors were struggling to drop the stage curtains on the last unfinished act. Father Harry's last starring role.

Quick As Winkie

When Detective Constable Frank Childers' mother picked him up from the plastic surgery department at the Prince's Infirmary, it was not to Roystonhill she took him back. Or any place as downmarket and dangerous. (Bloody Roystonhill, she, a woman who rarely used rough language, now habitually called it.)

She blamed Roystonhill (the traditional name for all of Mirkhill, including the lands of Mirkyknowes in old Mirkhill that housed the Convent of the Bleeding Heart), Roystonhill itself and Low Royston, and all the grimy hills and vales, excluding the nearby Bishopbirks neat little housing estate. It was to Bishopbirks that she was taking him, where she had kept on her half of a doll's house, even after her husband had died and after Frank had moved out.

"I'm taking you home, son!" she had declared, bundling him into her mini. "Stop crying!"

In vain, Frank had protested he was not in tears, it was simply the operation to repair his broken nose that made his eyes water. His Mammy only snorted in disbelief, then tut-tutted, in rueful maternal sympathy.

Mrs Childers grimly steered her car the long way round 'home', as she insisted Frank call the semi. She avoided Mirkshields Police Station, at the interchange, where his colleagues would still be having a laugh at her son's expense. She hated the cop shop anyway, she had

had plans for Frank to have got a position in the Royal Scottish National Orchestra, playing his violin, after all those expensive lessons and the practising she had endured. And some of those detectives were rough as badgers' bottoms, not what you saw on television at all.

So Vera Childers made quite a wide detour, swinging round by Royston cemetery, to avoid Mirkhill where Varrie Valentino lived. Vera did not like to think too much about that girl, who had seduced her son away from his own posh new build flat in the Merchant City, as well as from his Mammy's semi. It was a harder job to avoid the tower block dwelling of the misbegotten taxi driver, Liam MacNee, who had attacked Frank over a parking space. Instead, Vera started chatting loudly as the tops of the Brick Road towers came into view over the terraced blocks below. (The towers had had little red 'hats' of roofing attached as a postmodern attempt to modify their brutal profiles.) "This could be a good chance, son," she chirped, "to stick in at your violin, and do some auditions. For the RSNO, I mean, you'd be very suited to it!"

"How?" Frank at last put in a surly word, scaring his Mammy.

"Well after all, Frank," she back-pedalled, avoiding telling him how good his violin teacher had said he was, "After all, you are Scottish, born and bred! Does that not count?"

"Nuh!" Frank grunted, going back to morosely pondering the incident of his bloody nose.

Liam had attacked him over a parking space, it was true. But that was just the ostensible reason for the attack. Although Liam MacNee had been maddened by the fact that the cop had parked his BMW in what Liam had come to think was his spot (just round the corner from Varrie Valentino's flat), that was just the start. The explosive rage that had made him lash out and punch Frank Childers' nose had been more of a crime of passion.

If it had come to court, that is what Liam would have claimed. But Frank had made sure it never did. He said he had tripped over a cat that had dashed out from under his car, and he had bashed his nose off his own car's near front wing. Frank's car's shiny black wing had been bumped, too true, but by a karate kick from MacNee.

Frank had insisted no-one had punched him, and in a way that was true, since MacNee had only head butted him, in his fit of jealous rage over Varrie.

Liam had driven Marie Louise and her fiancée, Tiziano, all the way back to Glasgow from London, as per his contract. He'd had to watch them lovey doveying all the way. Then he had suffered the humiliation of having to serve as a witness at their subsequent wedding at Royston Registry Office. He had had to shower confetti over Marie Louise, the girl he loved, and her priestly husband, before they flew to Milan for the religious ceremony. Did that not count as bigamy, he wondered, if you had taken vows as a priest, even if just a trainee one?

He had begun to think more kindly of Varrie Valentino, whom he had had to dump during his infatuation with Marie Louise. However, with rolls of the Millionairess's notes stuffed in the back of his jeans, Liam thought he would drive round to Mirkhill and give Varrie a treat. Unfortunately, she was already being given a treat by Detective Constable Frank Childers.

At least he was just about to when Liam charged in, somehow having acquired a key for Varrie's flat, and caught them in flagrante delicto.

Frank's blood made an awful mess of Varrie's house. His nose bled and bled, and even MacNee had recourse to what his Mammy used to say would stop a nosebleed. Keys down the back of the neck. Which was unlucky for him, because he used Varrie's keys, and had the devil's own job, subsequently, to get them back.

She made him pay for his impetuosity, made a bit of a nerd out of him, made him bring her flowers. He was forced to phone her at all hours, and had to resort to waylaying her as she came home from her work at Saint Jude's. He finally won her over by turning up at the school, with Marigolds and pinny on, and helping her finish off her sinks. Varrie had laughed so much, she'd pissed herself, and had to accept a lift home.

As for Frank Childers, the head butting episode put him off, it has to be admitted. And when his Mammy picked him up and took him 'home', he let himself be picked up and taken. For a start, he did not want to be seen with his nose plaster on. And he thought if he had one more bloody interruption, on the point of consummation of his romance with Varrie, it would render him impotent for life.

The good side of his 'accident' as far as Frank was concerned, was that the lady surgeon (to quote the sexist term his mother used) had casually straightened Frank's slightly squint nose as she repaired it. She thereby fixed a blemish caused by a schoolboy game of rugby. And when the bruising and swelling finally went down, he was revealed as even more good looking than he had been before.

Mrs Childers made a novena to Saint Philomena in thanksgiving. She had blamed the saint for letting his nose get bashed in the first place, as well as his PE teacher at Saint Ignatius, where he was a half scholarship boy. He should never have been put in a match with boys so much bigger and uglier than himself. It might have been jealousy that had been responsible. It turned out it was the home team that had caused the nasal damage, not the opponents.

But Vera Childers knew she shouldn't dwell on the past. She should be thankful that Frank had been at last restored to his boyish good looks. And was more than 100 per cent perfect. Or in the language of the telly talent shows, 110 per cent. The lady surgeon was a dab hand with the scalpel, and quite interested in Frank's nose. Vera thought Frank might stand a chance with her. He seemed to have been given loads of appointments for check-ups.

As for Varrie, by the time Frank got rid of his nose shield, she and his attacker Liam MacNee had become a couple.

The truth was that Frank was beginning to make Varrie nervous, one way and another, and she wasn't sure if she could stand much more of his violin playing, either. And sexual jealousy had actually triggered off a proposal of marriage from Liam. She had no intention of accepting him, however. The excuse she gave Liam was that it would not be good business for a policeman Kissogram actor to be a married man.

Because Varrie had set up her sweetheart in his chosen business, with Martha helping financially. Liam had made himself useful in the little business that Martha and Varrie ran. They ran a small cleaning business called 'Quick as Winkie', a phone-in cleaning agency. Liam shared the premises, Martha's high rise flat, which she had snapped up for a song. He ran the 'Personal Services' side of it, providing Kissograms and other party surprises.

In spite of it being such a terrific success, Martha kept 'Quick as Winkie' small, refusing to expand into other districts. She serviced the Mirkhill flats of the big time operators in the drugs market, who lived in small ordinary, but luxuriously appointed, flats to bamboozle the authorities. Both she and Varrie knew how to keep their eyes lowered and their lips shut.

They also worked in the neat suburbs to the north, the douce enclave of Bishopbirks, where Frank's mother lived. Martha fell in love with a little semi in the same street, and put an offer in without having opened the door, which Varrie thought was pure stupid. But it turned out alright. It had belonged to an old lady, so none of the inside had been modernised, which suited Martha very well. It had a just enough of a garden to keep her twins Darren and Wayne busy when they were let out of Larkshields Offenders' Institution on the odd weekend on home visits. She told the neighbours they were at boarding school, and always referred to their visits as 'half term'.

Kansas, Varrie's little daughter, on the other hand, really was at boarding school. She and her pal Dakota had auditioned for ballet school in Sussex, and both had got in. Martha had bestowed some endowments on the school, and also paid for the girls' shoes, tights and uniforms. Varrie was pleased Kansas was away from Saint Jude's, although she missed the laughs they had had.

Kansas was just pleased full stop. She loved the school. With their Scottish accents, they could not be placed socially by the other girls. She and Dakota added some Gaelic words to their vocabulary, to make Gaelic not Glasgow accents. And they were soon fluent in posh English. They became bilingual, one voice for Mirkhill and one voice for Bexhill. When Varrie and Liam turned up at prizegivings, Kansas was very nice to them, calling them Varrie and Liam, giving the impression by her lack of sulks and tantrums, that they must be some kind of servants, and not parent and parent's partner. She told the other girls her parents were cold, uncaring celebrities who hardly ever visited her. The girls were sorry for her, and envied her.

School life would have been perfect, like something out of an old fashioned storybook, if out of the blue, Rory Robbie O'Donnell Lavery had not turned up at the ballet school with a full scholarship and a posh metropolitan accent. Wee Rory had become Big Robbie as quick as winkie, and had instantly become a macho star attraction. To audiences as well as all the young girls, and, to be honest, some of the young boy dance students. Kansas and Dakota were crushed to discover that he really did not recognise them from Saint Jude's, and that it was not necessary to keep snubbing him. (He hadn't recognised the snubs either.)

"Must have been that blow on the head he got with the crucifix, Kansas." said Dakota. "And to think it was your wee Auntie Martha saved him with her miraculous medals."

Despite all her good works, which Martha did stealthily, as advised in the Bible, and since she had made only modest changes to her own life style, she had disarmed her friends and former neighbours. They no longer maintained that her lottery win had been massive. She still went to the same hairdresser in Mirkhill Road, who still gave her the same curly perm. And the fact that her sons were still being 'trained' in a secure youth unit, made folk believe the contrary, that her win had been relatively small. Anyone who had won millions, they reckoned, would have enough to bribe their boys' way out of Larkshields. It was well known that the boys had her heart broken. Though she still managed to look pleased to see them when they came back on their 'holidays' and rampaged through the house and straight out to the back garden shed where she had stowed the drum kit she had bought them. She even let them rehearse their scary rock band 'The First Offenders' there.

Martha Dearie was never uppity either. She would take her turn cleaning at Saint Jude's if loads of her operatives at 'Quick as Winkie' had phoned in sick. The turnover of part time cleaners at the school, and especially the art department was always rapid. It was said that Martha always wore the same big red gloves she had worn as a Polisher, although she had been forced to give that up, sadly, when she won the Lottery. Polishers had to be full time. Still she had the big red gloves, the badge of her promotion. And the Polishing team still saluted her as they passed the classroom she was cleaning, as they went by, singing in close five part harmony, on the days she filled in for a shift or two.

Martha never learned to drive either. So no-one could accuse her of buying Rolls Royces or BMWs. It was rumoured that she had bought Liam MacNee's cab for him, though, as part of a pre-nuptial agreement. Varrie was wrangling over it daily. If he ever had the temerity to apply for divorce, even if Varrie was the guilty party (Martha was nothing if not realistic), the taxi would go to Varrie. Martha was just a little bit suspicious of Liam, although he always made himself agreeable to her, cracking rude jokes to make her blush, practising his various Kissogram routines on her, snapping handcuffs on her, or bending her over in tangos.

She still relied on Liam to ferry her about on 'Quick as Winkie' business, either as one of the cleaners, or as an executive, when his kisses were not required.

But Kansas was getting used to her mother, Varrie's, boyfriend, Liam. Kansas had begun to quite like him, and his funny ways. For instance, he occasionally let her drive his cab, giving the drivers of oncoming vehicles heart attacks. And he let her shave all his hair off once, for a dare. So she began to call Liam Daddy, and her Dad, Paddy, Uncle Paddy. It hurt the poor man's feelings. But there you go, if you will try to be a big time crook, and then go and get caught. Kansas was afraid Paddy would get caught again, when he got out of Barlinnie. She thought her chances of retaining a permanent daddy were better with Liam.

Lena Wallace, the big erstwhile art teacher who had been responsible for most of the mess in the art department of Saint Jude's, offered her services to 'Quick as Winkie' after she had given up teaching on the birth of her cute baby boy. She showed a new side of herself to Martha and Varrie. She was obsessive about cleanliness when not being harassed by wild school kids, and brought her own polish and polishing cloths in, which was always a good sign in a cleansing operative, Martha noted.

In a surprisingly quick period of time since his murderous dealings, a myth began to grow about Father Harry. About him not being as black as he was painted. About the Whizz of Oz debacle being an unfortunate 'happening' when Father Harry himself was the only victim. In spite of Frank Childers bringing proof positive against the priest on all counts. He had amassed evidence from so many sources, he really annoyed his superiors. The man was deceased now. It was costing money to continue his posthumous prosecution, Doubleday said. They would be coming out of the woodwork for compensation. Let sleeping dogs lie.

But Varrie Valentino had eagerly given evidence. And, reluctantly, so had Martha. The detective also had got forensics from Sky's ragged fur coat, where Father Harry's and Sky's blood intermingled. Although Tam Tam's evidence alone convinced Frank Childers.

But Frank seemed to get no help in tying up the loose ends of Harry's diabolical reign as the guardian of the poor souls of Royston. It took ages for him to get a warrant to break open Father Harry's rosewood desk. And then he was doubled up in excruciating nervous indigestion, when all it disclosed was hundreds of lottery tickets, and lists of names.

Father Seamas was pained too. It was obvious that Harry had been off his head for ages, he thought, reaching for his pipe, as he showed Childers out, in embarrassed silence.

A little stash of grass Father Harry had left in a rosewood tobacco bowl, Father Seamas with his own plug, taking it to be an upmarket mix, and really enjoyed it in his pipe. Especially after a chittering early mass. Though it sometimes made his eyes sting.

Coming Clean

Mother Agnes sat in a high backed chair in the convent kitchen, being martyred. Sister Mary of Perpetual Succour and Sister Mary of the Angels called it being pampered. Agnes knew better. Sister Angel had Agnes's towel-swathed head in a vice like grip, while Sister Peppy was grimly plucking the eyebrows that sprouted, black or grizzled, in a straight line across Mother Agnes's large weather-beaten face.

"They make you look pure ferocious, Mother Agnes. Like an escaped criminal. You wouldn't want to look ferocious at your interview with the police. They might think you had something to hide," Peppy bullied her.

Mother Agnes gave a little gasp.

"Sorry, Mother Agnes! Nearly done now, and then we'll do your peppermint face mask. There might be TV cameras at the police station, and you wouldn't want to let us down."

"Sure, how do poor women stand this pain? Do they have to go through this often?"

"Keep still!" Sister Peppy went on relentlessly plucking. "It's a good job you never had to go through childbirth, Mother!"

"Is it really as bad as the women make out?" Sister Angel asked Peppy, she being the authority on the subject, having five younger siblings. Peppy hesitated. She was not exactly sure that Angel would make it as a nun. Apart from her stunning good looks, Peppy didn't think Angel had totally given up on men. And there was the convention of not warning young women what they were in for.

"Not really!" Unable to cross her fingers to mitigate the fib, she conceded, "As long as they make sure they get an epidural!"

"Anyway", said Sister Angel, "I think the whole process is pure disgusting!"

Well, maybe she would make a nun after all, Peppy thought.

"That's you done, Mother Agnes, but hold still till Angel slathers this gunk on you. This will remove all impurities from your complexion."

Imelda nearly had a heart attack when she came in to find Mother Agnes, motionless and green faced, corpse like, in the chair. The young ones couldn't stop laughing, the more so since Agnes wasn't allowed to laugh in case she split the mask, and all she could do was make little screams of anguished mirth.

The carry on reminded Agnes of the daft times she and Sister Philomena had had, before Philly lost her wits. She felt her face within its mask fall into stupid tragic lines. Which, thank God, the girls didn't notice. Agnes pushed them aside and rushing to the sink, doused her face under the tap, drying it roughly with the roller towel.

"And look what you've done to my good peignoir!" She held out the beatifically stained working habit that she had worn for her beautification, now encrusted with peppermint paste. The two young nuns drew back, a little bit aghast. They certainly didn't seem to have prettified Agnes, as she stood there, red nosed from the cold water, her eyebrow pruning giving her a kind of comically enquiring look.

But in her festive day white habit, newly back from the cleaners, and with some tinted cream that Sister

Angel had dashed on, calling it ointment, and with a little more painful adjustment to the eyebrows, and then a little pencilling in, Mother Agnes was a picture.

"Sure you've got me like Marlene Dietrich!" she complained. "What will Benigna say?"

But she was more like the Virgin enthroned in one of those early renaissance pictures, the erudite art historian, Sister Mary of the Angels, thought. When the artists weren't really into drawing as we know it today.

When they took her into the sewing room to look in the cheval glass, Agnes was stunned and shy at her comely image. She put her hands up in wonder to her smooth face, framed in the floating wimple.

"Nails!" screamed Peppy. "Would you look at her nails!"

Agnes held out both work stained hands hopelessly, in surrender.

It was all worth it in the end, though. Mother Agnes floated through the massive doors of Mirkshields Police Station like a queen. And when the cameras flashed in her face, she held up her newly daintified hands to shield her eyes. It felt lovely.

Detective Inspector Doubleday, also in full fig, presented her with her Good Citizen medal several times for the benefit of the cameras. The paparazzi were keen, maybe because of Sister Angel hovering in the background. They got some of their best shots ever that day.

But Doubleday felt he had done his duty. He wasn't really into nuns, and handed them over to a young policewoman to give them tea.

"Detective Constable Childers wondered if you would take tea with him, ladies. May I take you to his office?" she said, leading them off as if she was directing a parade.

Mother Agnes took one look at the clever, considering look on the young man's face and decided to get rid of

244

Angel. She felt she was in for more than a nice wee cup of tea.

"Wait in the truck, kid!" she said out of the corner of her mouth, Country and Western fashion, and Angel disappeared to repark the jeep, that she'd left kind of squinty.

Frank was a bit thinner than when Agnes had met him before. Not surprising since he'd got a hospital infection in his wound, which had caused bleeding at an awkward moment. He'd got over it quickly, though, and had no intention of letting it get him down or hold him back. Otherwise he would be stuck at his present rank forever.

"Earl Grey or Ordinary?" he enquired. "Shall I be Mummy?"

"Oh please!" Agnes was the world's worst at pouring out tea. "And ordinary!"

While she drank, she gave Frank the once over, and he returned the compliment. Plain clothes? Agnes thought to herself. Is that what they mean by plain clothes? (Frank was wearing a fuchsia pink shirt with a smart silver mohair suit.)

Frank was wondering if he was speaking to the same Mother Agnes who had greeted him in muddy dungarees on his visit to the convent about the chickens.

"No more trouble about the chickens?" he enquired, putting his bone china cup down. "I know you phoned me on my mobile about it, and then at the station. Sorry I wasn't available." Involuntarily his hand went to his wound, now practically painless. "No further trouble from the fox?"

"No, none, thanks. Sister Mary of the Angels managed to wring the poor hen's neck."

"And we have to thank you for your action in attempting to resuscitate the criminal, Henry Xavier Brown. And in guarding him in a lockfast room till the police arrived. Of course we didn't want him pulled to pieces by an angry mob. Ideally, the man would have recovered enough to stand trial." He looked at her shrewdly.

Mother Agnes's new expression of mild surprise did not change.

"Just one little question, Mother Agnes." Frank squirmed in his chair, easing his waistband over his scar. "Excuse me!"

"In giving the criminal mouth to mouth, as you say here you did," Frank consulted a form in front of him. Her testimony, she gathered. "Is it possible you may have caused some further damage to the man's body?"

"It's just possible, officer, though I have extensive training, and I know how light a touch one must use on already damaged tissues. In externally massaging the heart, one must use a degree of force, unfortunately."

Frank opened a drawer, and slammed the form in it.

"The shotgun, Mother Agnes?" Frank asked mildly. "You left it on the balcony. Your prints were all over it."

"Yes, it had been left in the trap by our gamekeeper. I took charge of it to keep it safe."

"You would not have dreamt, I suppose, of using it on a deranged person?"

"Only in self-defence, officer."

"And that condition would only have obtained after the man shot and injured Mrs O'Donnell, I think."

"No, he threatened the children too. I would have used it if I had had to."

"Yes, a judge would see it that way, certainly. But if I may, Mother Agnes, forgive me if I broach a sensitive subject. Did you ever suspect, in regard to the young boys being looked after in the Convent, that Father Harry ever used inappropriate behaviour to them?"

Agnes was taken aback. She never had. But now, she remembered. She recalled coming into Rory's room, and finding him watching Scooby Doo, sitting on Father Harry's knee, shouting out with laughter at the funny bits. Jumping up to point out things on the actual television screen, and then jumping back on the priest's knee. Rory had hardly noticed her presence. Harry had grinned at her tenderly over the boy's head. She'd even felt a bit sentimental over the encounter. Now she saw it in a different light.

Agnes felt herself grew cold, shivering all over.

"No I did not!" she said. "Crass idiot that I was, I did not!"

"Now, if you'll forgive me bringing up terrible memories, Mother Agnes, did you believe Henry Brown, a.k.a. Father Henry Xavier was guilty of the murder of your friend, Sister Philomena of the Sorrows? Did you have any reason to suspect this?"

The last rays of a red frosty sun caught the vertical slats on the dingy windows at just the exact angle to catch Mother Agnes with stripes of ruby light.

Agnes, who had managed to keep her composure, while lying through her teeth, suddenly lost it. She flushed, her face glowing pink, matching the luminous tints playing on her white habit. Frank leaned forward eagerly waiting for her to speak, but keeping himself always in the shadows. Still Agnes, would not, could not reply.

"Tell me, Mother Agnes, did you suspect it? And if so why did you not report it? "

Mother Agnes stood up, now towering over her slim young interrogator.

"Yes I suspected it. I was just too big a fool to realise I did. And of course I suspected the man was a villain. In spite of his charm."

"And did Sister Philomena appreciate his charm? It has been insinuated in the press that she did. Mother Agnes, was Sister Philomena in love with Father Harry? And did you object to this?"

Agnes collapsed into the spindly plastic chair again, looking at Frank in outrage.

"No, she was not in love with him. She thought he was a lovely man, which is different. And I don't think Sister Philomena was in love with anybody ever. And Father Harry was a real charmer. It would have been hard for anyone to withstand his charm."

Into her mind came the charm Harry had handed out to her. How near the wind he had sailed with her.

"He went so far with me as to summon up a comic pretend family that the two of us might have had, had we met at the right time. He had names for them too. Angusina, with the pointed skull. Wee Willie Winky, with the really big nose! His jokes made me hysterical with laughter. So you see, Mr Childers, what a clown I was! It was I who loved Harry!"

The sun had mercifully dipped below the Mirkhill tenements and no longer intruded into the dusty grey room, setting it ablaze with dust motes and colour. A kind of sepia light pervaded the room as Agnes shrank back in her chair.

"So Philomena did not love Harry, Mother Agnes. And you did not resent it. And you did not use undue force in resuscitation manoeuvres. It's academic now. But I thought it might be useful to know the truth. Useful for both of us!"

"You're right, of course, Detective. I should have known that. But you've got it wrong, as even a clever young man like you sometimes will. Philomena did not love Harry. She only ever loved me. That is until she lost the use of the higher domains of her brain. Our love was confined and defined by the chaste protocols of convent life. A spiritual bouquet left beside the plate on a name day. Making a face behind Benigna's back when the other was getting a telling off. Mistakes covered up. I had to do that a lot at the end, trying to protect her. But I failed in that big time, don't you agree?"

"You won't ask, but you're wondering if there was anything physical between us. In a way there was. The touch of chilly fingers on an arm, to say how cold it was outside, when we were under silence. Warm hands on a flushed cheek to say how roasting hot it was in our heavy habits on a blistering sunny day. We kept going on that."

"With Harry it was different. He had the devil in his eye. I don't know what I wouldn't have done for him if he had really asked me, and really meant it. But of course he hadn't and he didn't. Why would he? He was using me, as he used so many others."

"Mother Agnes, let me ask you again. Did you injure the man deliberately?"

"Now you wouldn't really want me to tell you, would you? But I'll say one thing! If Harry was sitting there where you are now, I would reach forward and I would kill him with these two hands. I would pull him to pieces, even if he was in the full flush of strength. And that, at last, is the truth I'm telling you, as God is my witness, Detective Constable!"

When Sister Mary of the Angels came into the room, she saw Mother Agnes, like the Virgin enthroned, rigid in her chair, her face transfused by some lofty passion, her arms extended towards Frank Childers. He, like the patron in a Flemish painting, leant towards her in supplication, his face worldly, but humane and compassionate. They might have been chiselled from marble or brushed onto canvas centuries before.

The image dissolved as Frank jumped up to put on the light.

Aftermath

If Father Harry's selfish spirit, lingering on in his decaying corpse, had thought to take comfort from the laughter of children in the nearby play park, it was in for a disappointment. For the adventure playground, in the damp dusks, was occupied by wild boys and girls, all dressed wickedly in white. And all out looking for action, shrieking and hollering crudely.

And in the velvet darkness that hung over the humid place, in some warm spell, in the depths of the night, cynical heterosexual rent boys (Father Harry's bugbears) took their tremulous clients there to go through the motions of love and desire.

On just such a night, though, they were scared off by a large cloaked figure who made for the unhallowed ground near it. Not a ghost, as they perhaps thought, but Agnes, on foot. Though she was usually driven there by Sister Peppy, in daytime, armed with her plastic gloves and apron, to pick up the dented beer cans and used condoms that were chucked over into the unhallowed ground, from the gangs in the adventure playground.

Not that the corner was unhallowed now. It had been hallowed by Father Seamas, with holy water and hyssop. He had sung the 'Asperges' in his pleasing baritone, while Mother Agnes had intoned the descant, as he flicked water over the grass and bracken. And the archbishop had liberally given permission to bury poor suicides there.

She had returned alone that sultry, breathless, night, to tend Father Harry's grave. It was the last night for the poppies, which had sprung up in a sudden flush from the barren lands disturbed by Harry's burial. They were already hanging their heads. And who knows if they would reappear next year, or centuries later. She had tried picking some, to put round his identification stub. But they had faded to mere smudges, like obliterated moths.

Agnes had a little school jotter in her hand. The one that Sky had given her in return for cheese sandwiches. She had soon realised that Sky was not able to make even the casual attempts at work that her other tramps made in return for food, which she had stage managed to save their pride. But she had always liked poetry anyway, especially the Romantics. Especially Byron.

"Fare thee well! and if for ever, Still for ever, fare thee well!" she murmured.

She had found most of Sky's poems a bit weird, but one she really liked. She had thought Harry would have liked it too, but had always been too shy to read it to him. She determined to do so now, approaching his grave with the papers fluttering in her hands, from her trembling. A kind of love poem, called 'Bleeding Hearts'. Agnes intoned it to distant, threatening, rumbles of thunder.

> *"People like what they like*
> *Like what they think they like*
> *Some guys and lassies like thinkers*
> *Some like stinkers alas*
> *Romance is a lottery*
> *Chance is constant*
> *Constancy in Romance*
> *Fat chance!*
> *Some people find pure love a pain*
> *Some won't endure the profane*
> *With some you are in for a chilly season*
> *But the poor heart surely still has its reason"*

"These are my last words to you, Harry, my love." The words croaked from Agnes's tight throat, through her livid cracked lips. She bent to kiss the iron marker of the grave.

A second later there was a fierce explosion, as lightning struck the numbered metal plate. It seemed as if Harry's spirit, imprisoned in the creaking wicker coffin below, gave up then on the crumbling remains. And in a burst of cynical manly rage, exploded the coffin and escaped in earthly gasses of decay, in a crack of thunder and doom. As before her eyes the compacted earth disintegrated, and fissures appeared as the cement casings round the marker collapsed. And Agnes was forced to stagger back from the spewed up debris, and make an awkward leap to safer ground.

The heavens opened as Mother Agnes limped home, sending her cascades of rain to wash away her sins, and to rid the air of the odour of sulphur that had seemed to her to hang in it. Her rough brown habit became sleek and black, as it clung to her. Agnes's face creased into its grimace of mirth and grief. The explosion from Harry's tomb had sounded for all the world like an enormous, derisive belch that Father Harry was blowing at her, in response to her dainty gesture of would be reconciliation. She raised her noble profile to the skies, laughing aloud in defiance of Father Harry, and of the storm.

And, to reward her bravery, a glossy pink dawn came at last, as the rain clouds, scudding in a freshening wind, made the bleak townscapes of Royston, spread out beneath her, look ridiculously pretty and glamorous. A bit too much of a good thing, Agnes thought wryly. Maybe a wee bit over the top, she muttered aloud, grinning again to an imaginary companion, as she splashed her way noisily homewards. She gave voice to a "De Profundis" loudly and with bravura. As if she was performing as a soloist, somewhere huge. Maybe the Albert Hall. Better still, in Milan Cathedral, before the Pope with all his cardinals in cyclamen. Maybe with ranks of white clad nuns behind her in a choir. Although black would be okay, with just herself in white.

> *"Out of the depths I have cried unto thee, O Lord!
> Lord, hear my voice!"*

A flock of jackdaws, disturbed from their breakfast chats, came to join in, squawking and flapping round her head, putting in their own weird modern harmonies. But the golden-toned bell from the convent chapel began to toll, summoning her to matins. And the pagan birds flew off, jeering, just as Mother Mary Agnes of the Holy Child reached the enclosed mossy footpaths that led her back to the Convent of the Bleeding Heart.

Maybe things would be alright now, Mother Agnes thought. Only yesterday Sister Mary of the Angels had told her she was expecting good news. Something exciting, she'd said.

But as the convent itself came into sight, Agnes was forced, for the second time that morning, to jump for her life, this time into the rough hedgerow overgrown with stinging nettles, bramble and briar.

"Mother of God!" Agnes cried aloud for help, picking herself up, "Do they want to destroy me entirely?"

An enormous van lumbered on uphill, scraping the hedges on both sides.

She peered after it, pulling weeds off her soaked habit. The van had some sort of lettering on the outside, and aerials sticking up from it in all directions. As she watched, three young guys, stylishly dressed in denim and leather, with headphones and other equipment slung around them, leapt up the front steps and rang the doorbell. Agnes saw Sister Peppy appear, still pulling on her brown sleeves, and eagerly welcome the young men.

Then Sister Mary of the Angels made her appearance, causing quite a stir, as she usually did, in her glittering white feast day habit.

I wonder what feast she's celebrating, Agnes asked herself cynically. The Chinese New Year, maybe. Then Agnes got it. Of course, the Docudrama on the convent that Peppy had been angling for. Well, that was quick work! As she watched, the technicians and the nuns all stared at their watches and then stared down the drive, where she reckoned they had caught sight of her unkempt figure, as she made her way reluctantly towards them.

Then, as if reassured, the young men started unloading equipment from their van, helped by a couple of young women who now emerged from it, smoking roll-ups. It was almost as if they had all been waiting for her.

Mother Agnes cracked her iconic smile at last, finally having to stand still and laugh, hanging on to an elaborately wrought iron gatepost.

"I'm not quite ready for my close up, Sister Peppy!" she shouted, striking an attitude.

But then, she reflected, would she ever be, if she had until Doomsday?

Lightning Source UK Ltd.
Milton Keynes UK
UKOW02f0252011014

239423UK00003B/30/P